MURDER ON GOOD FRIDAY

MURDER
on GOOD FRIDAY

Sara Conway

Mystery
Conway

Cumberland House
Nashville, Tennessee

Published by Cumberland House Publishing, Inc., 431 Harding Industrial Drive, Nashville, TN 37211

Cover design: Unlikely Suburban Design

Library of Congress Cataloging-in-Publication Data

Conway, Sara, 1962–
    Murder on Good Friday / Sara Conway.
        p. cm.
    ISBN 1-58182-188-3 (alk. paper)
        1. Great Britain--History--Henry III, 1216–1272--Fiction. 2. Hexham
    (England)--Fiction. 3. Jews--England--Fiction. 4. Bailiffs--Fiction. I. Title.

PS3603.O68 M8 2001
813'.6--dc21

                                                                2001017241

Printed in the United States of America
1 2 3 4 5 6 7—05 04 03 02 01 00

For Richard

Acknowledgements

I am deeply grateful to my mentors and friends, Dr. Robin Stacey and Dr. Robert Stacey, Professors of Medieval History at the University of Washington. In addition to reading the manuscript and offering valuable criticism, they provided unflagging support and encouragement during my years under their tutelage.

Special thanks also to Ron Pitkin and my editor, Lisa Taylor.

And finally, my warmest thanks and gratitude go to my mom, for always believing.

Map of Hexham

River Tyne

The Haugh

1. The Priory Cathedral of St. Andrew
2. The Moot Hall
3. Market Square
4. The Keep

N

R. Conway

GLOSSARY

Augustinian Canons (also Austin Canons): Monks who followed the Rule of St. Augustine—based on community service, respect for authority, care of the sick, and self-discipline. Commonly called "Black Canons" from the color of their habits.

Corrody: A pension or annuity in the form of lodging at a monastery, or an allowance of food, clothing, etc., granted to a lay person.

Croft: A small piece of arable land, oftentimes next to a house.

Demesne: The part of the lord's manorial lands reserved for his own use and not given to his serfs or free tenants. Serfs worked the demesne for a specified number of days per week. The Royal Demesne was all land in the realm which had not been put into private hands.

Eyre: (Latin *Iter*): The right of the king, or his justices, to visit and inspect the holdings of any vassal. This was done periodically, usually at intervals of a few years.

Franchise: A grant of royal judicial authority to a private individual or body of persons (such as a monastery).

Hospital: Especially common in towns, these were places for the elderly and infirm to live out their days in relative comfort.

The Hours: The monastic timetable for daily liturgy.
Matins: 2–3 am winter, 1–2 am summer
Lauds: 6–7 am winter, 4–5 am summer
Prime: 7–8 am winter, 5–6 am summer
Tierce: 9–10 am winter, 7–8 am summer
None: 1–2 pm winter, 2–3 pm summer
Vespers: 4–5 pm winter, 6–7 pm summer
Compline: 6:15–6:30 pm winter,
         8:15–8:30 pm summer

Hue and Cry: The requirement of all members of a village to pursue a criminal with a horn and voice. It was the duty of any person discovering a felony to raise the hue and cry.

Moot (Anglo-Saxon *Mot*): Assembly, court, or council.

Obedientiary: Monk, canon, or nun who has been assigned particular administrative responsibilities in the running of the monastery.
Almoner: Distributed alms to the sick and poor.
Cellarer: Responsible for all property, rents, and revenues of the house.
Hosteller: Responsible for guests and guest houses.
Infirmarian: Oversaw the welfare of the sick and elderly in the infirmary.
Kitchener: Oversaw preparation of all meals.
Novice-Master: Prepared postulants and novices for taking their vows.

Precentor: Responsible for liturgical books, psalters, missals and choir books and for leading the chant at services.

Sacrist: Responsible for the safety and cleanliness of the monastic church and the provision of vessels for the altar.

Oblate: Child placed by parents in a religious house with a view to taking vows when he or she reached the required age.

Priory: Any monastic house administered by a prior or prioress. A smaller monastic establishment than an abbey.

Tourney: Mock combat for knights. Regulated by the 1270 Statute of Arms, which aimed to prevent such tourneys from turning into the rape, pillage, and murder of the villages and towns where the tourney took place.

MURDER ON GOOD FRIDAY

PROLOGUE ✠

It was the thirtieth day of March in the year 1220, the day after Easter, when young Gwyn found the body. She came upon it in the meadow just south of town, where she had been sent by her mother to collect an herb needed for treating her ailing younger brother, Siward.

"Betony will be difficult to find so early in the season," her mother had warned as Gwyn eagerly prepared for her outing, bundling herself in a heavy woolen cloak and taking up her gathering basket. "It will only be a tiny stalk growing among the grasses."

Their stores of remedies and decoctions were low, for it had been an unusually harsh winter, and most had been consumed treating the many maladies that accompany the wearying cold of that season. Nor it seemed was Winter yet inclined to loosen his chilly grasp. As Gwyn made her way into the nearby fields to begin her search, the bitter March wind continued to blow, scudding and puffing over the landscape, bullying a pale sun, whose newly dawned rays did little to warm her as she stooped over the stunted grasses. She hunkered down to scratch at the earth with a tiny finger, her practiced eye roving over the ground.

Feeling suddenly daunted, she looked up and stared across the wide meadow. The early hour and biting cold made for a deserted pasture, with only gusts of wind for company.

Then she recalled Siward, sick and needful in his bed near the hearth, and was roused to mind her task. And to stave off the oppressive solitude, she decided to sing a song as she hunted—a rhyme to accompany her, one of many Gwyn had memorized to help in learning the healing properties of herbs. Her tiny child's voice was barely audible in the remote expanse, even in her own ears, as the words were cruelly snatched away by the wind:

> *Betony, betony*
> *O virtuous betony!*
> *Guards against evil*
> *In amulet form.*
> *Mends cuts and sores*
> *As a poultice worn.*
> *Headaches and coughs*
> *Will surely flee*
> *When virtuous betony*
> *Is sipped as a tea.*

She ended with a few skips, then pondered singing another—the hymn to horehound maybe? But she halted after the first verse, finding the songs were doing little to bolster failing spirits, her solitary voice only underscoring her aloneness. Time to get on with the task, she decided, knitting sandy-colored brows in earnest concentration. Once the betony was found, she could leave this dreary place and return to the warmth and comfort of home. Eyes carefully trained to the ground, she took one slow step after another, like a fox stalking prey, ready to pounce the moment her quarry was within plucking distance.

She halted in frustration. Not a single shoot located, and if she didn't return home soon her mother would begin to worry. She tried to recall the place where last summer they had discovered a large patch of the herb. Gazing across the expanse of stubbled green, she remembered that it had been somewhere near the eastern edge of the meadow, where grasses meet woodland, that threshold-like place where the illuminated world gives way to the shrouded and secretive realm of the forest.

That day, as her mother had gathered for her stores, Gwyn had rested in the coolness of the sun-dappled shade, while peering into the shadowy woodland realm. Children were cautioned by their elders to keep away from the forest. Young ones might become lost in the vast woods, starving to death before they could be found. Thieves and vagabonds were also known to hide there, and little ones would be easy game for desperate outcasts. The children knew, however, that much worse than mere mortals dwelled in the forest. The Wild Huntsman stalked its murky depths, accompanied by his troop of unbaptized souls, and children were especially longed-for prey.

Studying the gloom, she had sensed a quiet watchfulness inside the forest, a presence that made her at once uneasy and curious. She had wandered in a ways, reassured and emboldened by the presence of her mother, daring herself to go farther. And the deeper into the woods she had gone, the quieter and more guarded the forest seemed to become. Yes, she had thought, it would be easy to become lost once the comforting edge of the meadow was out of sight.

Then her mother had called, and it was with relief that she had turned from the forest's stifling interior. But once her back was turned to the dimness, she was seized by a desire to run, headlong, as though the unseen presence were now chasing her, bent on capturing the impertinent child who had dared enter its domain. It bore down on her, and Gwyn had sprinted for her life, stumbling and lurching through the leafy deadness of the forest floor. She was almost within its grasp, feeling moist, hot breath on her back, hearing the whoosh of demonic arms beating air as they strained to reach her. Finally, she had broken free of the woods, springing forth into the safe warmth and blinding brightness of the summer sun.

Now the memory added to Gwyn's anxiety, and she decided to keep looking for the betony in the open meadow. She didn't want to go near the forest. She resumed her methodical, step-by-step search, but did not find the elusive herb. Instead, Gwyn found Alfred, the brewer's son, one of her playmates.

She stared down at him as he lay on his back, arms splayed. He was lying amongst the tall brown stalks of a long-dead plant, and she recoiled at the sight of his piteous body; for it was immediately apparent by the frozen look of terror on Alfred's colorless face, by the weird stiffness of his limbs, that he was dead. Gwyn jammed a fist to her mouth, dropping her empty basket. She shook her head violently, rejecting the sight. Then, with nightmare-like slowness, she began to back away, anxiously scanning the meadow around her, eyes pulled to the dark line of trees in the distance. Had the Wild Huntsman of the forest killed Alfred? Could he still be near, stalking her now? In an instant she was running, making for home and hearth with lightning speed, driven by the certainty that once again she was running for her life, knowing that poor Alfred had not been able to run fast enough.

O n e ✝

Lord Godwin sat at a large plank table occupying one corner of Hexham's great Moot Hall, an imposing stone structure situated on the east side of the Market Square, directly opposite the priory church dedicated to St. Andrew. Erected long ago to serve the needs of the bailiff, keeper of justice on behalf of the archbishop of York, the Moot Hall uncompromisingly dominated the marketplace, a potent reminder of the shire's powerful overlord, Archbishop Walter de Grey.

With arms propped on the table, dark head held in his hands, Godwin sat staring at a large pile of documents—writs delivered last week by an agent of the archbishop. He could ignore the directives from his lord no longer, and with weary fortitude took one up and cracked open its seal to scan the contents. But his eyes quickly strayed from the tight cursive script, reading no more than the formula salutation. Loath to go further, he knew he would find the order disagreeable.

He had held the office of bailiff for eight months now, assuming it upon his return from crusade, still finding certain of its duties difficult to bear. At times he questioned his impulsive bid for the post and was well aware that others, too, shirefolk and kin, puzzled over his motives. Why does the lord of Dilston Hall, nephew of Earl Patric, crave to be bailiff? A sheriff, he is, collecting fines and fees for that greedy man, the archbishop. Why does he break up tavern brawls and run down petty thieves and knaves when he could be at tournament, winning honor, or serving the earl? Silver aplenty he has, so why take the job?

It was true that many men of Godwin's stature would contemptuously reject the office. Before the crusade to Damietta, Godwin himself would not have considered becoming a bailiff. What skills had he in justice? His training was in war. At thirty-five years old, his rugged looks and weathered features attested to a life spent out-of-doors, in the saddle hunting, tourneying, and campaigning. Middling in height and compact in form, his sturdy yet supple body bore witness to wide experience in the physical labors of armed conflict, while a calm composure and easy assurance marked him as a natural leader.

Yet fourteen months in the East with the endless battles and deaths of so many valiant men, Christian and infidel alike, had left him reconsidering his lifelong aims and pursuits. Rendering justice had seemed a noble course to follow. Besides, these were quiet times. The civil war between King John and the barons was well over, Magna Carta won: the king's will was now subject to predictable and customary law. A boy, John's thirteen-year-old son Henry, sat on England's throne, his regents busily putting matters in order at home; campaigns abroad to recapture lands lost to the French king would be a long time in coming. And here in the north, the Marches, too, were quiet, a wary peace in force between England and Scotland. Yes, a time for new beginnings, for tending to household and tenants and lands under the plow.

With a heavy sigh, Godwin forced his attention back to the writ.

All at once, he was on his feet, chair careening across the floor behind him. "By God's eyeballs, I won't do it!" he roared, banging a fist on the table. The pile of letters jumped and toppled. His eleven-year-old nephew, Eilaf, who had been dozing near the hearth where he tended its fire, jumped as well. Godwin looked his way and gave the boy a weak smile, as if to apologize, but Eilaf thought it a grimace and went to fetch more wood. It seemed that letters from the archbishop never heralded good tidings; rather, they ushered in periods of perturbed gloom for Godwin, times when Eilaf found it best to stay clear of the bailiff; for his uncle's frequent disgust with directives from his overlord sometimes compelled him to give rein to an already quick temper, making him unpleasant company.

Godwin retrieved his chair and banged it back into place. Regretting his outburst, he watched Eilaf sidle out the door. The archbishop, or rather his agents, for such a noble man of the Church would never soil himself directly with such base matters, had just ordered the bailiff to seize the goods and property of a tenant who had failed to pay a debt. The man was Guthlaf, one of the town's fullers. Godwin knew that a recent spell of bad luck had left him unable to pay most of his debts, forcing him to pawn virtually everything he owned. All that did not pertain to his craft of scouring and cleansing newly woven cloth, that is. Godwin knew he could never bring himself to seize the man's remaining possessions, for these were his only means to recovery. He would simply have to stall in responding to the writ, though he was acutely aware that another would soon be fired off demanding to know what action the bailiff had taken.

Experience told Godwin that it was no use trying to reason with the archbishop's agents, explaining, as he once had tried, that by leaving a man his trade, the debt would eventually be paid, impoverishment averted.

"Such charity," they had sternly reminded, "would make the archbishop a pauper himself. He cannot save every Christian from disaster. Besides, the income from his liberties and franchises benefits the entire English Church. Matters must be viewed from this larger perspective, Lord Godwin. As a man of the archbishop, your duty is to put his interests first."

Godwin had come to understand his duties very well indeed. As a liberty of the archbishop, all pleas of the crown and common law matters were dealt with by his court and its chief executive officer in Hexham, the bailiff. Godwin had been drawn to the prospect of dispensing justice, righting wrongs. But more often he was required to perform tasks that were quite unjust, to his way of thinking, as in the seizure of goods and chattels and the imposition of onerous fines. He hadn't, of course, expected exceptional Christian munificence on the part of his new lord simply because he occupied a Church office. Godwin was well aware that high Church offices were conferred by the king, these days his regents, as a reward to secular men for exceptional services rendered. Piety was not a consideration.

Yet he had been unprepared for the ruthlessness and ceaseless dedication with which the archbishop and his court exercised authority over the liberty of Hexhamshire. An agonizingly close account of all rents and taxes due was kept, as were accounts of all pleas and petitions to the archbishop's court. The business of justice, Godwin had quickly discovered, was a lucrative one as countless small filing fees and amercements added up to considerable amounts of silver. Never a single shilling due escaped the archiepiscopal court's attention.

He sat down again, determined to dispense with the unpleasant business of the writs as quickly as possible. The directive concerning Guthlaf was placed at the bottom of the pile. He would delay action against the fuller for as long as possible, until he could help the man find a way out of his predicament. No sooner had Godwin picked up the next writ, though, than the big oak door of the Moot Hall was thrown open. Fara, Hexham's herbalist and healer, came blowing in like an unexpected gale.

She stood for a moment just inside the doorway, breathless, one hand clutching long woolen skirts hiked to her shins. Frantically she looked about, startled brown eyes wide and searching, then relieved when they lighted on Godwin. Quickly he came from behind his desk to meet her, concerned. Never had he seen the healer, always calm and composed, so distraught.

Youthful looks belied Fara's twenty-seven years, although a serene, almost grave, nature called to mind a wise and learned elder. Well schooled and practiced in the ways of healing, she had mastered the art under her mother's tutelage, just as Gwyn now learned from Fara.

"My Lord, I have dreadful news!" she cried, hurrying forward. "Gwyn has discovered a body in the town pasture! She says it is Alfred, the brewer's boy!"

Godwin listened as she repeated the tale of grisly discovery. Then he called to Eilaf, who was standing nearby, tightly clutching the pile of wood he held in his arms. Alfred was his playmate, Godwin realized, feeling a sharp pang of regret for his nephew.

His sister's son, Eilaf served Godwin just as Godwin and his cousin Aidan had served their uncle, Earl Patric. For most boys of good birth and lineage, at age eleven or thereabouts, entered the service of an honored kinsman to learn the ways of knighthood and lordship, of battle and command. Godwin remembered well his first year in service, his first time away from mother and sister. Still a child, but yearning for manhood, he had been at once excited and terrified, adventure hungry and homesick. Eilaf, Godwin thought, gazing at his lanky, fair-haired nephew, all angles and sharply protruding bones, was like that long-ago youth, fragile one moment, the next chafing for responsibility while still delighting in childish pranks and horseplay.

As gently as he could, Godwin said, "Eilaf, run quickly to the priory and fetch Bosa. He's delivering letters from the archbishop to Prior Morel. Then find Wulfstan. He should be just finishing his rounds and likely resting up at Watt's tavern. Send them both to the south fields."

Turning back to Fara, he said, "Will you accompany me? It may be that Gwyn is mistaken, that Alfred still lives and needs your skills."

"Of course, my lord." But Fara knew it was unlikely that her daughter was mistaken. Everyone recognized death, for it lived among them, a part of life, and the young were seldom sheltered from its indiscriminate harvest of souls.

While Eilaf dashed off in the direction of the priory, Fara and Godwin hastened through the quiet streets toward the common fields, attracting little attention, for it was still early, only an hour or so past Prime. Quickly they followed the tiny imprints of Gwyn's feet in the frosty grass to the body, but when they saw Alfred, they both knew that he was dead. Fara kneeled to gently press fingers against his small neck, noting that the flesh beneath her touch was cold.

"He's been dead for some time," she said, slowly drawing back her hand.

Godwin stood rooted, staring down at Alfred. He had fully expected to find the boy alive, sick perhaps, or even feigning to frighten poor Gwyn. He had not been prepared for this.

As a soldier, he had seen countless men die in a myriad of battles, had seen the innocent killed because they had the misfortune of being in the path of war's destruction. Yet he had never seen a child he knew brutally murdered. Choked to death it appeared, for Alfred's face wore the unmistakable expression of strangulation. Godwin felt a sick revulsion wash over him as Fara looked up, her eyes pleading the bailiff for an explanation.

With great effort, he suppressed his shock and tried to push away his last memory of Alfred—a carefree child capering about the streets of Hexham, reveling in the festivities that accompany Holy Week. Godwin kneeled down, like Fara, to feel the cold stiffness of the body and study the boy again. Calling on his long experience in battle, he guessed that Alfred had died two or perhaps three days ago, though the unusual cold made estimating difficult. Strange, he thought, that his folks have not come forward to report him missing. There was an explanation he was sure, for he could never imagine the couple capable of foul play. Godwin knew that they adored their son, and his stomach clenched at the prospect of delivering the news of Alfred's death.

His deputies, Wulfstan and Bosa, came running over, both short of breath. They stopped abruptly to stare down at the boy. Godwin looked up, suddenly anxious for Bosa. Studying his deputy's large, gentle face, he saw an initial look of horror give way to grieving pain as recognition of Alfred slowly registered. Godwin regretted summoning him and cursed his lack of foresight.

He did his best to shield Bosa from life's darker elements and was reminded once again that he had been an unlikely candidate to serve as vassal in Godwin's knightly retinue. His father, however, had been determined to see him enter the ranks, as was his right by hereditary tenure. And to Godwin's pleasure, taking Bosa into service had improved the relationship between father and son; the former was less embarrassed by his hulking boy, huge and strong as an ox, yet gentle as a lamb and as easily startled. Bosa himself, it seemed, had transferred all filial devotion to his new lord, likely grateful to be relieved of an overbearing father.

Yet Godwin had worried about the rough-and-tumble competitiveness of knightly conduct and its effects on Bosa. Thus, he had given his "ward" the additional rank of deputy with a mind toward keeping a closer watch on him, limiting his contact with the boon companionship of Godwin's other knights, good men all, but aggressive and prone to vigorous rivalries.

As a deputy, Bosa's duties were tame in nature, for in the quiet town of Hexham violent crime was rare; infrequent drunken brawls outside the alehouse and heated exchanges between customer and vendor on Market Day were more typical expressions of hostile behavior. But even in these simple cases, Bosa was useless and likely to be the victim of any abuse. He got on best with the town's children and could often be seen striding through the streets with several hanging from his huge limbs. He and Eilaf had become fast friends. Once, Godwin had asked how, given the choice, he would choose to spend his life, fully expecting him to admit a desire for the cloister. Bosa had only looked confused, then alarmed, as if Godwin were hinting he should consider another occupation.

Now he looked on the verge of tears, and Godwin stood up quickly, saying, "Bosa, go back to the priory and fetch a litter—discreetly. I don't want half the town out here trampling the fields and nosing around. Tell the canons we'll soon be arriving with a body that needs tending for burial."

Bosa nodded slowly, then turned and lumbered back across the field. The three remaining stood gazing sadly at Alfred, slowly crossing themselves, one after another, in a succession of genuflections. Godwin tried to memorize every detail of the body and its surroundings. As bailiff, he had had little experience with murder. There had only been two in the past eight months, both carried out by bandits who had waylaid wealthy merchants traveling the southern route to Hexham. Motive and means were immediately apparent: to acquire silver by means of a crossbow, in one instance, with bare hands in the other. Neither case had been difficult to solve, and both criminals were apprehended after a relentless search of the shire's forests. Public hangings in the Market Square had shortly followed.

But this, the murder of a townsman's child, was altogether different. Who could do this, his mind kept asking. Why? Carefully he studied Alfred for answers, noting that he wore no outer gear to protect against the bitter cold, no cotte or cloak. It was impossible to say, Godwin realized, whether he had been killed in the meadow, or somewhere else and placed here after.

Wulfstan, still staring in shocked disbelief, echoed Godwin's thoughts, asking, "Who could do this, lord?"

Godwin knelt once more, gently turning Alfred's head to examine his neck. "Look here," he said, pointing to an abrasion circling the child's throat. "I'd say he was strangled by a length of rope. And see his left side? There's a knife wound there, though it doesn't look as if the thrust was deadly. Perhaps it was put there after death—notice how little blood came forth?" Something else caught his eye as he moved on to examine Alfred's hands: they were pierced, as if heavy iron nails had been driven clean through. He heard a sharp hiss from Fara as she caught sight of the bizarre wounds.

"Murder," his deputy was saying slowly, warily, as if he had never uttered the word.

Godwin straightened, his face grim. Though it was not apparent, he, too, was shaken. There was something wholly disturbing about the ritualistic injuries marking Alfred. He said, "Let's look about the field carefully, Wulfstan. There may be clues to be found as to who is responsible for this wicked act."

Fara remained beside the body, shivering in the cold as the men hunted in the nearby grasses. But their search turned up nothing, and Bosa soon returned with the litter. Alfred, now wrapped in Godwin's cape, was solemnly raised between the men and carried from the meadow. In the tangle of crushed grasses and weeds where the body had lain, Fara noticed a little patch of newly sprouted betony, white-green and twisted in a futile effort to grow beneath the pressing weight. As she stooped to pick up Gwyn's basket, she plucked some of the fleshy stems, wondering what evil had befallen the boy. A bane so powerful, she reflected with a shudder, that even betony could not guard against it. She hurried to catch up to the litter.

Alfred was carried in slow procession to the priory church of St. Andrew. Across the Market Square they went, where more people were about now, opening shops and setting up stalls in preparation for the weekly market. Heads turned to stare at the small shrouded body, and a cluster of curious townsfolk soon gathered to trail the solemn bearers up Gate Street, along the priory's precinct wall to its gate-house. The inquisitive were stopped there, though, for Brother Michael was instructed by Godwin to keep them at bay. The thwarted onlookers shouted questions to the bailiff as he, Fara, and the deputies passed through the gates with their burden into the courtyard beyond.

Several canons awaited, alerted by Bosa, and they hastily led the party to St. Etheldreda's Chapel in the north transept of the cathedral. Godwin instructed them to prepare Alfred for burial, keeping an eye open for any clues on the body he may have overlooked. "His parents will want to see him," he added. "Tend him well, brothers, that they might remember their son as he was."

Then he set out for the brewery, to tell poor Gamel and Ada that their only child was dead.

Two

Rumor of the murder spread quickly, and an anxious crowd had soon gathered outside the Moot Hall, clamoring for details of the crime. Godwin, just returned from delivering the news to Gamel and Ada, sat inside mulling over what he had learned from the now stricken couple.

He had found them hard at work in the brewery, a roomy shop at the end of Bishop's Road near the East Burn, their source for water. They were tending fires roaring beneath vats of boiling liquid, with casks standing ready to receive the freshly brewed ale. The shop was spiced with the heady fragrances of yeast and barley malt, so richly pervasive that Godwin could taste the potent flavors in the air, every breath an ethereal sip of ale.

As they led him to a pleasant nook in the corner of the brewery, Godwin dreaded more than anything the next few minutes. It had been made into a cozy sanctuary, this corner, out of the way of the large vats that occupied the rest of the shop. The family clearly spent a great deal of time here while they waited for their ale to brew, for Ada's spinning wheel was nearby, and benches with brightly covered cushions were arranged around a low table.

They would not believe him at first, for they thought their son in Corbridge, a small town just across the river and to the east. As a special treat, they had granted Alfred's wish to spend the Easter Festival with some kin in the nearby town. Arrangements had been made for him to travel the short distance with a group of pilgrims on their way to the Holy Island. He was to meet them on the morning of Good Friday at the vintner's shop, where the party would be refilling flasks before resuming their journey north. Alfred left, they told the bailiff, shortly before the hour of Tierce.

Godwin told them, as gently as he could, how Alfred had been murdered, where he had been found.

The couple sat stunned, unable to take in the words.

"Ada," Godwin said gently, "can you tell me how Alfred was dressed? Did he carry anything?"

The question seemed to bring the truth home, and Godwin watched as anguish replaced disbelief on their faces. Ada, a tall woman with great muscles in her arms from hauling the huge cauldrons of their trade, was suddenly diminished, pared down by overwhelming sorrow. Her jovial face became pinched and pale. Gamel, not as large as his wife, though her equal in strength, with plump cheeks permanently ruddied from a lifetime of ale sampling, stared at Godwin through dazed, bewildered eyes.

Slowly, big tears rolled down Ada's face as she answered Godwin. "He was dressed for the cold in a heavy cloak. He carried nothing save a few pennies for his journey."

"I found no cloak, nor any coin," Godwin said.

"Could one of these pilgrims have robbed and killed our boy, lord?" Gamel asked, a small spark lighting his dull eyes.

"Nothing is known for certain," Godwin said, seeing an avenging fire beginning to smolder in Gamel. "But you can be sure I'll not rest until I find who is responsible."

Once back in the Moot Hall, Wulfstan was dispatched to the wine shop with instructions to find out from the vintner whether the boy had arrived for his rendezvous on Good Friday. Then Godwin hastily scrawled a note to the archbishop, describing the murder. "Go to Dilston Hall and alert my household knights," he instructed Bosa and Eilaf. "Give this to Osbern," he said, handing the folded parchment to his deputy. "Tell him to deliver it to the archbishop in York. He's to leave immediately. Then have Chadd gather all the knights, even those on their lands. They're to start searching the woods south of town. We may have a murderer on the loose."

Altogether, he had seventeen men in his service, including Wulfstan and Bosa. Ten belonged to his household retinue. Young and unmarried, as was Wulfstan, they served in exchange for training, and bread and board at Dilston Hall, Godwin's primary estate and patrimony. He was tenurial lord to the other seven, his knightly tenants whose ancestors had been granted lands in exchange for military service and other obligations to the Lords of Dilston Hall. Settled men these, with fields to till and children to rear. Some, like Bosa's father, had already passed the inheritance on to the eldest son.

Godwin himself had come to his inheritance young. He was only two years old when his father died at sea in a shipwreck crossing the Channel. A generation tragically lost, for the ship had been ferrying the finest of young northern lords and knights, hastening to the Aquitaine at King Henry II's summons. Hostilities had flared once again between the English and French kings, prompting each to call up their army of vassal knights and mercenaries. All converged at Châteauroux, yet war did not follow. A truce was won instead, and Godwin often pondered the meaning of the loss of those men, dutifully bound for a battle that never took place.

His mother was left to rear two children alone, for she refused to remarry, and though Godwin spent his childhood years at her side, he was placed in the wardship of his uncle, a powerful lord with one foot planted firmly in the Scottish royal court, the other in England's. Earl Patric saw to it that Godwin's lands and properties were properly managed, and upon his nephew's majority, at age twenty-one, had received his pledge of homage and service, girding him with sword and handing over his patrimony, including Dilston Hall.

Once called Devil's Stone for reasons no one could recall, it was a goodly place for a child to grow up—an open, sprawling settlement, not heavily fortified as some. On a rich plain east of Hexham, the manor house sits happily ensconced, attended by its barns and bakehouses, stables, smithy and workshops. Clustered about these are crofts of tenants and servants, a tiny church, more cow-sheds and a mill. Yes, he remembered, smiling fondly, an agreeable place for a young boy to grow up, to find adventure with a younger sister in tow . . .

Nephew and deputy hurried to the door now, and Godwin marveled at the marked contrast between them, like David and Goliath. As they opened the door, he called, "Once you've summoned the knights, come back to the Moot Hall straightaway. I may have other tasks for you." He did not mention that he wanted neither straying near the shire's woods, possibly at risk from a roving killer. Though he had no information yet pointing one way or another, Godwin was beginning to feel certain that their murderer was a stranger, an outlaw perhaps, hiding in the nearby forests. No one in Hexham, to his mind, was capable of so vicious a murder.

When they had gone, Godwin sat alone, pondering what he ought to do next. But outside in the square he could hear the crowd growing larger, the rising pitch in voices now edged with fear and excitement as people fed on each other's agitation. He had better start by calming his folk, he realized, and hastened outside to address them.

The nervous talk did not abate when he emerged, however, even when he mounted the large block of stone that served as a platform for addressing town assemblies. So ancient was the huge chunk of rock that it held two worn depressions on its smooth surface where countless men had stood atop, feet braced firmly apart to speak, or to preach, to warn, or to incite the people of Hexham. When he slipped his feet into the grooves, Godwin always felt a powerful sense of history. He wondered how he measured against all those who had stood there before him.

He waited, gazing at the townsfolk, once again finding it impossible to imagine one was responsible for Alfred's death. He knew them all well, and like any, each had their foibles, yet he could not find Alfred's murderer in the faces gathered before him.

His gaze shifted to the priory at the far end of the Market Square. From his vantage point, he could see beyond the high stone wall that cloistered church, monastic buildings, and ample grounds from the world; for though St. Andrews sat firmly anchored almost in the center of town, one had to travel up Gate Street, bearing northwesterly toward the river, to seek admittance to its grounds and buildings through the stalwart priory gatehouse.

The throng was getting larger with each passing minute as more and more wandered over to investigate the commotion, much larger and more animated than a typical Market Day crowd. Curiosity marked otherwise slack faces, and many looked around blankly, ignorant of why they had come. Those who joined the rear craned their necks and stood on tiptoe, trying to locate the object of everyone's attention. Others who were better informed filled in the less knowledgeable, and Godwin heard snippets of conversations, most of them inaccurate. As he continued to gaze, the crowd finally grew quiet, turning to stare expectantly at their bailiff.

"As many of you have already learned," he called out, "Gamel and Ada's boy Alfred has been slain."

But before Godwin could say more, a voice shouted, "Tell us, lord. Is it true the lad was murdered on Good Friday?"

The question sent a ripple of astonishment through the crowd, and people turned to stare at their neighbors in open-mouthed horror. *On Good Friday?* they exclaimed at once. Nay what! It couldn't be true! they said, shaking their heads in vehement denial.

The murder of an innocent child on one of the most holy days of the year was inconceivable to many in its wickedness. Such a damning act was beyond even the most evil of men. What then? they wondered fearfully. Was something more sinister at work?

The buzzing of anxious speculation continued to grow, and many crossed themselves as a fearful dread began to grip them like a tightening noose. Godwin heard the words *demon* and *Satan* murmured fearfully and struggled to control his impatience with such nonsense.

Why must it be demons? Did they not know that men are behind the worst crimes? Perhaps not, he supposed. These people had little knowledge, by and large, of the violent acts of men Godwin had witnessed in his lifetime. Most here knew little of war. The battles between King John and his northern barons had centered around castle strongholds, not towns like Hexham, and the devastating Scottish raids were distant memories for most. Calamity and hardship they knew, to be sure. These came in the form of disease, the failure of vital crops, the sudden unexplained death of a loved one—disasters sometimes hard to account for. But explain them they must, for people always need answers, something or someone to blame. Demons are handy that way, ready and ever-present foes. Yes, Godwin could understand, after all, their impulse to employ them now. Many could not imagine a man behind the deed, so it must be an evil spirit.

"Calm yourselves," he called out, his deep voice ringing over the mob, checking the rising tide of hysteria. "Make no mistake, those who would do evil care not what day of the week it is." When they had quieted once more, he said, "A search of the nearby woods is being conducted, for it may be that our man is a felon from other parts, hiding out in the forest." He looked around, seeing shocked faces, but was satisfied to see relieved ones as well. A mere mortal, though a vicious killer, they could contend with. Demons were something altogether different. "I myself will be coming around to speak with any who saw young Alfred near the time of his death. If there are any among you who saw the boy late last week, or have *any* knowledge of his last whereabouts, please make yourselves known to me.

"As for the rest of you, keep a close watch on your children, and report anything unusual immediately. That is all I can tell you now. Please, go back to your shops and stalls so that I can get on with finding the murderer."

"But lord," shouted another as Godwin was turning to step down from his stone perch. "What if the guilty one is among us, 'ere in town? With all yer men beatin' the woods, the evildoer might git away clean."

A murmur of agreement rustled through the gathering. Heads nodded and turned again to look at the Bailiff, awaiting his reply.

Godwin recognized the voice as that of Sigfrid. For reasons unclear to the Bailiff, the man often felt it necessary to offer advice on the administration of justice in Hexham.

"What you say may be true, but an outlaw hiding in the forest is more likely, and I have only a limited number of men at my disposal. They will search the forest first. I've sent word to the archbishop, informing him of the murder. Given its seriousness, he may see fit to send some of his retinue to aid us in our search."

"We 'avn't any need fer those blokes comin' 'ere, tendin' our business," called a surly voice from the rear. "We kin help ouselves!" it angrily declared. "Why don' ye draft sum of us into yer service, Lord Godwin? If the guilty chap's hidin' in town, we'll fetch 'im out." The voice had a nasty edge to it.

The last thing Godwin needed was an angry mob tearing through the town on a rampage. It had probably been unwise to mention the archbishop, he realized, for the speaker was voicing a sentiment many in Hexham shared. The townspeople cared little for their overlord. As a "foreigner," he was automatically suspect, though it was his repressive policies that fixed him permanently as an odious foe, forever thwarting their attempts at self-government. Everywhere towns and burgesses were gaining autonomy and independence, bargaining for the right to appoint their own officials, to hold their own court and collect taxes. The archbishop and other ecclesiastical lords, however, tended to be conservative with respect to such matters, unwilling to relinquish one jot of their jealously guarded power.

Godwin was sympathetic, understanding their frustration, yet Walter de Grey was his feudal lord; he had knelt before him, placing his hands between the archbishop's, swearing fealty. "It may come to that, indeed," answered Godwin. "But mind how you speak of the lord archbishop," he warned, searching for the owner of the hostile voice, finding Grendel, a sullen man and chronic naysayer. "I, too, am his man, and justice in Hexham is his concern by ancient right, as well you know, Grendel. This is his liberty and he keeps the law here. There are good men in his service who know their business, and we should be grateful for any help they might offer."

It was clear from the grumbling in the crowd that not all agreed, but finally people began to disperse, though reluctantly. Godwin waited to see if any would come forward with information, but apparently no one here had seen Alfred late in the week. It was not surprising, really, for Holy Week was a hectic time with much coming and going. A small boy would be easily overlooked.

Godwin returned briefly to the Hall before leaving for the vintner's shop to meet Wulfstan. The writs from the archbishop's court were unceremoniously dumped into a large wooden chest. Such trivial matters would have to wait, he thought, securing the trunk with a heavy padlock. Godwin supposed that when the archbishop learned that a child had been murdered in his liberty, he would be outraged, but probably not surprised. For it was well known that he considered all who dwelled in the northern provinces, excepting his noble brethren, Saxon barbarians and Scottish savages. The archbishop hated the wilds of Northumbria and considered Yorkshire only slightly more civilized, due to its proximity to the cosmopolitan south. He preferred to spend his time at the royal court in Westminster, hobnobbing with other magnates as they jockeyed for power, these days dispensed by the three regents who ruled in young King Henry's name. The archbishop was usually content to have his extensive holdings in the north governed by an extremely competent and exacting staff.

Certainly most in the north were of Saxon and Scottish descent, for blood mingled on the Marches. Welshmen, even Norsemen, were represented, too, but Godwin knew that the independent spirit that existed there, that set itself apart from the English who dwelled in the south, had less to do with tribal bloodlines, and more with a tumultuous history.

William the Conqueror successfully subdued the south in 1066, but when he bent his will to the conquest of the north, he met resistance unlike any he had yet encountered. Control was finally achieved by ousting the natives from their powerful positions as overlords; Saxon barons and Scottish magnates had been murdered and in their place came Norman lords. These men quickly took the daughters of native nobles as wives to legitimize and solidify their power. Over time, though, these *novi homines* became indistinguishable from their Saxon and Scottish predecessors, transferring their loyalty from a Norman king far away in the south to the land itself.

With the coming of the Angevins in the person of Henry II, followed by his sons, little changed, initially, for the northerners. Barons continued to exercise wide powers, essentially independent so long as they mouthed fealty to the southern king. The frontier counties were too large and distant to control from the south; the best any king could do was sway the balance of power, trying to keep it in his favor.

The situation changed drastically, however, when the despised John came to the throne. It was he who tried to integrate north with south, to check the power and wealth of the barons and seize it for himself. John was the first king to travel in the border counties on a regular basis. Even Richard the Lion-Hearted had gone no farther than Sherwood. And everywhere John went, he forced lords to pay for grants confirming their rights and privileges. A "greedy bloodsucker" is how he came to be described by northerners, a perception locally confirmed when once he visited Corbridge and hearing the age-old tale of Roman treasure buried there, made any who could hold a shovel dig until the place was riddled with holes, like a giant rabbit warren. But nothing was unearthed save a deep loathing for the king.

John, Godwin knew, was the root cause of the antagonism and suspicion his people felt for the king of England and those loyal to him. On a very local level, especially among the townsfolk and farmers who rarely traveled beyond their shire, this wariness extended to anyone dwelling in the south, often described as "foreigners." Thus, it chafed many in Hexhamshire that their overlord, the archbishop of York, was not native, but one such "foreigner" appointed by the king.

There was a time, Godwin recalled, when sentiments like these embarrassed him, thinking they arose from ignorance. As a warrior he had traveled widely—to Normandy and France, Italy and Spain, and finally, by way of crusade, east to Egypt. But what he had witnessed in distant lands, the wars waged, the battles fought, almost made him envy the simple ways of his fellow northerners. Besides, was it ignorance they displayed, or innocence? Was there even a distinction between the two? Were they not more content in their lives, he wondered; for his own knowledge of a wider world seemed not to benefit him or anyone, and only served to induce despair if he dwelled overmuch in his memories.

Nor were the locals far off the mark in their assessment of the archbishop, and Godwin wondered again how his lord would react to the news of Alfred's murder. He was a volatile and unpredictable man. He and his agents might pay it little mind. They were occupied with important matters just now. Hubert de Burgh, the regent who presided over the judicial arm of royal government, had come north to Yorkshire with the archbishop in preparation for a great council to be convened at York. The north had been chosen to make a political point: to show the unruly inhabitants that despite the fact that a mere boy was England's king and that three men vied for power in his stead, central authority would not succumb to the competing forces of regional magnates and petty local lords.

On the other hand, the archbishop might be so outraged by a murder within his own franchise that he would be compelled to take a personal interest in bringing the guilty to justice. Godwin shrugged off such thoughts, however, for it was impossible to predict the actions of his lord, and they would make little difference to him in any event. What mattered was that he act swiftly, before the trail to the murderer grew cold. He surveyed the table for any stray documents, then rose to leave for the vintner's shop.

As he stepped outside, he heard the bell pealing. Strange, he thought, for it was past the time for Tierce and too early for None. He debated investigating, then saw Fara hurrying toward the Hall. She had been assisting the canons with Alfred's body, and her exhausted appearance told Godwin it had been a trying task. Her pretty face was haggard, her tiny frame hunched, shoulders folded in, as if shielding against a shower of unseen blows. Wayward strands of long hair the color of ripening wheat, always neatly plaited, hung limp about her shoulders.

Godwin led her inside the Moot Hall to a bench. "Fara, you should take some rest. Let me see you home."

"I'll be fine, lord," she said, her voice low and hoarse with strain.

Sensing she had something to report, Godwin waited patiently.

"I only need a moment . . ." Her voice trailed off. "I can't seem to break free of the sight . . . the way he was murdered . . . it's so evil." She trembled and clutched at her fleece-lined cloak, pulling it closer to her body.

Godwin placed a hand on her shoulder. "You should be at home, Fara, with your children." When she remained seated, he asked, "Is there something more you want to tell me? Did you or the canons notice any-thing as the body was tended?"

"No," she said, voice barely a whisper. Then more clearly, "There was nothing more to be learned. You saw his . . . wounds. And the canons agree that he's been dead for several days."

Godwin told her about his meeting with Gamel and Ada, about Alfred's plans to travel to Corbridge. "They saw him last on Good Friday. I don't know yet whether he ever left Hexham."

She looked up suddenly. "If he did not, would that not mean someone in town murdered him?" She jumped from her chair, starting like a frightened animal, as if she might bolt home to her young that instant.

"It could mean a number of things, Fara," Godwin tried to assure her. "Remember, last week was Holy Week. Many were in Hexham from abroad."

"Yes, Holy Week," she murmured softly, returning to her chair. After a moment, she said, "He must have been killed elsewhere, lord, and only put in the field last night or early this morning. Easter Week is a busy time with folk coming and going through the pastures. Surely, if poor Alfred has been a-lying in that field since Good Friday, someone would have stumbled on him."

Godwin nodded. He had been wondering about this same thing, though the body might have been simply overlooked. Alfred was small, and much can be missed when the route is known, for thoughts wander when one is freed from the burden of minding the way. And the weather had been unusually cold; no one would have tarried long in the open field. Besides, Alfred had not been lying near one of the towpaths, and the weeds had partially hidden him.

Fara was staring down at her lap again, fidgeting with the long end of the leather belt that cinched her gown at the waist. Something else was troubling her, he knew. She looked up at Godwin, fear in her eyes, saying, "My lord, an innocent child was killed on Good Friday, the day of our Lord's crucifixion. He was stabbed in the left side and strangled, crucified one could say. His hands were pierced clean through. It's as if he was killed after the manner of Christ. This is no ordinary murder, if ever there was such a thing. The canons were very distressed. They whispered among themselves as I helped cleanse the body. Now they ring the church bell to ward off demons. Something evil is come to Hexham, Lord Godwin. I feel it, and it frightens me."

"Yes, Fara, the murder has been made to look as you describe, and I cannot yet say what this means, but I will find out. I promise you. In the meantime, do not be too quick to judge the meaning of events before we have all the facts. Now come, let me see you home."

He guided a weary Fara back to her home at the east end of town. There they found Gwyn, quiet and subdued, taking care of her brother. As she buried her face in her mother's skirts, Godwin wondered, as a healer, how many more deaths she would see in her lifetime. Never another like Alfred's, he hoped, then quietly took his leave to set out for the vintner's shop on Haugh Lane.

Crossing the Market Square once again, he headed up Gate Street, turning right opposite the gatehouse to plunge down a steeply descending lane called the Shambles. A dark place, for the upper stories of the decrepit houses and shops jutted out over their ground floors so that facing buildings almost met over the narrow street, creating a cave-like atmosphere. It was a rather poor neighborhood, most of the homes belonging to the priory, which let them cheap to unfortunates who barely earned enough to live on.

Reaching the end of the street, Godwin angled left onto Haugh Lane, a wider avenue running parallel to Gate Street above. Flanking a pleasant stretch of riverside meadow, prone to flooding in winter and spring, Godwin enjoyed this particular walk, for here, away from the busy, hive-like center of town, it was quiet, the pace more leisurely. Although Haugh would take a traveler to the town's only river crossing at High Ford, most preferred the more convenient Gate Street, becoming Gilesgate as it passed the hospital, to reach the crossing, for the higher road wound easily down to the river, crossing Haugh just before the bridge.

Heading briskly for the vintner's, Godwin glanced to his left, admiring how the town perched graciously above the river Tyne. Through gently undulating hills that bound the waterway within its valley, the approach to Hexham from the vale was made by climbing to the natural terrace upon which it sat overlooking the river and slopes of pasturage and farmland dotted with tofts and livestock. Some twenty leagues upriver from Newcastle and the furious commercial bustle of that seaport city, the town was fairly prosperous, but small in scale compared to the larger centers of trade and industry that lay on the coast and to the south. To the north and east loftier hills rose, accommodating vast forested lands of oak, hazel, and rowan with their undergrowth of holly and yew, Godwin's favorite hunting grounds.

Hexham itself was dominated by its magnificent cathedral, the priory church of St. Andrews. Built centuries ago by the great Wilfrid, it was one of many this saint-bishop constructed in the north. In those far-off days, Hexham's cathedral was considered the most glorious west of the Alps, though now it stood in a rather dilapidated state. Its former grandeur could not be denied, however, for it was reflected in its very bones, no matter how weathered they had become. Pilgrims still marveled from afar at its majestic beauty, just as they did centuries ago, but few veered off the north-south road, as they once did, to pay it closer homage. The holy relics brought from Rome by St. Wilfrid, to be enshrined in the crypt, were largely forgotten now, even among the local population. No longer did these saints make their presence known through miracles, attracting Christians from afar, and few could even recall the names of those once powerful intercessors. Even the cathedral's most prized relic, the arm of Wilfrid, suitably encased in a bejeweled reliquary, drew little attention or fuss.

The church had long been stripped of its designation as a cathedral as well. Augustinian canons, fondly called Austin canons, were housed at St. Andrews— men who followed a monastic rule not unlike the Benedictine, with an emphasis on community service instead of withdrawal and ceaseless, solitary prayer.

Godwin smiled wryly. Hexham's canons took "less strict" to new heights, or lows, depending on one's view. Monastic standards vary tremendously, of course, but by any measure these canons were quite lacking in religious devotion, being rather fond of food and drink, women and song. Most hailed from local families and, more often than not, had joined the monastery for reasons of convenience rather than having been stirred by a religious calling. The daily offices were rarely attended; for while the priory bell faithfully announced each of the seven monastic hours, the brethren were rarely chastened to bestir themselves from slumber or mealtime.

They were a merry, kindly lot, though, and generally well liked. The priory served as the town's parish church, and no one was offended by the lax brothers, especially those burgesses in the victualing trades. They always gave a good Mass and all rituals and sacraments were strictly observed, the sermons brief. The canons also dealt fairly with the citizens, buying and selling locally, while rents on the priory's vast holdings were very reasonable. All made for an easygoing relationship between town and church.

To the chagrin of the canons, however, their relaxed way of life was fast becoming a thing of the past, for all was now in turmoil at St. Andrews. The archbishop had recently installed a new prior, Archil Morel, who had been instructed to reimpose discipline and bring the dissolute flock back into line. Morel was bending his reputably considerable will to accomplish his assigned task, and Godwin had heard that the canons were quite miserable. Shaking his head and smiling again, he felt only a little sympathy for the canons.

He was getting nearer the vintner's shop now and could see Wulfstan striding purposefully toward him.

"My lord," reported his deputy, "the vintner never saw the lad on Friday, nor did any of the neighbors I've spoken with."

Godwin thought for a moment, then said, "It's likely Alfred never left Hexham, but we must be sure. It might be that a small boy amongst a large company was overlooked by the vintner, or that Alfred arrived late and set out alone. Fetch your horse, Wulfstan, and ride over to Corbridge. See what you can learn about this party of pilgrims. They're sure to be long gone, but find out where they lodged and whether they arrived with a small boy in tow.

"Find Alfred's kin," he went on. "See what they know. And ask after any strangers who arrived around the time Alfred was due. If the boy decided to make the journey alone, he could have met up with a thief. His father gave him a few pennies for the journey. Perhaps he was murdered for these and the cloak he wore, for it is missing as well, then the body gotten rid of in the meadow."

Godwin did not voice the objection his scenario

immediately raised: If Alfred had been murdered on Good Friday somewhere on the road to Corbridge, why had his body been taken to the fields south of town? Why not leave it in the dense woods bordering the road and river?

"I'll leave straightaway, lord," Wulfstan said, meeting Godwin's eye. "If anyone in Corbridge has knowledge of Alfred, I'll find it out, you can be sure of it." The deputy's lips curled to reveal pointed canines.

"Wulfstan," Godwin said sharply. "Mind your manners. I want no rough stuff this time. You're to gather information, not round up suspects. If someone seems suspicious, alert the sheriff and send for me. Apprehend only if you must, but no summary justice this time. Understood?"

Wulfstan gave him a curt nod then strode off stiffly, hauberk chinking. Godwin watched him march off toward the stables, thinking how his deputy was never without his knightly garb. Being a small man and acutely aware of his diminutive physique, Godwin suspected he donned the leather padding and cumbersome chains to enhance his slender frame, to beef up narrow shoulders. Even during the hottest days of summer, Wulfstan could be seen trudging about town covered head to toe in mail, sweating profusely beneath his helm.

Yet, unlike gentle-hearted Bosa, Wulfstan made a very effective deputy, so long as Godwin kept him on a short leash. Despite his small stature, he had a threatening quality that cowed most everyone. Hard-bitten and cunning, Wulfstan could root out vice like a terrier hunting coney, and like any of that breed, he was fearless, no matter how large the prey. Petty thieves and wrongdoers usually froze in their tracks when they knew he had their scent. A mere scowl and snarl compelled most to make a full confession.

Staring thoughtfully at Wulfstan's retreating figure,

Godwin considered the bizarre circumstances of Alfred's murder. He was very troubled, for while he was drawn to the notion that a wandering outlaw was responsible, he knew it was unlikely that a common robber would kill in the fashion Alfred was slain. And this, of course, was the most puzzling aspect of the crime: the ritual-like slaying of the boy. Why would someone murder a child that way? It had to be the act of a person gone mad, a lunatic loose in the country-side. He could think of no other explanation.

Yet news of such a person roving about would likely spread quickly, and Godwin had heard no reports. Still, if a madman was hiding in the forests, he could remain concealed for some time, in which case, his men might have a chance of making a capture.

Or was the murder made to look like a ritual slaying to confuse, to throw the law off the murderer's tracks by making it appear as something other than a common killing? This seemed closer to the truth, for he refused to consider the other possibilities still being floated by some townsfolk: that the murder was an act of God meant to punish Christians for some as yet unknown transgression; or it was the work of demons. Godwin was convinced that when the murderer was found and the motive uncovered, the hand of man, albeit likely a madman, would be revealed, not God's.

He resumed his course for the wine shop. He would start with the vintner, then work his way back toward the brewery in hopes of finding someone who had seen Alfred on Good Friday. If he could mark the location where the boy was last seen, perhaps he could uncover a clue that would point him in the right direction.

Worry clutched at him. Did he truly know the best way to proceed? He had no experience with a murder like this. What if he had already missed something vital, something that had allowed the murderer to escape? He tried to push the doubts from his mind, for they did him no good, and concentrate instead on different courses of action. Once he had questioned the residents here, he would check with Hexham's two inns and the priory to find if anyone suspicious had arrived in town last week, especially toward the latter end. For if Wulfstan confirmed that Alfred never left town, then it meant the murderer had come to Hexham.

Running down every stranger, however, might prove difficult as events that accompany Holy Week attract people from all over the countryside. Passion plays, holy processions, and festive rituals are a welcome break from the usual toil that subsistence in the countryside requires, and few miss out on the festivities. Merchants from all over come as well, plying their wares, trading trinkets. No, it wouldn't be easy, Godwin realized, but not impossible either. Hexham is small enough that all are well known and new arrivals, aside from peddlers, are usually someone's kin visiting from abroad. A stranger would have a difficult time simply blending in with the locals.

The vintner, Ranulf, a man with fair looks to match an agreeable disposition, had little to add to the statement already given to Wulfstan. He never saw Alfred amongst the party of pilgrims on the morning of Good Friday.

"Yes, it's *possible* I overlooked the lad," he said in reply to Godwin's question. "They were a lively bunch, my lord, some ten or twelve pilgrims, and more interested in merrymaking and seeing the sights than pious devotion, if you know what I mean. But no harm in that, after all, and they seemed like good folk. Ordered Gascon wine and paid in honest silver."

Godwin thanked the vintner, then questioned the other residents and shopkeepers who dwelled on Haugh, working his way back toward the square. But he could find no one who had seen Alfred come this way on Good Friday.

Then, just as he was beginning to think that he should go back and start at the brewery, the boy's point of departure, he arrived at Master Swynburn's, a weaver who worked a goodly shop situated on the corner of Haugh and the Shambles. Here the bailiff finally found his first witness.

The weaver had not gathered with the mob outside the Moot Hall. He rarely left his looms while they were in operation, though a sketchy account of the murder had reached his ears. He had not learned the victim's name, however, and was shocked and dismayed to hear it was Alfred. When he realized he had important information for Godwin, he screwed up his pudgy face, and put forth a concentrated effort to dredge forth every memory of the morning in question.

Godwin was pleased in his witness, for he knew the weaver to be a shrewd and observant man, though prone to gossip. He was short, thickly made, with sharp eyes that constantly cast about, roaming and surveying, missing little and storing much for future tavern talk and street-side chats.

"Yes, yes, my lord, I did see little Alfred come this way," he said after expressing his sorrow. He gripped a straw broom as he spoke and began pecking at debris on his doorstep, twitching it into the lane.

Conversation and physical activity were oddly connected in Master Swynburn; one stimulated the other in a kind of nervous accompaniment.

"About the hour of Tierce it was . . . I remember hearing the priory bell. I'd gone out to see a party of travelers, pilgrims they called themselves, on their way to Lindisfarne. They asked me directions to the vintner and I pointed the way. I was hurrying back inside my shop." Now the broom attacked some cobwebs sticking in the corners of his thickly paned windows. "You know how it is, my lord . . . these apprentices . . . any chance they have to slack off, they grab it! I must keep a constant eye out!" he cried. "It was Good Friday—we ought not to have been laboring, but work's backed up and must get done somehow!" Cobwebs under the eaves were now his target. "Business is good, you know. Too good I sometimes think—"

"Where did you see Alfred?" cut in Godwin, knowing the weaver could digress to eternity.

"Well, as I said, the pilgrims had just passed by. When I turned to go inside, I saw someone coming down the Shambles." A rag was plucked from a pocket in his leather apron and set to vigorously polishing the panes of glass. Then he stepped back to proudly admire the luster, for glass was a luxury many could not afford; most made do with oiled parchment or cloth.

"It was Alfred, I'm sure of it. Seen him the day before, too, on Thursday. Sent by one of the canons he was, Brother Mark, I think, to fetch an altar cloth— work I did for the priory. Fine piece of weaving it was, I might add. The boy did a fair amount of errands for the priory, especially for that knight, the one lately come to Hexham, the priory's new tenant."

"Did you speak to the boy?" asked Godwin.

"No . . . he was far an' away up the lane, as I recall, and I had business to attend. Can't spend the day gossiping in the street, you know. He gave me a wave and I hailed him back, then I went inside my shop."

"Did you see him pass by?"

The weaver thought for a moment, leaning on his broom in an exceptional moment of repose. "No . . . I never saw him pass. As I recall, that was about the time a spindle broke on one of the looms, young Nob's. The boy is always daydreaming when he should be minding his work. Well, seeing to that took a bit of time. It was a while before I had a chance to go outside again. As I was saying, I can't turn my back on matters, even for a moment—"

"Thank you, Master Swynburn," Godwin interrupted

again. "You've been very helpful. If anything else should come to mind, you know where to find me."

Godwin turned up the Shambles to resume his door-to-door inquiries, but could find no one else who had seen Alfred on the morning of Good Friday. Back on Gate Street, he went over to speak with Brother Michael, keeper of St. Andrew's gatehouse. The road widened to form a small square or courtyard before the impressive passageway with its vaulted entrance, high and wide enough to allow heavily laden carts to pass beyond the iron gates, through the double arches. Godwin approached the canon, for the second time that day, asking after any visitors who may have arrived late last week for a stay in the priory's guest lodgings.

He often wondered if Brother Michael ever left his little stone abode adjacent to the gates, for it was a rare occasion to approach the priory and not find the canon's kindly, welcoming smile. He had arrived at St. Andrews as a child, an oblate given over to the monastery by his poor widowed mother. Well past middle age now, he had seen priors and canons come and go, yet he stayed on, content in his fate and faith. The lodging was equipped to his satisfaction with cot, small hearth, and numerous jars storing his favorite victuals. One usually found him either sleeping or supping, but he minded not interruptions, always welcoming chats with visitors and news from abroad.

"No, my lord, we were full up early on," he answered Godwin, after washing down his last morsel of bread with a liberal draught of wine. "Most arrived on Palm Sunday, before the procession of the blessed sacrament. We squeezed in a few more on Monday, but after that, latecomers were sent to the inns."

"Can you recall any stranger in search of lodging that you had to turn away? Perhaps someone a bit out of the ordinary?" asked Godwin.

Brother Michael pursed his lips and furrowed his

bushy brows. "Well, my lord, there was a great deal of coming and going, right up to the Compline bell on Skyre Thursday. Many come to see the washing of the feet, as you know, and the courtyard was packed with worshipers trying to make their way into the church. Still, I don't recall any strangers. Been at this post for many a year, have I. There's few faces in the shire I don't recognize."

Godwin asked, "Tell me of Alfred, Brother. Master Swynburn says he did errands for the priory, and I believe he came this way on Good Friday. Did you see him?"

"Oh, I couldn't say for certain, Lord Godwin. It was sore hectic last week, and Alfred came and went often. He worked mostly for our new corrodian, Sir Havelok." Brother Michael fidgeted with the braided rope that circled his wide girth, then lowered his voice, saying, "The knight worked the boy hard. Paid him a pittance, too. And what an ill-tempered man to labor for! Many a time poor Alfred had to dodge his fist, and when we brothers tried to intervene, he'd turn on us, too!"

Godwin waited, for it was clear that the indignant canon had more to report on Sir Havelok. Brother Michael did not disappoint, saying, "Why, not long ago, Havelok took after Brother Mark! The poor canon ran for the church, believing its sanctity would never be violated. But the knight followed him right in! Around and around the baptismal font they went with Havelok waving his sword, ranting about his honor!" Brother Michael's face was pink with outrage, recalling the scandalous event. "Lucky for Brother Mark the knight grew weary of the chase!" He snorted, saying, "Calls himself a Christian soldier, one of Christ's warriors, but naught in his actions says it's so, save that he spends much time in the church praying. Bent as a sickle, is he. Taken one too many blows from a lance, I'd say.

"Anyhow, Lord Godwin," he finished, "you might speak with the knight concerning Alfred. He's sure to have been among the last to see the boy alive."

"Indeed I will, Brother," said Godwin. "But do this for me also: ask among the canons whether they remember someone seeming out of the ordinary late last week, and send word if any can recall such."

"I'll do that, my lord," he assured Godwin, his face puckering with distress. "It's an evil business, this murder. The brothers are quite upset. They'll be glad to help in any way they can." Brother Michael lowered his voice again, leaning forward. "My lord, there are many here saying it's the work of demons, or those under their influence. I don't know what to think myself. I've never seen an evil spirit. Why would one take after young Alfred?"

Godwin heaved a sigh. It seemed the whole town was convinced that dark forces were at work in Hexham. "I've yet to see one myself, Brother, save those that take the shape of men."

With that, Godwin left the good brother to call on Hexham's two inns, both located on Gate Street. But neither innkeeper could recall a guest who appeared suspicious or unusual, yet there were many people about and much work to be done. Both inns were filled to the rafters by Tuesday night and even storerooms had been converted into makeshift accommodations.

Growing weary, Godwin returned to the Moot Hall to see if any messages awaited, noticing as he entered the square that the Monday Market had been abandoned. Only a few people remained, exchanging gossip and rumors instead of wares. Normally humming with brisk trading and activity, the empty square made him unaccountably uneasy. Then he chastised himself. Is this not what he had ordered, that the townspeople return to their homes and shops? Market Day had been given up, no doubt, out of respect for Alfred's death.

He was surprised to find that Bosa and Eilaf had not yet returned to the Moot Hall—another cause for worry. He stood debating whether to go to look for them, or continue questioning the townspeople.

But there was no need, for just then, the door burst open, the second time that day. Godwin spun around to see Bosa bounding in, wide-eyed and frantic, filling the room with his giant presence. Eilaf followed closely, a dwarf in his counterpart's great shadow.

"My lord," his deputy cried, "they have them! They have Alfred's murderers! The townspeople have captured them! They're in the Keep! You must come!"

"Who, Bosa? Who's in the Keep?"

"The Jews, my lord! The Jews of Hexham!"

THREE ✟

Ivetta led the chain of frightened women and children down Hawk's Lane toward the Market Square. As they frantically fled the Keep, the sound of a jeering mob followed, chased them along the narrow lane to echo off the houses lining it. For one terrifying moment, Ivetta feared the townspeople were after them once more, had them cornered in the tight quarters of the southern end of town. But no, she realized, with a feeling of relief that hit her like a drenching wave, the clamor was lessening as they gained some distance from the Keep.

They had been spared the townsfolk's sudden wrath—for now. The Jewish women and children had been allowed to leave the town prison, unmolested, to return to the homes they had been brutally seized from, along with their menfolk, only a short while ago. A fervent appeal to his fellow citizens, now his abductors, from Ivetta's husband, Jacob, had won their release, and she had wasted no time in gathering them to flee, lest the angry mob abruptly change its collective mind. She had thrust her three-year-old daughter, Florin, into the arms of her stunned mother-in-law, Judith, while pulling her two sons close to hustle them down the

Keep's steep rise. Her sister-in-law, Mirabella, came last, clutching baby Solomon tightly in her arms.

They had stumbled through the parted crowd, past faces Ivetta knew well but hardly recognized, so twisted with hate had they become. Threats and abuses were pelted at them as the women crouched protectively over the children. Once they were clear of the cloven horde, it had fused once more, turning its fury on the Jewish men. Recalling the nightmarish scene brought Ivetta to a sudden halt, and she half-turned, ready to hasten back to the Keep. She could not leave them, could not leave her Jacob. Yet what *could* she do? There was no reasoning with that mob, that flock of horror. She stood in the middle of the road, rooted by panic and indecision as Judith and Mirabella caught up to stand beside her, panting with exertion.

Ivetta knew that she had to get help, had to find the bailiff. She sprinted forward once more. Yes, she thought, get the children to safety and find Lord Godwin. And pray that in the meantime the lives of their men would be protected. Her fear subsided a little, and her rising panic stilled as she fastened all thought and bearing on these present aims, like a floundering survivor in a terrible shipwreck at sea, desperate to reach some floating debris of hope, not thinking beyond the immediate threat of drowning. She would not now contemplate how the Jews of Hexham might be saved from the raging sea they had suddenly been cast into; she would attend to their present peril only, then the next. . . .

But her sister-in-law, cradling the baby, could go no faster, nor could Ivetta's own children. She glanced down at six-year-old Isaac and seven-year-old Aaron. Each were clasping one of her hands in a white-taut grip, eyes wide and staring as they struggled to keep up with their mother. Judith, too, was lagging, struggling under her granddaughter's weight. Ivetta stopped once more and waited for the two women to catch up, crying out when she saw Judith stumble as her legs became tangled in her long woolen skirts. Down she went, falling forward while one hand instinctively reached to cradle Florin's head, the other her back. She saw Judith struggle to keep from landing atop the child, coming down hard and square on her knees. She stayed that way, a slim, graying woman kneeling in the street, as if in prayer, little Florin held tightly in her arms.

Ivetta and Mirabella ran to her. "Mother!" Ivetta cried. "Are you hurt? Can you stand?" The pain must have been excruciating, yet Judith did not utter a sound, only handed the child carefully up to Ivetta before struggling to her feet. They helped her to a low wall enclosing a tiny garden in front of a vacant house. The plot was rank and choked with dead weeds and grasses. There they huddled, while Ivetta glanced nervously about. The streets were eerily quiet now that the turmoil at the Keep was well behind them. She caught sight of shadowed faces here and there, peering from dark windows; those unwilling to involve themselves in the sudden chaos that had descended on their quiet town, like a bolt of lightning hurled from the heavens, aimed at Hexham's tiny Jewish community.

It made no sense, none of it. In the midst of their terrifying seizure, Ivetta had gathered that the brewer's son, Alfred, had been murdered, that the townspeople thought the Jews were responsible. Why would they think we murdered poor Alfred?

The day had started like any other. The children had awakened, as usual, before she and Jacob, creeping to their parents' small bedchamber with the first light, tugging mother and father from sleep. Ivetta had tried to coax them to snuggle under the thick, warm blankets, hoping to win a few more minutes sleep for herself and Jacob. But Isaac, Aaron, and little Florin were wide awake with other plans, and she had sleepily pushed herself from Jacob's side to quickly don a wrap, for the morning air was very cold and gusting mightily outside, forcing its way through every crack and fissure in their timber cottage. Ivetta hastened to rekindle the fire in the hearth.

Water was put on for the morning ablutions, then Ivetta set to work on the first meal of the day. The children recited their morning prayer, washed and dressed, then sat to eat a breakfast of warm porridge. Jacob finally emerged to join them, still sleepy, his dark hair tousled. She remembered how fetching he had looked, wearing only his white shirt and dark woolen breeches. Cold rarely troubled her husband, and he seldom wore a tunic or surcoat in the house.

Yes, it had been a typical morning, pleasantly predictable. After the meal, Jacob had taken Isaac and Aaron to synagogue for their studies. They had only to walk next door, to the home of Jacob's father, Isaac, where an upper chamber in his great stone house had been set aside for communal use by Hexham's extended family of Jews.

When Jacob and the boys had gone, Ivetta spent time playing with Florin before getting on with the daily work. A lively, happy baby, her daughter's features mirrored Ivetta's. Thick black hair crowned a delicate face, framed dark eyes, while petite limbs belied surprising strength.

A short time later, as Ivetta stood sweeping the stoop, she saw Samuel rush by, late for synagogue again. Ivetta had smiled, thinking how unlike the two brothers were. Jacob took his studies very seriously, devoting much of his free time to reading Hebrew scripts and to discussions with his father over points of Jewish law and interpretation. Samuel, though, always looked a bit nonplused by the lively debates that ensued between brother and father, and Ivetta suspected he would much rather be in his shop on these frequent occasions, working with the wares and pawned goods that were sold from the street-level floor of Isaac's house.

Late in the morning, she had stood at the hearth once again, beginning her preparations for the noon dinner. She had been pondering what supplies she needed to purchase from the market. She never went early on Mondays, like most, for she loathed the crowded jostling in the square and shopped for goods instead during the afternoon when the pace was less frantic, though the selection was somewhat poorer.

Then, without warning, the rhythm of daily life had been shattered by an angry mob bursting into her home. Looking crazed and unrecognizable, the townspeople had rushed at her, the obvious object of their wrath. Ivetta quickly snatched up Florin, and the two were roughly driven from the house amidst an angry barrage of accusations and curses.

As she was pushed into the street, Ivetta saw that the men, along with Judith, had already been seized from Isaac's house. They stood surrounded by furious townspeople, and Jacob was shouting something, but Ivetta could not understand his words. She had anxiously looked for Isaac in the throng, for he was old and growing weak, and she feared what this sudden shock might do to him. Then a terrified Mirabella, holding her baby tightly to her breast, came running toward her from the other direction, chased by another knot of angry Christians.

Once the Jews had been forced from their homes, they were driven through the streets of Hexham to the Keep. Ivetta had noticed that Grendel, the town's jack-of-all-trades, seemed to be leading the assault, giving orders and directing others in the seizure of the Jews. The women were not harmed, only hounded relentlessly, but their husbands were kicked and beaten.

Now, standing by the stone wall, Ivetta shook her head, outraged and bewildered. Bitter anger welled up, too. Her husband's family had lived in Hexham for several generations, dwelling peacefully amidst the Christians. They did not deserve this treatment, this summary judgment. No one did.

They knew, of course, that they had enemies, those in town and countryside who hated Jews, not any individual in particular, but all the children of Israel. Grendel was one of these. He dwelled farther along on Jewry Lane, not far from the Jews' small enclave of three houses. Ivetta often saw him standing on his front step, staring contemptuously their way, eyes hostile and accusing. There were many like Grendel, yet many also accepted the presence of Jews, dealt fairly and honestly with them. Friends, too, they had among Christians. Jacob and Lord Godwin passed much time together, hunting and hawking and holding discussions, sometimes far into the night over several flasks of wine. And Ivetta also had companions among the Gentiles.

Yes, they understood well that, like anywhere, attitudes toward Jews ranged from open hostility to tolerance to genuine friendship and respect. They had learned to accept their mixed circumstances, and so long as they kept mostly to themselves, quietly pursuing the patterns of their communal life, they found that conflict was easily avoided. The unexpected shove by a passerby on the street, the curses, the cold glares were simply endured.

News from abroad reached them from time to time of savage punishments meted out to Jews by Christians, and the Jews of Hexham counted themselves lucky to be living where such incidences were, until now, unknown. Some of Ivetta's own kin had experienced the violent wrath that sometimes gripped Christians, for she came from a wealthy family of moneylenders, and these were often the favorite targets of Christians.

The Jews of Hexham were not wealthy, though they were not poor either, and their middling position, she realized, probably accounted for their peaceful existence here.

Finally, Ivetta urged them from their temporary respite at the stone wall, though they walked now, with Judith hobbling between herself and Mirabella. They reached the Market Square without incident, and like the streets, found it strangely deserted, aside from a few latecomers to the fracas, seemingly ignorant of the spectacle ongoing just a few blocks away. They headed straight for the Moot Hall, and Ivetta fervently hoped to find Lord Godwin within. As they approached the great door, his deputy and nephew came flying out and ran madly past the astonished women. They headed south across the square, turned a corner and disappeared from sight. Then Godwin appeared in the doorway, hurriedly girding his sword.

Ivetta sagged with relief when she saw him, feeling the first stirrings of hope. If anyone could right this matter, it was Hexham's bailiff. As she watched him cinch the scabbard tightly around his waist, she wondered what it was about him that inspired such confidence. He was not a large man, only average in height and build. Nor was there anything about his dress or manner that spoke of high-born lordship, unless it was his confident expectation that men would follow his command.

"Thank the Virgin!" Godwin cried when he looked up to see the women and children hastening toward him. "I just learned of the arrest," he said, hurrying forward. "Did they harm you, Judith?" he asked, taking her arm and helping her through the door of the Moot Hall.

"I took a fall is all," she quietly assured him.

"Your menfolk, are they still in the Keep?" Godwin asked. "Bosa could tell me very little."

"Yes!" Ivetta cried. "You must go to them, Lord Godwin! We were let go, but I fear what may happen to Jacob and the others! The townspeople—they think our husbands murdered the brewer's son!"

Godwin ushered them inside the hall and urged them to the hearth; for they were all shivering with fear and cold. Quickly he brought a chair over for Judith. "Yes, Bosa has told me. And I have an idea how the notion came about, but I can't take time now to explain. I must get to the Keep. Some have obviously decided to take the law into their own hands." He strode quickly to the door, adding, "But they will not dare act without my knowledge or authority. Fear not—your men will be safe. Bosa has gone to fetch my knights from the woods. They will meet me at the Keep. You will be safe here, so long as you bar the door after I leave. Open it for no one, save me!" Then he was gone, and Ivetta ran to heft the heavy wooden brace securely into place across the door.

It was a long and tortuous wait. Godwin was gone for nearly two hours, but finally he returned and hailed the women inside the Moot Hall. Ivetta rushed to remove the bar, and Godwin quickly strode in, followed closely by Bosa and Eilaf. Ivetta, Judith, and Mirabella looked anxiously past, searching for the faces of their husbands. "Your men are safe and unharmed," Godwin quickly assured them. "But I have asked them to remain in the Keep for their own safety. My knights stand guard outside its walls to protect them."

The women let out a collective sigh of relief, for they had been imagining the worst. "What happened when you arrived?" Ivetta asked.

"Most of the townsfolk were already regretting their roughshod ways," Godwin answered. "They left willingly, even before my knights arrived. But it was hard going getting a few to give over. It took a drawn sword to persuade them. These I do not trust. I saw a thirst for vengeance in their eyes. Your men are safest in the Keep, for now, until wits have returned to the ruffians who led the seizure."

"Why do they need protection, Lord Godwin?" Judith asked from her chair by the fire. "Why do the townspeople accuse our husbands of murder?" She looked drawn and very tired, resigned almost, Ivetta thought, as if a long-expected tragedy had finally come to pass.

Godwin hesitated, glancing at the children. The women grasped his discomfort and came away from the hearth to where the bailiff was standing. Bosa went to a chest alongside the wall to rummage within, pulling out an armful of carved wooden figures. He took these over to Ivetta's children and settled down to play a game with them. The figures were exquisitely wrought, each a work of great craftsmanship. There were ships and horses, knights and courtly ladies, castles and cathedrals.

"I have already explained matters to your husbands," Godwin was saying, keeping his voice low. "You know that Alfred was discovered this morning, murdered. Have you learned of the manner of his death? Heard tell of the wounds marking his body?"

The women shook their heads slowly, frowning.

"His death resembles a crucifixion . . . Christ's crucifixion." Godwin went on to describe the boy's wounds, his pierced left side, the punctures in his palms.

Mirabella's plump arms tightened around her baby. Ivetta covered her mouth and squeezed her eyes shut as though trying to ward off the appalling image. "Who would do such things to a child, Lord Godwin?" she asked.

"That is what I aim to discover. And the sooner I do, the sooner your husbands will be cleared from all guilt in the minds of townsfolk."

"But why blame the Jews at all?" Ivetta cried. "It makes no sense!"

"It makes perfect sense, child," Judith said quietly. Ivetta and Mirabella turned and stared at her, puzzled. "A thousand years ago," Judith continued, "Jews murdered an innocent man, their own Savior. They have repeated the crime many times since, wickedly reenacting the crucifixion. Is that not what Christians believe, Lord Godwin?"

"Many ignorant Christians believe this, yes," he answered, feeling awkward. "But many as well do not."

Then he told them to gather the children so that he could see them safely to their houses. "I have knights posted there as well. There will be no more raids on Jewish homes," he said. "But I urge you to stay inside for a few days, until this insanity has passed. My men can fetch any goods you require."

They left the Moot Hall, finding the square bustling once more with eager gossipmongers. News of Alfred's terrible death was still flying about, like a raven on the wind. Only now, stuck in its claws were the Jews, and talk of the murder was ominously linked to their seizure. The Jews were given dark looks and a wide berth as Godwin led them across the square to head down Hall Stile, a wide avenue that stairstepped down to the river before cutting east toward Dilston.

About halfway along, a much narrower street, called Jewry Lane, branched right to form a rough semicircle, looping around to reconnect with the main road farther down. The three homes of Hexham's Jews were located near the lower intersection. Isaac's imposing stone house was closest to Hall Stile, situated on a large lot that once accommodated three small timber cottages. Long ago, his grandfather Aaron had purchased the plots from the priory, then he had the houses razed to make way for his new stone house.

His story was well known to the natives of Hexhamshire. Aaron had moved his family from Newcastle to Hexham, hoping to extend his kinfolk's thriving moneylending enterprise. In those days, Hexham had seemed about to emerge as a major center of commerce in Northumbria. Its burgeoning market and location on the Tyne promised an economic boom, and Aaron wanted to be there when it happened. He had caused quite a stir, for many in the shire, especially those in the rural outreaches, had never had dealings with Jews.

Others followed in Aaron of Newcastle's wake, and for a time Hexham's population of Jews rapidly increased. Yet the sudden burst of commercial growth was short-lived. Even worse for the Jews, the gentry of rural Northumberland, unlike Newcastle, had less need to borrow and when they did it was in small increments. Thus, there was not enough business to go around and eventually most Jews moved on to more promising locations until only Aaron and his family remained. Upon his death, the house and business passed to Isaac's father, Jacob, called Jacob of Newcastle. Eventually, these had passed to Isaac, though he did not inherit the epithet, and the connection with Newcastle was finally severed. Now, the aging Isaac was slowly turning over his moneylending and pawn trade to his sons.

On one side of the great stone house, at the corner, lived the widow Lioba. On the other, in a much smaller house, dwelt Jacob and Ivetta, while two houses away from them were Samuel and Mirabella. As they traveled around the bend, past Grendel's house, Godwin watched to see if the man would show his face. He had been the most reluctant to quit the Keep, the most adamant about the guilt of the Jews. Godwin had exchanged harsh words with the man, and it had taken three knights to convince him that he had lost the day. He braced himself for another confrontation, but no one stirred within the shuttered house as he led his party past.

They decided that all the women and children should stay with Judith; for the stone house would be the most difficult of the three to breach and easiest for his knights to defend. Godwin waited while Ivetta and Mirabella went to fetch food and clothing. "Gather also things your men might need for a night away," he told them. "I will deliver them to the Keep."

When they returned, Godwin made ready to leave, armed with a bundle of goods for Isaac, Jacob, and Samuel. As he turned to go, Ivetta came over to put a tenative hand upon his arm. "I know you have much to do, Lord Godwin," she said. "But may I come with you? I must see Jacob, if only for a minute or two." She watched his face anxiously, waiting for his reply, not at all sure he would understand her need. But she saw his eyes grow sympathetic, anguished almost, and she wondered at the meaning. She knew that Godwin, many years ago, had lost his wife in childbirth. Did memory of her still bring him pain? Or was the source more recent?

But the sorrowful look was gone in an instant, and so fleeting was it that Ivetta thought she must have imagined it. Godwin was nodding to her, saying, "Of course you may see Jacob, but you must be brief. I am running out of men and need to round up some trusty souls who can help my knights search the forests."

"You think Alfred's murderer is hiding there?"

He did not answer immediately. "I fear he may be long gone by now, Ivetta, yet there is a chance we may find him skulking in the woods, waiting for the uproar to die down."

She looked troubled. "If the murderer escapes, will not many in Hexham go on believing the Jews killed Alfred?"

"It would be best if the murderer is captured, for your sakes and for the sake of justice. Still, if he is not, we should be able to establish your innocence easily enough. I have already learned from Jacob that none of you stirred from your homes during Holy Week, except to go to synagogue at Isaac's."

"That is true enough," she said. "It is not safe for Jews to be about, for Christian passions run high during this time. We plan ahead and stock up supplies to last the week, and emerge only after your Easter is passed."

"And Alfred was last seen at the north end of town, a fair distance from Jewry Lane," said Godwin.

"Poor lad. I still can't believe he's dead," she said. "He came often lately to Isaac's house. He was a sweet boy and so hard-working."

"What business did he have at Isaac's?"

"He did errands for the priory. Fetched and returned hawked goods. That sort of thing."

Godwin nodded, saying, "Come, we must go." Sensing no relief to Ivetta's anxiety, he added, "When this madness dies down, the facts will prove your innocence. The townspeople will see that they have sorely wronged the Jews of Hexham."

Ivetta was not convinced that it would be so simple, but said no more as she and Godwin quickly retraced their steps to the Market Square. The townspeople were still gathering here, the place growing thick with bodies. Rank as nettles, Ivetta thought angrily, wondering why they were not tending their own business. Godwin pushed his way through, holding her arm tightly. She walked erect, resisting the temptation to cringe from those who glared balefully as she passed, their loathing as palpable as the smell of rotting flesh. A few, though, reached a tentative hand toward her and gave her a kindly smile, telling her to be strong.

Then they met Master Guthred, the town's only tanner. He was directly in their path, standing toe-to-toe with a man she did not recognize and in the midst of a violent debate. Ivetta had had frequent dealings with Master Guthred, as did any in Hexham who required leather goods, and she always found him friendly enough, though in his gruff sort of way. He was a reserved and dignified man, rarely inclined to include an amiable chat with a patron's purchase. Still, though outwardly solemn, there was a flicker of warmth in his eyes, especially when he gazed at her children. Two weeks ago, she had gone to his shop to purchase a pair of gloves, and he had given Florin and the boys some candied ginger as a reward for their good behavior while Ivetta was fitted. Now, as she stared at the tanner in the square, heard the bitterness in his voice as ugly words spewed forth from his mouth, she could not believe that he was the same man. Guthred turned, and when he met her eyes, the tirade halted abruptly and he looked momentarily embarrassed. Then he clenched his mouth shut, thrust out his chin, and turning on his heel, marched away.

Godwin was tugging her forward once more, and they finally reached the far side of the square. But just as they were about to head down Hawk's Lane toward the Keep, something, a rising intensity in the voices behind, made them both turn back to nervously eye the crowd that was now bunching together at the other side of the square. It was difficult from their vantage point to see what the new source of disturbance might be and Godwin jumped onto a low wall to get a better look.

"I see a canon," he told her. "He is shouting something to the people, but I cannot . . . Wait! Now they are leaving, making for the priory! What can be afoot now!"

They watched the square empty, the crowd pouring out to spill down Gate Street. Godwin said, "I must find out what this is about, Ivetta! Come, let me get you back home—"

"No!" she cried. "I must come with you to the priory! This may concern the Jews!"

"If it does, then it may not be safe for you. Please, Ivetta, we have no time to argue!"

"Then let us go!" she said firmly.

Godwin hesitated. He could order her to return home, but was reluctant to do so. If this did concern her fate, she had a right to learn it firsthand, yet her safety was his chief concern. But surely, no one would dare attack Ivetta with the bailiff at her side. His mind made up, he took her arm to keep her close by his side as they scrambled to catch up with stragglers heading for the priory. When they reached the gates, they saw that they had been thrown wide, either by the people storming through, or by canons wisely yielding to the overwhelming onslaught. The gatehouse was closed up tight, and as they hurried by, Ivetta wondered if Brother Michael was concealed within, avoiding the turmoil.

Beyond the priory gates, before the cathedral's west entrance, lay a courtyard. Those lately in the Market Square were now crowded here, joining others to make the assemblage surprisingly large. Five deep steps led up to the church's grand west doors, huge wooden portals of elaborately carved oak. At the top stood several canons, nervously milling and fidgeting with the ropes girding their black robes. A knight suited for battle was present also, staring severely at the people, sword in hand, as if prepared to take on the entire mob should it become riotous. He stood a little apart from the canons, who seemed anxious to maintain the distance.

Ivetta said, "That knight, is he your man, Lord Godwin?"

"Nay, he is not mine," he answered, thoughtfully eyeing the man. "I think he must be Sir Havelok, the priory's new lodger."

It was a loud and clamorous gathering, pervaded with a sense of excitement and anticipation. Ivetta noticed that eyes constantly strayed to the canons, as if expecting an announcement to be issued at any moment. She heard the word *miracle* repeated over and over, like a chant.

Godwin led her around the edge of the crowd toward the west doors, and she assumed that his intent was to address the canons gathered on the steps. But before they could get close enough, another canon emerged from the church to stand awkwardly before the mob in the courtyard. Ivetta did not recognize the brother, and guessed he was Brother Elias, the canon newly come to St. Andrews with Prior Morel. He glanced nervously over his shoulder, into the church, as if looking for strength in its quiet recesses. Then he held his arms high, silently asking for quiet.

It took several minutes, but finally silence won over the excited chatter, and any errant voices were irritably shushed by others in the crowd. Brother Elias gazed out over the people, and Ivetta thought he looked at once ecstatic and terrified. Like a bird, he seemed poised for flight, and she grew more curious about his impending announcement. She glanced over at Godwin and saw that he remained tense, his eyes roving about, as if plotting the safest course should they need to make a hasty departure. "Ivetta," he said, speaking in a low voice close to her ear. "It is too late for us to leave, yet something about all this troubles me. If anything should happen, run for the church."

She nodded, but was not nervous or fearful. The people seemed excited, happy, not dangerous or threatening, and she no longer worried that the event somehow spelled more trouble for the Jews. She looked at Brother Elias again. He was strangely compelling in his appearance, though no one characteristic demanded attention; rather, distinct features, separately plain and unremarkable, came together to form a striking whole. From a distance, he could well be taken for a youth of thirteen or fourteen years. A small man, he possessed exquisitely delicate hands and fingers, so refined and elegant that Ivetta felt her own to be large and clumsy by comparison. His feet, too, were as fine as any woman's, seemingly assaulted by the heavy rope and leather sandals. The canon's skin was pale, luminous almost, contrasting sharply with his coarse black habit and raven hair. The eyes that gazed out at the people were dark shimmering pools, the color of spiced wine held within a mazer of mahogany.

When he spoke, his voice was sweetly innocent, ringing out over the gathering at his feet: "St. Andrews has been blessed by a miracle," he shouted, then waited for the cheering to die down before continuing. "Young Alfred, the innocent child slain on Good Friday, has wrought a miracle. He has cured a crippled man of a lifelong affliction."

Now there was a great commotion in the courtyard as everyone began to talk at once. A Christian miracle, Ivetta was relieved to hear, nothing to do with the Jews.

Some in the crowd began shouting questions to Brother Elias, who held his arms up for peace again. "Some of you are asking what meaning this miracle holds, how it is that a boy murdered has come to possess divine favor." An affirming roar issued from the crowd. "It is obvious to me, for I have seen the answers in a vision. Alfred was foully murdered by the enemies of Christ. He is a holy martyr to his faith—the miracle confirms it. Now he seeks his vengeance." Brother Elias's gaze moved to Ivetta, and all heads turned to follow. "Alfred is pleased with the arrest of the Jews," the canon cried. "Why else would he bestow a miracle so swiftly on the heels of their seizure?" The mob shouted its agreement and moved as one to encircle Ivetta and Godwin.

FOUR ✝

Constance sat on a wide stone windowsill in the manor kitchen, staring out at her garden, a gray and dreary place on this cold March day. The steaming cup of ginger tea that had been placed beside her went untouched, then grew cold as she continued to gaze, motionless and solitary. Around her, Cynwyse bustled industriously, yet for the figure at the window, the cook's activities were mere flickers of sound and motion from a faraway place.

How desolate the world looks. Will spring ever come? It had been a long and wearisome winter behind the stone walls of Bordweal Manor. She yearned for the brightness and warmth of the sun, for the gaily colored flowers that crowded her borders in summer, for days unlike those just passed, unlike those that stretched ahead.

She turned from the dreary scene as her two-year-old son, Aldwin, came tottering into the kitchen, squealing with delight when he spied his mother. Her melancholy began to fade as she scooped up her child, hugging him to her. But he soon wriggled out of her arms, his attention already diverted. He eagerly rushed to the carved horses and knights that lay scattered on the floor in a corner of the large room.

"What shall we play, my sweet?" asked Constance, coming over and lifting her skirts to settle with her son on a mat of woven herbs and rushes. A sweet, wholesome fragrance wafted up from the dried stalks as they were crushed, the redolent aroma calling to mind the simple pleasures of summer: harvest feasts and bonfire revelries, apple gathering and wildflower bouquets of gillyflower and gorse. "Shall we go a-hunting?"

They played until Aldwin grew tired, then Constance put him down for a nap in his cradle, placed out of the way in a warm nook by the hearth. The alcove also housed Cuthbert, her terrier, who lay curled in his basket, a tight ball of wiry black fur. He twitched his ears to acknowledge her nearness, though he did not raise his head as she stepped to and from the cradle. Then she sat in a nearby rocker and took up a book of poetry. It was one of three books she owned, prized possessions all, and this her favorite, a collection of verses by the pagan Roman poet Ovid.

She opened the volume to an exquisitely lettered page, but her thoughts kept returning to Aidan. Aldwin had his features, Constance reflected, as she did often lately; for they were coming into sharper focus as he grew and shed the jolly plumpness of infancy. His tawny hair was the exact shade Aidan's had been, and she felt a sharp stab at the thought they would never know each other, father and son.

"Lady," said Cynwyse from across the kitchen, and in a tone that told Constance advice was imminent. She braced herself and looked warily at the cook who was vigorously kneading a massive ball of bread dough with the heels of her palms. Tall, thick-set, and very strong, Cynwyse radiated vigor and competency. A careworn face, graying locks, and shrewdly intelligent eyes bespoke a vast experience with life's obstacles and uncertainties, while a forthright disposition and decisive optimism attested to an even vaster supply of answers and strategies to overcome them. "Long enough have ye grieved," she announced, not taking her eyes from the smooth, elastic dough. "'Tis harmful to carry on so. A change of scenery is what you need, to my way of thinking. Why don't ye take Aldwin to Wells, to see your family?" She looked up finally to gaze directly at Constance.

Constance suppressed a surge of irritation, knowing, as she once had not, that the cook spoke out of deep concern and devotion. How could Cynwyse understand? She was not, to her mind, grieving, for it had been a year since Godwin's messenger arrived from Egypt, carrying the devastating news that Aidan had been killed during a siege against the Muslims.

A whole year gone by and in its passing Constance had finally come to terms with her husband's death. Yet the effort had cost much, had brought her life to a listless standstill, a kind of impasse, one that she had not the will nor strength, it seemed, to overcome. No, it was not *grief* that made her suffer still, she wanted to tell Cynwyse, but an overwhelming lack of purpose, a feeling of aimlessness so intense it all but immobilized her.

They shared only one year together, after marrying in May of 1217, in the midst of the civil war with King John. Older than most brides, she was twenty-five, Aidan seven years her senior. She met him at a tournament held in Wells—a grand affair drawing knights from all over Christendom. They were married shortly thereafter, and Constance, with mixed feelings of trepidation and excitement, had bid farewell to her lifelong home in the south.

She took to Northumbria at once, though. The wild landscape matched the proud disposition of the native Saxons, exhilarating her in a way the tame, Norman south never had. They were suspicious of her at first, these fiercely independent northerners, her new kin and fellow shirefolk, but slowly she gained their friendship, once they were satisfied Constance would not be demonstrating any of the imperious behavior they associated with Normans. A year later, Aidan departed for Egypt, taking the cross with his cousin Godwin. They were away many long months before she received word that the crusader army was making for Egypt. Why were they not going to the Holy Land, she had wondered. The next message from Godwin reported that her husband was dead.

Cynwyse could not understand the numbness and uncertainty that now filled her being; for the cook, her dear friend, was a woman of action. She did not wait for answers, for healing to come in due time. No, Cynwyse wrested answers from the world, ruthlessly chased them from their secret places to serve her needs, tore at Future's thick curtain to find what lay in store. She was famous locally and widely sought for her skills, for her powerful cures and charms. These came from a myriad of sources, many plainly pagan, Constance had once pointed out. This mattered not to Cynwyse, who gladly received and put to the test any bit of lore or wisdom that aided in mastering fate.

Now Cynwyse had bent her mighty will to "curing" Constance. Every charm and drawing potion, every lucky talisman and amulet she could lay hands to had been employed. Constance glanced at the cup of tea on the windowsill; it, too, was no doubt laced with a curative.

Constance wearily endured the cook's ministrations, unable to explain that the life she had eagerly anticipated when she came to Northumbria three years ago had been cruelly snatched away, casting her adrift. In its place had come an existence that was oppressively unfamiliar, burdensome to negotiate, her son providing the only tether to a strange new life. She needed time to find her way, to learn what was expected of her, what she wanted. And in this pause, this interval that was her life, she hesitated over basic considerations:

Should she move back to Wells, to be with her kin? But what of Aidan's kin, now her son's?

Constance looked up to see Cynwyse watching her. "Nay, we will not travel yet," she said. "The roads are sodden, and the air's too cold for Aldwin. But perhaps when it's warmed up a bit, Cynwyse." Constance hoped this vague answer would satisfy the cook, forestalling argument, if only temporarily.

Cynwyse pursed her lips. "Aye, yer right on that score, lady," she conceded, looking past Constance to the frosty world on the other side of the thickly paned window. "'Tis cold and damp as the grave out there." She looked back at her mistress. "But Sidroc says the weather'll soon fair up. Warmer air is a-cumin' in," she said, jerking her head westerly, as if the longed-for milder weather sat just over the horizon. "Ye won't have no call to put me off then," she warned.

Constance was happy to postpone the issue, counting herself lucky, for Cynwyse was not always so easy to deny. She was sure she knew best, and usually did— an irritating combination at times. In contests of will, the cook had an infuriating habit of referring her opposition to St. Peter: "Mind what I say or take it up with St. Peter" was an oft-repeated phrase, leaving disputants at a confused loss. How did one "take it up with St. Peter," Constance once asked, but got no answer, only a steady gaze that told her not to pursue the question.

Besides, when the weather warmed, perhaps she *would* feel like making a change, a permanent one even. She would find a comfortable familiarity in Wells, on the wide, fertile lands her family farmed and leased to tenants. She might even find the remnant of an old life left behind, one that she could take up again, her son at her side.

For one hundred and fifty years, Constance's folk had dwelled in the south of England. The first of her kin to leave Normandy was a young, adventurous knight with no hope of an inheritance. He pledged his loyalty to William the Bastard, and his brave military service won him a generous grant of land after the Conquest.

She looked outside again, wondering, not for the first time, what Sidroc saw that she could not; for though the thick glass obscured the distant view, it seemed to Constance that more of the same cold lay in wait: dark clouds gathered ominously to the north like a hostile force, issuing forth strong winds that fiercely whipped the tall, barren trees circling the manor.

Yet she did not doubt that Bordweal's beekeeper and chief gardener was correct. Sidroc, she had come to learn, was uniquely attuned to his natural setting, to weather and seasons, to moon and stars, to animals and all living things that pushed roots into soil. However, he was especially sensitive to his bees. He could readily recognize his own, and regularly spoke with the creatures, treating them with the gravest respect. Once, he had burst into the kitchen, anxiously inquiring whether a bee had strayed indoors, for one of his had gone missing. When she first arrived at Bordweal, Constance had thought the man cracked as a broken pot, that her husband kept him on out of pity. But she had quickly learned otherwise.

Her attention was diverted by a flurry of motion from Cynwyse, who had moved briskly from bread-making to preparations for today's dinner—pork pie. She was stalking around the big kitchen, efficiently gathering ingredients and utensils. "The Easter Feast was magnificent, Cynwyse," Constance said, recalling yesterday's sumptuous repast. "I'm afraid I over-indulged, the dishes were so delicious."

"Aye, ye could stand more of that, to my way of thinking," she answered, critically eyeing Constance's waistline. "Slim as a gate post are ye!"

True, she was slenderly made upon a small frame, yet Constance possessed a wiry strength that denied her fragility. No delicate beauty, she scorned idleness. Before Aidan's death she preferred active pursuits to sedentary ones, save reading and studying, though even these were done with much pacing and with frequent interruptions for walks or gardening when the weather was fair. Long thick hair the color of Sidroc's clover honey was kept piled atop her head, where it could not hinder, accentuating a tapering neck. Limbs, too, were slim, yet lean and firm from handling both horse and spade.

Constance watched now as the cook sliced gleaming black prunes and yellow disks of hard-boiled eggs to garnish the pastry, which would then be painted with saffron and baked to a deep gold. Cynwyse, she knew, was luxuriating in the passage of Lent, and fish, to everyone's relief, would not be on the menu for quite some time.

Still, for those who dwelled at Bordweal, the Lenten season was quite bearable; for Cynwyse's especial talent lay in making the days of fasting, not merely endurable in their absence of meat and dairy, but positively delightful culinary experiences. The six-week season of Lent presented her with a particularly formidable challenge, one that she approached with the fortitude of a saint doing penance. Constance had never missed meat or eggs as Cynwyse had presented one delectable meal after another. Her hoarded stores of dried figs, currants, dates, and almonds were finally ransacked for the occasion to flavor exquisitely prepared fish recipes: fish that was baked, grilled, simmered, and attended by a host of subtle sauces. Almond milk had flavored stews and soups and, substituting for the forbidden egg, had bound pastries filled with dried fruits and nuts.

However, her pièce de résistance this year had been a "mock egg," a delightful and delicious novelty that Constance had never before experienced. "Tell me,

Cynwyse," she said. "Were they difficult to make, these mock eggs? However did you get the idea?"

"'Twas the priory cook who gave me the recipe," she answered. "The canons, poor souls, have many restrictions to mind. Brother Peter must always be cumin' up with new dishes to tempt their appetites."

Constance laughed wryly. Leave it to the canons of St. Andrews to find a tasty way around one of the most fundamental of their dietary restrictions.

"As easy as sin to make they were," Cynwyse went on, stopping her work to explain. "First, ye ground some almonds and simmer them in water 'til ye have a nice broth. Then ye draw off the milk so yer left with a mash. To that ye add sugar, then divide the lot in two. Leave one half white and color the other yellow with a bit of saffron, ginger, and cinnamon. Next, take an egg and blow it out, good and clean, then stuff it with the yellow and white paste. Last thing ye do is roast it in the ashes, and that's all there is to having a hard-boiled egg on Good Friday."

Constance and Cynwyse smiled together over the ingenuity of Brother Peter, then looked over as one of the cook's assistants, Thecla, came hurrying into the kitchen.

"And what kept ye so long?" demanded Cynwyse, her amusement gone. She aimed her great bulk at the young girl, folding arms over her hefty bosom. "I'll not send ye to town for me goods if ye can't stir yer stumps from the market before noontime!"

Thecla, a spindly girl with small, darting eyes, ignored the cook, turning to face Constance. "Lady," she cried. "Hexham's astir! No one is mindin' the stalls in the market square—that's why I'm so late." Over her shoulder, she gave Cynwyse a defiant look, then turning back to Constance, went on breathlessly, "Folks are on fire about the murder! The brewer's son was found in a field this morn, dead as a hammer!"

"Young Alfred?" Constance said slowly.

"Aye, lady. Murdered he was, by the Jews!"

"Nay what!" cried Constance, leaping from her rocker. "What nonsense is this?"

"'Tis the truth, lady! Everyone knows it!"

"Thecla," Constance said sharply. "Tell us the tale, or what you know of it—from the start."

"Aye, lady," she said, taking a deep breath, pleased to be the center of attention. "Gwyn found him this morning in the common pasture. They think he was murdered on Good Friday. Strangled he was! On his head he wore a crown of thorns, and in his left side, they found knife wounds! His palms were pierced by nails, and a cross of two broad beams was found near the body. He was *crucified*, lady! They've rounded up the Jews; they're holdin' them in the Keep for the murder."

Constance was stunned. She knew the Jews of Hexham well; they were not capable of the violent murder just described by Thecla. "Why have they arrested the Jews?" she demanded. "What evidence is there?"

"Why, it's clear as day the Jews did it," she answered immediately. "No Christian would murder on Good Friday, lady. Besides, the boy was killed by way of a mock crucifixion. Who but a Jew would crucify a Christian?"

It can't be true, thought Constance. Thecla has got it muddled somehow. "You say they've arrested *all* the Jews?" she asked. "Surely not the women and children?"

"Well, no," she admitted. "They were set free, but it may prove that the women were in on it with their menfolk. In that case, they'll be condemned just the same." She sounded hopeful at the prospect.

"You may go about your chores now, Thecla," Constance said, sharply dismissive. "And I want no gossiping about this with the staff," she warned. "The whole tale sounds fantastic . . . ridiculous even, and I won't have you spreading vicious rumors."

Thecla left, plainly disappointed by their reactions. In the square, she had stood with the other women, going over the details of the story several times, dissecting every tidbit, speculating and theorizing with the rest. She had looked forward to doing no less at home.

When she had gone, Constance paced about the kitchen, deeply troubled. "What do you make of all this, Cynwyse? Do you think there's any truth to what Thecla says?"

The cook had gone back to her cooking, but she wore a deep frown as she sliced the pork, tender from long stewing. "A grain mayhap," she answered. "But ye can't lay much store by what Thecla says, lady. A bad 'un, she is, always settin' things about. Likes to stir up strife she does." Cynwyse eyed the cutting edge on her knife, adding, "And what's Lord Godwin's part in all this, I'd like to know." She began sharpening the blade on a small whetstone that hung from her belt, scraping it across the grainy surface. "Like you, lady, I'm hard put believin' the Jews are mixed up in this. So why are they a sittin' in the Keep?" She pointed the knife at Constance. "We need to hear the story from someone a far piece more reliable than Thecla."

As if on cue, the steward arrived, his lean frame hovering in the doorway as he stiffly awaited acknowledgment. Cuthbert lifted his head and emitted a low growl, and Hereberht shot him a disdainful glance down his patrician nose, then lifted his chin and gave a little sniff.

"Hereberht," said Constance, moving toward Cuthbert, ready to restrain him lest he become more ambitious in his dislike of the steward. "I was just about to send for you. Have you any news of the murder in Hexham?"

The steward briskly came forward, his loosely fitting gown, properly buckled at the neck, billowed out below a knee-length, belted tunic. The movement brought Cuthbert to his feet. A show of canines now accompanied his warning growls; attack was imminent. Constance scooped him up before he could charge. "No, Cuthbert," she scolded.

They did not get on well, her dog and Hereberht. They never had—it was dislike at first sight. The steward considered Cuthbert a useless household addition, consuming without ever contributing, a serious affront to his business-minded nature; for Cuthbert had no interest in hunting, in rooting out and keeping at bay the rodents and pests that human dwellings always attract. No, he had little interest in working for his bread and board, preferring to spend his days dozing in warm places. Nor was he terribly handsome to behold, looking more like a wild creature just wandered in from the woods with his tufts of coarse, soot-colored hair sticking out in all directions. Yet Constance adored her dog, a wedding gift from Godwin. Why Cuthbert detested the steward, she had not a clue.

"I've only heard rumors, mistress," he was saying tersely, wisely keeping his distance. "Nothing that makes any sense." He stood erect with hands clasped behind his back, looking put out by his lack of information. Hereberht was usually very well informed—his network of highly placed sources brought news from all over the countryside. He never gossiped, merely collected information to stay abreast of the news. He was an extremely conscientious estate manager.

"You know nothing? Well, that *is* a first!" Cynwyse cried derisively. She slapped her hand on the kneading table, sending up a cloud of flour. Hereberht gave the cook a quick, cold glare, then watched in silent outrage as she walked over to give Cuthbert a generous piece of hard-boiled egg.

The steward did not get on well with Cynwyse either. At some point in time, before Constance's arrival at

Bordweal, they had declared war on one another and were disinclined to ever call a truce. They did not quarrel openly—that would be far too boorish for the prudish Hereberht. They simply pelted verbal darts at each other in a ceaseless, wearying volley of pointed remarks and insulting retorts.

Constance tried to keep them separated as much as possible, but once a week Cynwyse had to account to the steward for her kitchen expenditures. This, Constance suspected, was the root of all evil for the cook: to have to justify her spending to a man who was constantly trying to cut her costs, and worse, had no regard for her talent. Her itemized account of ingredients, usually lavish, elicited tightly pursed lips and exaggerated sighs as Hereberht recorded the numbers with formality. She was always over budget, and though she had two assistants, she often drafted servants from other parts of the manor to help in the kitchen. Once, the steward had been outraged to find the stable boy working as a turnspit, reclined in deep contentment beside the cooking hearth.

He had looked, in vain, to his mistress, expecting Constance to impose some limits on the cook. Yet she had not the mettle to contradict Cynwyse when it came to matters of the kitchen. Besides, she adored Cynwyse's cooking and minded not her extravagance. The steward, Constance judged, could never be won over by such carnal pleasures. He looked like an ascetic, a genteel monk on the straight and narrow, living on bread and water in a rigorous mortification of the flesh. Hereberht probably fasted every day of the year.

"Mistress," he was saying. "There's someone here to see you. It's the Jewess Ivetta."

A shaken Ivetta was led into the kitchen by the steward, who hastily departed, made uncomfortable, Constance guessed, by Ivetta's distressed state. They helped her to a chair near the hearth, and Cynwyse fetched cups for wine. Then, in a voice that was sometimes tearful, sometimes angry, Ivetta described the arrest, how a mob of townspeople had stormed the tiny Jewish quarter to haul them off to the Keep.

Constance reached out to clasp one of Ivetta's small, cold hands, holding it tightly between her own. She counted Ivetta among her closest friends, though Constance knew she had neglected their friendship in the last year. One of many ties, she suddenly realized, that was selfishly forsaken.

In Ivetta, Constance had always admired the blending of strong resilience with delicate beauty, like the graceful iris that elegantly sways in the wind. She possessed a beauty that was rooted in healthful vigor and flowed from a generous spirit. Now, though, Ivetta's face looked etched from white marble, rigid and colorless, dramatically contrasting with her plaited ropes of thick black hair.

She interrupted her tale to sip the wine Cynwyse had urged into her hands, while Constance sat beside her, considering the events just described. They were beginning to make more sense, and she was even a bit heartened. It was obvious that a mob of townspeople had been responsible for the arrest of the Jews, not the bailiff. The bizarre "crucifixion" of Alfred had prompted some to attribute the murder to the Jews, just as Thecla had described, leading to an attack on the small community. Surely, once Godwin stepped in and sorted out the matter, he would release the unjustly held prisoners. With hope, they would have recourse in the law for their false arrest.

But as Ivetta resumed her account of the morning's events, describing the scene in the church courtyard, the miracle and the canon's interpretation of it, Constance felt her optimism quickly drain away.

"They've gone mad!" she said when Ivetta told how the people had turned on her and Godwin, how he had been forced to draw his sword to keep them at bay until his knights arrived to disband the vengeful crowd.

Ivetta suddenly clutched at Constance's arm. "Please help us," she pleaded. "We have no one else to turn to, lady. You have been my good friend, and your kinship ties are powerful. Please! You must help us!"

"Ivetta," said Constance, hoping her calm voice would lessen the woman's increasing panic. "You must trust in Lord Godwin. He will help you. A miracle is no evidence in a court of law. You must give him time to set matters right."

"No," Ivetta said, her despair complete. "The Jews have been accused of murder, and the Christians have called their God as witness. They claim He speaks through an innocent martyr: The Jews are guilty; the miracle confirms it. Lord Godwin can do nothing. Isaac, Jacob, and Samuel are to be hanged."

FIVE✝

Prior Morel gazed sternly at the obedientiaries humbly seated before him in his private chamber. Ten officials, he thought irately, for a priory that housed only twenty-five canons!

This was but one of the many abuses he had been confronted with upon taking up his new post as prior of St. Andrews. Most of his time thus far had been spent studying the monastery's accounts and ledgers, and though they had been carelessly kept, the house's poverty had quickly become apparent. Mismanagement was at the heart of the evil: rents on priory property were far too low, its extensive farmlands had been left to lie fallow for years, flocks had disappeared. Worst of all, the laxness of the canons and their idle ways had infected town and countryside. The Christians here were detached, only going through the motions of following their faith. Where was passionate devotion, the zealousness that brought generous contributions to the earthly symbol of their dedication?

Morel straightened his lean frame, squaring his shoulders resolutely. It was time to reinvigorate souls, to trim the fat and set this monastery back on the road to piety, productivity, and profit. The archbishop had chosen wisely, he thought, supremely confident. The prior would not rest until his task was accomplished, God as his witness.

"Brothers," the Prior said sternly, bringing the meeting to order. "I would like first to discuss our one corrodian. Sir Havelok is his name, I believe," he said, glancing at a parchment document before him. "Brother Cellarer," he said, addressing Brother John. "Please describe the contract you negotiated with this knight. The records of the transaction are very poor," Morel said pointedly.

The canons looked even more uncomfortable, shifting in their chairs.

"Is there a problem with Sir Havelok, brothers?" Morel asked sharply.

Brother John was the only canon with courage enough to answer. "It's only that he's very ill-natured, Lord Prior. The brothers try to stay clear of his path. As bad tempered as a nettle, that one is."

"I'm not interested in his disposition," the prior said impatiently. "What has he given St. Andrews in return for lifelong board, lodging, and a share of charitable donations to the priory?"

"Well, it went like this," Brother John readily answered, oblivious to the displeasure in the prior's voice. "Sir Havelok was quite indebted to the Jews, you see. He was in sore danger of losing everything—his lands and all possessions." The canon looked momentarily pained, as if embarrassed to discuss another man's financial misfortunes. "When Sir Havelok came to us for help, we felt obligated to assist, as is our duty as servants of Christ. Had we known about his evil temper, though, we may have thought twice. Anyhow, the harvest was profitable last year, for a change, so the priory had the funds available. Land is always a useful investment, is it not?" The canon looked pleased with himself now, recalling his investment savvy. "His debts were paid in exchange for his lands. Havelok also received a lifelong pension of room and board plus a cash income based on a percentage of the priory's annual income. We thought the terms quite fair, yet Sir Havelok is an embittered man for having lost his patrimony. I fear his pride has taken a severe blow, and he is not inclined to hide his resentment, though his hostility is aimed mostly at the Jews."

Morel's lips tightened with exasperation. How typical of this establishment, he thought bitterly—to take a rare windfall and invest it to the priory's disadvantage. "Quite fair for Havelok, Brother," Morel answered in a bitter tone, gesturing to the contract. "From what I can gather, most of his lands are out of production and therefore worthless. The expense of lifelong support and a guaranteed income will far exceed the value of his lands. He should be grateful to us for so generous an agreement." The prior glared accusingly at Brother John, then, with a disgusted sigh, set aside Sir Havelok's contract to address the matter of the priory's bloated staff. Heads were about to roll, he thought with delighted satisfaction, his thin lips curling into a cold smile.

"Brother Sacristan," said Morel, crisply addressing one of the cowed canons. "You shall keep your position as keeper of the church and its sacred ornaments." The sacristan, Brother Mark, perked up hopefully.

"However," continued the prior, his gaze resting on another fearful face. "We shall dispense with the position of sub-sacristan. Brother Mark, you will take on the additional responsibilities of caring for the liturgical books and leading the chant at services."

Brother Mark slumped back into his chair. *Two* offices to maintain, he thought morosely. And how would he lead the chant? He didn't even know it!

"And Brother Sacristan," added the prior. "A recent inspection of the church has left me most distressed. Many items do not appear in their proper place. I want an immediate accounting of all altar vessels, crucifixes, altar frontals, reliquaries, and vestments."

"Yes, Lord Prior," said the sacristan, while looking nervously at the cellarer.

"Brother Hosteller," said Morel, shifting his gaze to Brother Thomas, who started in his chair as if struck. "As a monastery, we are obligated to provide for guests, thus, you shall continue in your duties as keeper of the guests and guesthouses. However, since we are a small establishment and our guests few, you shall also take on the offices of kitchener and refectorian."

The two canons who had until that moment held these positions sat up in alarm, though neither of the newly ousted dared to ask what their new assignment might be.

"I myself will take on the duties of bursar and cellarer," Morel continued. "The management of priory funds will be my express concern until fiscal matters are sufficiently in hand," he decreed. "My sub-prior, Brother Elias, whom you have all met by now, will assist me in these matters. The offices of novice-master, infirmarian, and almoner shall be eliminated." He paused before making his final pronouncement: "I've dismissed most of the serving staff as well."

The room suddenly erupted, the last proclamation propelling the canons from their seats, all protesting at once. "That will do, brothers!" Morel thundered. "If you have a criticism to offer, do so in a civilized manner, one at a time."

The canons huddled together as the prior looked from one to the next, daring a reply. All protests died on their lips under his unnerving gaze.

Save one. Brother John, now the former cellarer, plucked up his nerve, for the sake of principle and propriety, and addressed the prior. "My lord," he said, "are not the monastic offices prescribed by the Rule under which we all strictly live? And does not the same Rule dictate that all the brothers have a vote in elections to those offices? I fear to lightly cast aside that which we have solemnly pledged to obey." Brother John did his best to look a meek and servile canon.

Morel was silently incensed. To his mind Brother John, as cellarer, had been the worst offender, spending lavishly on food, brew, and wine, while allowing revenues from the priory's extensive properties to steadily decline. When short of cash, he had simply borrowed the needed funds or pawned one of the many precious items that adorned St. Andrews. Why, even the reliquary containing the arm of St. Wilfrid had been pawned! Upon his arrival, the prior had headed straight for this holiest of objects to pay homage to the saint he most revered, only to find the precious relic gone, unredeemed and forsaken in the Jew's shop. Brother John's sweetly feigned innocence incited a rage in Morel he could scarcely contain.

"Brother John," he said. "Your devotion to the Rule is commendable, and your commitment to the monastic life stands as a sterling example to us all. Nevertheless, I have the well-being of this establishment to consider. This house is deeply in debt. Many of the buildings are crumbling because they have been sorely neglected, and money to repair them is not at hand because revenues are insufficient." The prior's accusing eyes rested on the former cellarer. "I'll not assign blame for this deplorable state of affairs—I leave that to God. But I expect all to cooperate in the rehabilitation of this house. The situation is desperate enough to warrant drastic action. Such is the archbishop's opinion, and he has put wide powers at my disposal. I am not fearful of wielding them."

"But Lord Prior," said Brother John, impervious to Morel's threatening glare. "A monastery without an almoner, infirmarian, or novice-master? It's unseemly. And no servants? How shall we manage?"

Prior Morel took a deep breath, struggling to contain his wrath, to cast out thoughts of throttling Brother John. "What is *unseemly* is three servants for every canon," he exclaimed. "We can do without an almoner because this house has no alms to give. We need no infirmarian because we maintain a hospital in town that can fill our needs adequately.

"As for the novice-keeper," Morel glanced at his notes, "that would be you, Brother Paul. How many postulants are you currently instructing in the Rule?"

"None at this time, Lord Prior."

"And when was the last time you had a novice?"

"I've not had one since taking my office, lord."

With that, Prior Morel considered the matter closed and dismissed the canons with an impatient wave of his hand. As they shuffled out of his chamber he added, "Those of you who are now without an office will serve God in the fields."

As the dejected canons filed away, Brother Elias scuttled into the prior's chamber, then obediently waited to be acknowledged. Experience told him this could take a while, but he did not mind. He was thrilled to be in the prior's presence, near this man of God so clearly marked out as one of *His* most powerful servants. From the imposingly tall and gaunt man, a forceful potency emanated that Brother Elias found breathtaking. Like God, Prior Morel brought order to chaos, light to darkness. And he worked with a serene confidence that Brother Elias found at once disturbing and awe-inspiring.

The prior finally finished arranging the parchments on his desk, making a note to speak next with the priory cook. The meals prepared by Brother Peter were absolutely decadent, though at least now they were served in the proper place—the frater. When he had first arrived, Morel discovered that the canons were taking meals in the upper story of the infirmary. The infirmary was heated, for the sake of the ill, while the frater was not. But warmth was not their only motivation. The Rule dictated that those who ate in the infirmary should not be held to the stringent dietary requirements and fasting that went with monastic life. The intent was to keep the infirm from becoming weaker through deprivation, but the devious canons of St. Andrews had seen it as a means to ease their dietary restrictions by eating in a room that was technically a part of the infirmary. So accustomed to the depraved habit had they become, it was not curtailed when the new prior arrived. On his first day as prior, he had heard such a commotion coming from the infirmary that he had interrupted his own meal in his private chamber to investigate. He had nearly swooned at the sight, so appalling was the spectacle confronting him: canons lolling in chairs, eating meat and drinking ale served up by women. There had even been a minstrel capering about, playing a ribald tune for the brothers' enjoyment.

The prior shuddered at the memory. The punishment he had meted out for such gross transgressions of the Rule had been severe, and the brothers, he was sure, had seen the evil of their former ways. Yet the priory cook was still providing meals excessively rich and generous in their portions. It would have to stop. Shaking his patrician head in disgust, he motioned impatiently for Brother Elias to come forward. "Come in, Brother," he said sharply. "Don't hover in the doorway like a penitent before God. Speak your purpose."

"My Lord Prior," said the sub-prior. "Lord Godwin is here. He wishes to speak with you."

The Bailiff was shown into the prior's chamber, declining an offer of wine. Morel dismissed Brother Elias, then settled himself behind his massive desk, looking across at Godwin with a politely inquiring look.

Godwin briefly studied the prior. He had met with him only one other time, and had yet to assess his impressions. He knew that Morel was native to Northumbria, but had served many years in the south. Godwin also knew that he had taken the position of prior of St. Andrews as a special favor to the archbishop, and that the townspeople were not pleased by the choice; for although Morel hailed from an important local family, his long absence in the south had rendered him suspect in their minds, and his arrogant ways were confirming many of their suspicions.

Godwin himself was reserving judgment. The task set before Morel was a daunting one, and it undoubtedly had been difficult for this obviously proud man to assume so obscure a post. He had even been forced to give up the title of abbot because St. Andrews only ranked as a priory. Yet this priory could be great again, Godwin reckoned, given enough time. Its assets were considerable, requiring only wise management and hard work.

"Lord Prior, I'll come straight to the point," he said. "Yesterday in the church courtyard, your Brother Elias claimed that a miracle took place at Alfred's tomb, one that confirms the guilt of the Jews in the murder of young Alfred. I want to know how the notion came into his head and why you let him announce it. Surely you knew it would create needless havoc? The situation was grave enough for the Jews, Prior, and the reckless words of your canon have made it far worse."

The prior's eyes flashed, and Godwin guessed he was unused to reproach.

"Lord Bailiff," Morel said, "when God speaks, His words cannot be hidden, nor is it for you or I to decide when or how *His* message is heard." His voice resonated, stirred by passion. He raised one arm, pointing a long, bony finger at the heavens. "That is not the way of our faith," he cried, waving the arm. "God communicates His will through a chosen few. We listen fearfully and humbly obey." His oration over, Prior Morel subsided back into his chair, regarding Godwin coolly, as if the matter were now settled.

Godwin heaved a sigh. "Lord Prior," he said, trying to keep his voice neutral. "Brother Elias spoke in the courtyard yesterday, not God. If Alfred wrought a miracle, then I am as moved as the next man, but why connect it to the Jews? Your canon's reading is absurd and dangerous. Please, Prior, can you tell me what happened here yesterday? How did all this come about?"

Prior Morel sat for a moment, gathering his recollections of the events, Godwin supposed. He finally said, "A large number of townspeople gathered in the church yesterday afternoon, wishing to pay their respects to the dead boy."

And to satisfy a bit of ghoulish curiosity, thought Godwin.

"They could not be turned away, for it is their church as well." Morel seemed reluctant to admit this, a look of distaste crossing his genteel face.

"The boy is laid out in St. Etheldreda's Chapel," he continued. "And I instructed the brothers to allow a few in at a time, for as you know the chapel is quite small. A crippled man was brought before the body to pray. He was miraculously healed when his hand touched the cloth upon which Alfred lay. Cured, he walked from the chapel without assistance.

"Word of the miracle spread quickly, and there was a great commotion in the church. I ordered Brother Elias to clear it at once." The prior pursed his lips. "Such disturbances are quite improper in a house of God.

"People gathered from all over town to join those in the courtyard, wanting to know the cause of excitement. You know the *ignoranti*, Lord Godwin," he broke off, now addressing a social equal. "They gather though they know not why, like sheep to their own slaughter. They act, guided by a simple nature."

The low esteem held by the townspeople for the prior was obviously returned, Godwin reflected dryly.

"Then I sent Brother Elias to announce the miracle to all."

"But why claim it as evidence against the Jews?" demanded Godwin. "Did he conjure up this absurd notion himself, or did someone tell him what to say?"

The prior's face darkened. "Your words border on blasphemy, Lord Godwin. Tread carefully! Brother Elias was divinely inspired of course. Words came in a vision and he spoke them as God's mouthpiece."

Godwin strove to keep his temper, though the discussion had taken on a circular quality that was infuriating him. He tried to tell himself that, from the Prior's perspective, the matter probably was as simple as he described it. "With your permission, Prior, I'd like to have a word with Brother Elias before I leave."

The prior inclined his head, then asked, "What of your investigation of the boy's murder? Have you turned up any evidence beyond the divinely manifested?"

Godwin looked sharply at the prior, expecting to see a twinkle of amusement in his eyes. There was none. "Very little," he answered. "But of course, I've only just begun."

"And will you keep the Jews in custody?"

"No," Godwin answered. "I'll release them when I know they will be safe." He shook his head, sadly baffled. "What has come over the people of this town?" he wondered aloud. "Jews and Christians have lived together in Hexham for years. I've heard of disturbances and attacks on Jews in distant parts, but I never thought to see it here.

"There are jurisdictional issues as well," Godwin

continued more briskly. "I'm sure you know the Jews are not under my authority, even though I am the archbishop's secular arm in matters of justice. Jews fall under the writ of the royal justices, despite the fact that they reside in the archbishop's liberty. Any action against them must be taken by representatives of the crown."

"Then it's likely the matter shall be taken from your hands?" the prior asked.

"Only if they stand accused," said Godwin. "And there is no reason to believe they will." He gazed directly at the man seated across from him. "A miracle, Prior, is no evidence for the king's justices, nor any secular court. The days of the Ordeal and of temporal courts calling on the spiritual to judge guilt are long past—the two spheres must and will be kept apart."

"That is true, Lord Godwin, in theory at any rate. In practice, however, matters are not so easily defined, and the boundary between secular and spiritual is difficult to draw in certain cases, especially in a liberty whose lord is the archbishop of York. And, of course, one must not forget the court of public opinion—its sway is very great, is it not?"

Godwin gazed steadily at Morel. "Public opinion may have the power to indict, Prior, but where *I* see to justice it will never have the power to condemn the innocent."

Godwin took his leave and set out to find Brother Elias, thoughtfully reflecting on his conversation with the prior. His annoyance with the man gone, he passed slowly by the cloister garth, watching the brothers as they hoed, turning the soil over for the March winds to dry. Arrogant and proud was Morel, secure and unshakable in his faith. The miracle and its reading by Brother Elias, these were not questionable events for him, nor for many. But in Godwin's mind they were immediately suspect, and he wondered why. What set his thinking apart? His friendship with the Jews?

Indeed, familiarity assured him they were incapable of murder—made him certain of it. Yet Morel could come to the opposite conclusion, and with the same clarity of perception, as secure in his knowledge as Godwin. It was an unsettling thought to contemplate. Judgments could vary according to the individual, each borne out of particular beliefs and experience. A different bailiff, Godwin realized, might have arrested the Jews of Hexham.

But, no, it was not as precarious as that, surely! Laws determine how we judge, how we are judged. Yet law, too, is a creation of man, a mere compilation of experience and custom, vulnerable to partiality and unfairness. Common consent then determines right from wrong, he decided. And if an individual finds his judgments at odds with the common will? What then?

Spotting Brother Mark, Godwin followed his billowing robe around the corner of the refectory. Upon inquiring after Brother Elias, he was told to try the scriptorium and went back to the vaulted passageway circling the garth to enter the small rectangular room attached to the east wall of the chapter house. Here the canons copied ancient manuscripts and holy texts, preserving and perpetuating the words for future generations. Brother Elias stood poised with a wax tablet and stylus in hand, preparing to take an inventory of manuscripts in production, Godwin guessed.

The room had a musty smell to it, though, as if it hadn't been used for a long time. There was a film of dust on the sloping desks that lined the east wall beneath the high windows. Heavy vellum sheets used for copying were scattered about in disarray while ink horns, quills, and ruling sticks lay carelessly abandoned on the work surfaces.

Brother Elias stood in the middle of the deserted space. He, too, looked forsaken.

"I'm sure it won't be too difficult bringing order here, brother," Godwin said encouragingly. "Are you fond of the scribe's work?"

Surprised, Brother Elias swung around, a sweet smile lighting his face when he saw the bailiff. Pleased to have company in this ghostly place, no doubt, thought Godwin, peering into the dark recesses of the room.

"Oh, yes," the canon answered. "I'm a scribe by training you see. I've always loved this work." He gestured to the dismal surroundings. "The peace and fulfillment," he continued dreamily. "I've often felt as if my hand was being guided by God. . . ."

There was an uncorrupted quality to this canon, a guileless simplicity that seemed almost childlike. Godwin could well imagine Brother Elias sitting hour upon hour, toiling in contented bliss over his manuscripts, working only by shafts of light that streamed through the windows, illuminating the holy words.

"May I ask you about yesterday's miracle, Brother?"

The canon looked perplexed an instant, then a dreamy smile crossed his face. "Of course," he said. "It was extraordinary . . . a vision from God . . ."

"Brother Elias," Godwin said. "You know that I am searching for young Alfred's murderer?"

"Yes . . ."

"And do you know that your announcement yesterday has put the Jews of Hexham in serious jeopardy?" Godwin watched Brother Elias, making sure his words were getting through. "You've also made my task much more difficult. Every moment I spend protecting the Jews is time for the true murderer to get away. "

"I don't understand . . . the miracle . . . do you not believe its meaning?"

"Brother, what makes you think that yesterday's miracle has anything to do with the murder?"

Brother Elias hesitated, saying slowly, "Does it not make perfect sense? Is it not evident?"

Godwin said, "Was it your idea, Brother, or did someone give it to you, tell you what to say?"

Brother Elias considered for a moment before responding earnestly, "I cannot say how the notion came to me. I have . . . visions, you see, moments of perfect clarity offered in times of confusion. For a brief time, the many voices become one, the disparate forms a whole . . . a revelation."

"How can you be sure it was a true vision, Brother, a *revelation* as you call it?"

Brother Elias blanched. "The only alternative is demonic delusion!"

"Perhaps there is another possibility," Godwin suggested gently. "Could someone else have put the idea in your mind? Think carefully. There were many people around you and much commotion."

"Yes, there was a great stir about me," said Brother Elias. "The visions, they often come, as I have said, when I am engulfed. The prior says they are a mark of my holiness." He lowered his eyes demurely, as if he had been caught boasting.

Godwin stared thoughtfully at the young canon, thinking what an odd pair they made, the formidable prior and his mystical counterpart. He considered the canon's vision, recalling an event he had almost forgotten, one that took place two years ago in Egypt, when he was a part of the crusader army trying to take the port city of Damietta on the Nile.

It was the first winter after the siege of the city had begun, and the first serious setback for the crusaders; for the winter was severe and they suffered intensely from floods that had destroyed their provisions and tents and carried over to the Muslim bank a floating fortress they had labored long and hard to construct. Spirits were downcast, and there was even talk of withdrawal.

Then one day a storm blew in, but instead of reading it as Godwin had, as another miserable strike against the wretched Christian soldiers, the others saw a wonderful portent unfolding in the sky above. Great white clouds came from the west, passing overhead to clash with more great clouds, these bespattered with darkness, looming over the Muslim mainland. The crusaders pointed excitedly at the heavens, seeing in the whirling storm clouds the movements of knights and armies. They saw ordered lines of battle with left-wings locked together. They saw skirmishers, attacking on right and left, then springing smartly back into line. Finally, they saw the white clouds thrust forward in a mighty offensive, routing the darkness, so that only a few dark wisps remained, appearing to be in flight toward the city. "Behold our cloud has conquered!" they cried, their fighting spirit renewed.

Godwin had looked in vain for the glorious battle in the sky. He saw only the swirling clouds of a squall passing quickly by, pelting him with fat drops as he searched the heavens. Like every other man, he wanted a sign, reassurance that his course was true. But he did not share in the vision, and was left feeling like an outsider to the holy brotherhood, or worse, a false member, a pretender. A poisonous thought had entered his mind, one he could not voice: that the heavenly battle was a collective delusion, borne of a longing for hope.

Godwin studied Brother Elias once more. Perhaps his vision was an expression of what most people in the church had already concluded. Even before the miracle, many believed that the Jews had murdered Alfred, and with that conviction held, it was not a far leap to interpret the miracle as further proof of it. The idea was in the air, so to speak: Brother Elias's "voices."

Ah, well, he told himself, enough time spent on this strange turn of events. "Brother, I want no more proclamations when they bear on matters of law. Do you understand?" Godwin tried not to sound too over-bearing.

"Yes, my lord," he said abjectly. Then he looked at Godwin and asked, "What of the miracle? And my vision? If it *was* false, why did I utter such things?"

"A very good question, Brother. Let us hope the answer is soon revealed."

Six

Godwin left the priory, giving Brother Michael a friendly nod as he passed beneath the arched way of the gatehouse. Heading down Gate Street, he made for Jewry Lane to ensure that all was well at the homes of the Jews. Plunging through a throng of people, he was enveloped by the teeming life and diverse industry of town dwelling.

As he strode along, Godwin marveled at the normality of the scene surrounding him: men and women were plying their trades, hawking wares, coming and going, gossiping amongst neighbors. Children ran about, and everyone shouted greetings as the bailiff passed by. It was difficult to imagine that many of these people, nonchalantly going about their business today, had yesterday been seized by an irrational fury aimed at their unsuspecting Jewish neighbors.

When Godwin reached the corner of Hall Stile and Jewry Lane, he met the widow Lioba, a small, vigorous woman, not yet forty and briskly good-natured. She was standing in the street, opening the folding shutters that covered her shop's window. He stopped to help her raise the higher one that sheltered the other, which let down to form a table for her merchandise. One of

Hexham's metalsmiths, the widow had carried on her husband's trade after his death. Next door, Godwin could see his man standing guard outside Isaac's great stone house, and beyond him, the knights who stood watch over the homes of Jacob and Samuel.

At one time, Jews had occupied the entire street, whence came its name. Now the neighborhood was a mixed population of Jews and Christians, and it suddenly occurred to Godwin to wonder why the community had dwindled. Where had they all gone?

"Come to see that all's well on Jewry Lane, Lord Bailiff?" Lioba asked.

"Indeed, I have," he said smiling warmly, for he liked this woman. Her husband had been a domineering brute, forever keeping her under his thumb. After his death, she had blossomed. Having won a bitter court battle with her brother-in-law over possession of the business, she had taken on the trade of metalworking with astounding success. Her two apprentices did the heavier labor—repairing armor, swords, and the like—while she concentrated on finer work such as jewelry and engraving, which required more skill and creativity.

Her specialty was engraving seals, and her work was much sought after. From all over the shire, landholders, merchants, religious houses, and individuals of all ranks employed her skills to render their device, or to create one anew, into a seal. She had recently made one for Godwin, engraved with his family's ancient tokens: the letter "G" overlaid with an oaken leaf, symbol of bravery, entwined with ivy, the mark of fidelity and friendship. It was exquisitely wrought, and Godwin still marveled at the fineness of detail and artistic rendering. The ivy gracefully looped around the seal, in and out of the "G," lovingly embracing its brave counterpart.

"Everything looks as it should," he said, glancing around. "There's been no more trouble, Lioba?"

"Thank the good Lord, no!" she cried. "I hope to never again witness the likes of what I saw here yesterday, Lord Godwin! Good folk dragged from their homes!" Lioba clucked her tongue and shook her head sadly. "Some even dared a bit of looting, when they thought all eyes were on the Jews!"

"Looting!" Godwin cried sharply, for he had heard no reports. "Did any get away with Jewish property?"

"Nay, sir!" she assured him. "As soon as I saw the townspeople gather and caught wind of their purpose, I told my boys to lock up the shop and meet me at Jacob's house. I took up my blade and ran there, fast as I could, fearing there might be some thievery. Sure enough, once they had the Jews in the street, a few tried to weasel back into their houses, aiming to snatch a few goods, no doubt. But I drove them off with my sword." As if to prove her story, Lioba reached around the corner of the doorway and took up a small, stout blade, honed deadly sharp.

Godwin laughed, clapping her lightly on the shoulder. "Good work, Lioba! I should take you on as a deputy! What of Isaac's house? Did any try to enter his?"

"No," she answered. "His is as safe as a fortress, being built of stone. I didn't worry of any looter gaining entrance there."

Godwin looked at Isaac's imposing house. Yes, he thought, a tough one to break into once buttoned up. Handsome, too, he realized, seeing how it contrasted markedly with the timber structures surrounding it.

Lioba followed his gaze, saying, "Isaac once told me that Jews have learned from the bad fortune of others. They try to always build in stone, when they can afford to, for it offers the best protection against fire and riots. He has many valuables stored in there, you know."

Godwin nodded. Isaac the patriarch was the wealthiest among the small community, and his wealth,

Godwin realized, could be a source of jealousy for some Christians.

As if reading his thoughts, Lioba said, "Many take issue with Jews having more wealth than Christians. But they've not been given many choices in their livelihoods, have they? They're barred from farming and the craft guilds—what does that leave?" she asked. "Commerce, artisan work, and moneylending," she said, answering her own question. "And when they make a success of these, Christians are jealous. They can't win!" Lioba threw up her arms in disgust.

Godwin nodded thoughtfully. Christians were prohibited by the Church from lending at interest, thus, Jews had come to dominate this vital occupational niche, a trade that often worked hand in hand with pawnbroking. Typically, someone in need of a loan pledged a security, land or chattels, as a guarantee that the cash and interest would be repaid. If the borrower did not meet the terms of the loan, the lender took legal possession of the pledge. All loans, large and small, were arranged by contract or bond, copies of which were safeguarded in the town *archa*, kept in the Moot Hall. As defaults on loans were not uncommon, the Jews usually had a wide variety of items in their possession for sale, sold from the shop located on the ground floor of Isaac's stone house.

"You're a good neighbor and friend, Lioba," said Godwin. "The Jews are grateful to you, I'm sure."

"They're fine folk and good to me as well," she said. "They send business my way whenever they can— mostly hawked wares in need of repair before they can be sold."

Godwin wished the widow a good day, then headed down the lane to speak with his men on watch. They stood at attention when they saw him approaching.

"There's been no further trouble here, Lord Godwin," reported Burchard, a doughty knight who had accompanied Godwin on the crusade to Damietta.

Satisfied, Godwin retraced his steps back to Hall Stile. At the corner, he turned to survey the Jewish enclave once more. Like a tiny ship, it seemed to him, adrift in a Christian sea. The waters were usually calm in Hexham, but yesterday an unexpected storm had raged.

Jews were not required to live in any particular area of town. Godwin knew that Isaac's grandfather Aaron had been the first to come to Hexham, and his great stone house had formed the nucleus around which others had settled. Space within had been given over for a synagogue, and others had naturally wanted to live near the center of communal worship as well as their fellow Jews. Yet, security must have been a factor as well; the Jews no doubt felt safer by drawing together.

As Godwin stood gazing back down the lane, he was struck once more by the ordinary picture of workaday life that met his eyes, his knights standing guard the only element of the portrait that did not belong. And yet, he was not convinced that all was back to normal, for he sensed an undercurrent of tension amidst the flurry of everyday activity. For the first time Godwin wondered what day-to-day life was like for Jews in this sea of Christians.

Jews and Christians lived and worked elbow-to-elbow. Bought and sold from one another, often employed each other as servants, formed friendships. Of course, the Church did not approve of close relations between Christians and Jews, and from time to time proclamations were handed down from Rome or Canterbury: Jews must wear a distinguishing badge; they must not take Church property as pledges; Christians must not mingle with Jews as their servants and wet nurses. But such commands were rarely heeded let alone enforced, and Jews remained an ordinary part of life in Hexham. Godwin had always thought them well liked, or at least accepted, never seeing signs to the contrary. But perhaps he hadn't been looking. Yesterday's swift attack made him wonder whether he had mistaken unreserved acceptance for grudging tolerance.

Godwin now understood that conditions were far more uncertain for Jews than he had ever imagined. No doubt some Christians accepted them without reservation, like Lioba, but a deep well of resentment and suspicion obviously resided in another segment of the population, needing only a catalyst to bring it gushing forth. Godwin felt a deep sense of shame that he of all people had been unaware of the seething hostility.

But he would not be caught off-guard again, he resolved, heading for the Keep to ensure that all was quiet there as well. He came to Gate Street and turned left into the Market Square, devoid of its Monday Market stalls and booths. He crossed to Hawk's Lane and advanced down the narrow street to the Keep. Here he had posted four of his men to guard those within. The remainder of his retinue, aside from those on Jewry Lane, continued to search the forests, though hopes that Alfred's murderer might be found in the woods were fading. As Godwin approached the stronghold, he noted with satisfaction that his men were standing sharp and alert.

The Keep was the only structure in Hexham capable of withstanding a siege. Hastily built during William's conquest of the north, it was a stout building with high walls, virtually impossible to scale. The northern defenders had plundered a nearby Roman ruin to build their makeshift fortification. Inscriptions of dedication to pagan gods could still be traced on the precisely cut blocks of stone, which had been hauled to the top of a small, natural incline. The northerners had not been successful in holding out against the determined attacks of the Conqueror, but had bequeathed a sturdy and useful monument to their proud descendants.

During the years of border warfare and frequent Scottish raiding, the Keep had been further fortified, but in a haphazard manner so that now it stood as a rather ungainly edifice, perching ungracefully above its neighbors. Battlements had been added in a slapdash way, using stone from wherever it could be scrounged. A watchtower was erected to squat heavily on the northwest corner, the weighty asymmetry giving the illusion that the awkward citadel might topple down the rise at any moment, end over tower.

Godwin gave a nod to the two men posted outside the high walls as he started up the short, steep climb to the Keep's gatehouse: a long, slender passage designed to narrow and limit an attacker's approach. At the end of the passageway hung a portcullis of oak and iron, which could be dropped in front of the entrance to the Keep by operating the pulleys from a small watch chamber above. Lookout slits lined the walls of the chamber so that a guard could detect approaching threats and quickly lower the portcullis. The bailiff had assigned Wulfstan, now back from Corbridge, to man the pulleys, confident his sharp eyes and quick wits would keep the people inside the Keep secure.

When he had passed through the long, dark corridor, lit only by sputtering oil lamps hung intermittently, he looked up into the portcullis chamber, barely making out the shadowy outline of his deputy, whose eyes and chain mail glinted in the faint light. Godwin sensed Wulfstan's alertness as he hovered, poised and taut like an animal ready to spring. Then Godwin called out and thumped on a heavy oaken door, the Keep's final defense, and was let in by Eoban, another trusty comrade of the crusade.

No modifications had been made to the interior of the stronghold; it had been left as a single large hall. The three Jewish men were gathered near its primitive hearth: a fire pit in the middle of the room with a hole cut out of the ceiling above. There was no chimney, and only a rudimentary hood over the vent kept the rain out. The large, drafty room was smoky and cold, despite the roaring fire. Samuel and Jacob were kneeling beside the fire, preparing the noontime meal. Earthenware pots sat on a grate placed over a corner of the fire, and the simmering food gave off a delicious aroma that made Godwin's stomach rumble as he approached.

They looked up hopefully when they saw him come through the door, the younger men rising to their feet. They took up positions behind the old man's chair— Jacob, dark and slender, with thoughtful, intelligent eyes beneath narrow brows; Samuel, stocky with a kindly face, a good-natured, easygoing man. Isaac remained seated, at their urging, the younger men gently pressing a hand to each bony shoulder. He resisted at first, his proud face set, then gave in, looking tired and frail.

Sorrow and shame washed over Godwin as he watched the learned Isaac struggle to maintain his dignity in the humiliating conditions. It was so unjust, this situation. Those who led yesterday's attack on the Jews ought to be here, not these good men. But, of course, Godwin could not arrest all those involved in the raid, though their actions had been unlawful. There were simply too many of them. Besides, Godwin knew he would find very few witnesses willing to come forward to testify against their fellow townsmen on behalf of the Jews.

He was beginning to suspect, too, that many joined yesterday's attack, not because they thought the Jews murdered Alfred, but because it provided an opportunity to vent their hatred without fear of accountability; for he knew that large numbers often carried out the worst injustices, taking refuge from the law, from moral principles, from their own consciences perhaps, in the anonymity of a dark fellowship.

He had once been part of such a fellowship. As a Christian soldier in a crusader army, Godwin had found himself fighting alongside men who seemed to have abandoned their normal code of behavior, or had left it behind in the West. Like his comrades, he had taken the cross firm in the conviction that the Holy Land should be in the hands of Christians, had been willing to die freeing it from the Muslims. But in the end, the way to that conquest had been too brutal; he could not partake in the slaughter, could not justify it, despite the large numbers of Christian soldiers who were dedicated to its cause.

The turning point, he remembered, came at the siege of Damietta. The crusaders had finally won the city, but it had come at the expense of many lives, including his cousin Aidan's. Christians now had a foothold in Egypt, the first step in their roundabout re-conquest of Jerusalem. All were celebrating the triumph, and the prospect of killing more infidels. But to his surprise, Godwin found that he did not share in his comrades' euphoric sense of victory. The bloody, ruthless brutality of crusading had somehow emptied his soul, leaving him bereft, like a burned-out castle, whole and sound from afar, but ravaged to those who cared to look closer. The core of faith that had compelled him to take the cross was gone, in its place doubt and bitter regret. Aidan was dead and Godwin would have to send the news back to his wife and parents. His son would grow up without a father. Was his death a noble one, a great sacrifice for Christendom? He wanted to believe it was, and not confront the dark conviction forming in his mind: that Aidan died a senseless death far away from home in a war that had nothing to do with honor and faith in God.

He felt like a barbarian raiding a foreign land, ruthlessly killing the valiant men who called it their home. And Muslims were not the crusaders' only targets: Godwin had seen countless Jews slain as well. In the

West, they were protected, not always successfully, of course, by Church and king, but in the Holy Land, he saw them helpless before the fury of crusader knights who called the Jews Christ killers, another enemy of the Faith.

Sickened by the slaughter, by his own complicity, Godwin had sheathed his sword, and gathering the knights who had taken the cross with him and Aidan, he returned home. With reinforcements arriving daily, all departing lords and knights were given a hero's hearty sendoff for bravely honoring their pledge.

Now, as he looked upon Isaac, Jacob, and Samuel, he vowed the same brutality would not reign in Hexham.

"What news have you, Lord Godwin?" Jacob was asking. "Is it safe to return to our homes?"

Godwin described the situation outside the Keep, assuring the men that their families and property were safe. "All is quiet now, yet I think another night or two in the Keep would be wise." Their expressions showed their disappointment and frustration. Godwin added, "Of course, I cannot force you to stay. You are free to go at any time, and should you decide to return to your homes, I'll give you all the protection I can manage. My men are trustworthy—should an attack come, they will stand for you. Yet, their numbers are small, and for this reason I think you are safest here, until this business of Alfred's miracle has died down."

"And if it doesn't, Lord Godwin?" Jacob demanded. "We cannot stay here indefinitely. Besides, is this not what our enemies desire? To see us locked away? I say we take our chances and leave this prison now." He glared at the walls of the Keep, at the iron manacles and chains strewn about the hall.

"I did not say your stay would be indefinite." Godwin could have predicted that Jacob would object to cautious counsel. "I am only asking you to consider another night or two. My men will be searching the woods through tomorrow, at the latest. If three days of scouring doesn't turn up a suspect, I doubt the murderer will be found that way. By Thursday, then, I'll have more swords at hand to ensure your safety."

Jacob's face was stubbornly set. Samuel only looked to his father-in-law, as did Godwin, knowing that Isaac would have the final say.

After a few moments' consideration, the old man said, "Lord Godwin, you have kept us safe and treated us with honor. If you advise us to stay, we will heed your words."

Jacob started to protest, but turned on his heel instead and stalked to the far end of the chamber. Prowling amongst the heavy shackles and fetters like a cornered animal, he kicked at a set of leg irons. Godwin felt sympathy for his friend, but was relieved by Isaac's pronouncement. The old man and Samuel ignored Jacob, accustomed to his outbursts. Holding a bony hand to his back, eyes amused, Isaac said, "But I must tell you, Lord Godwin, your accommodations are sorely lacking in creature comforts! How I miss my soft bed!"

Godwin smiled, marveling that Isaac could keep his humor. He quickly sobered, though, noting again how frail the old man looked. His body was racked from time to time by a dry, rasping cough. "Are you well, Isaac?" he asked, suddenly anxious. "Should I send for Fara? She might have a remedy for your cough."

But Isaac waved away his concern and Godwin took his leave. On the way out, he instructed the competent Eoban to keep the fire well stoked, day and night. "There's a cold wind blowing," he said. "I'll send Eilaf with more blankets." He gave the room a final glance, saying, "See to their needs, and keep alert!"

Constance paced the floor of Moot Hall as she awaited Godwin's return. Her flowing gown of pale blue wool, with its folds girded about her waist with a leathern belt, flapped against her legs as she strode back and forth, unease adding a jerky quality to her step. Seated upon stools at the far end of the hall were Hamo, Constance's young groom, Eilaf, and Bosa. They were playing at dice, oblivious to her nervous pacing, interrupting their game only to add wood to the fire when it burned low.

Her apprehension was driven by concern for Ivetta and the rest of the Jews, and she had come to ask Godwin how matters stood with them. However, the prospect of seeing him added to her nervousness, a realization that brought an ironic smile to her lips.

She recalled that once she had seen him most every day, for he and Aidan had been almost inseparable, so close was their friendship. Bordweal Manor was just across the river from Godwin's own at Dilston, making it easy for the cousins to spend much of their time together, retinues in tow oftentimes.

Arriving in the north three years ago as Aidan's new bride, she had been somewhat dismayed by the relationship. There was no jealousy on her part, for her husband was very attentive. Nor did the constant presence of Godwin and his trail of boon companions trouble her. She had been raised with four brothers, and it seemed only natural to live in a household bursting with men. No, her early uneasiness had stemmed from the great contrast apparent between the two men.

Aidan was quietly reserved, thoughtful and easily overlooked in a large gathering—a peaceful man of letters and learning. Constance had been drawn to his gentleness and to the serene composure he radiated. Godwin, on the other hand, burned with a powerful and compelling personality. Without arrogance, he commanded attention, and people were drawn to him as they were to a glowing fire on a frosty day.

Constance had been filled with resentment, seeing

her husband paled by Godwin's presence, thrust in his shadow. But as a newcomer, she had not understood the workings of their friendship, one that stretched back to childhood. It did not take her long to realize, though, that here was not a relationship of dominance and subordination; rather, the two men complemented one another, each seeming to value in the other what he himself lacked: Godwin, like Constance, was calmed and soothed by Aidan's gentle nature, while Aidan was supported and encouraged by his cousin's potent presence.

Once her initial reservations had vanished, life at Bordweal had been joyful, charmed it seemed now, as in the stories sung by bards and minstrels of Arthur and his court at Camelot. Then the call to crusade had come, and the cousins valiantly pledged to go, though only a year had passed since Aidan and she had wed. Yet crusading was strong in Constance's family, as it was among most Normans, and she did not dissuade her husband from taking the cross, for she knew that he wanted to prove his worth. The two had looked bold and invincible on the day of departure, she recalled, mounted in proud armor, setting out to reclaim the heart of Christendom. But only one had returned from the quest.

She had never asked Godwin about the circumstances of Aidan's death, and he rarely came to Bordweal now, nor did Constance encourage him. His presence was a painful reminder of the enchanted life they had all shared, like a dream in its fleeting bliss. When he had taken the bailiff's position, shortly after his return, she had been surprised, in a distracted sort of way. But her curiosity had quickly passed, his actions noted dully, then dismissed as she walked in her haze of grief.

Now, as she stood in the Moot Hall thinking back on all these things, Constance realized she had been very selfish, dwelling on her own loss without a thought to Godwin's. It must have been like losing a brother, and Constance only added to his grief by silently deterring him from seeing his godson, a precious link to the man now lost. She thought how disappointed Aidan would be at her lack of compassion, especially as Godwin had no one close. His wife had died in childbirth many years before Constance came to the north.

She looked over as the wide door to the Hall swung open. Godwin strode in briskly, only to stop mid-stride in surprise when he caught sight of Constance.

On first sight he looked to her the same as always— hair cropped short and face clean-shaven. He still dressed like a huntsman, she thought with a faint smile, ever disdainful of the pomp and finery that went with lordship. Ruddy and handsome, he looked like a seasoned campaigner who had spent much time in the saddle. Yet he seemed different in certain small ways, and the eyes that gazed at her were more somber than she remembered, holding less gaiety than before. The smile that had always lurked upon his lips was not there, and he seemed older to her now.

"Hello, Godwin," she said, with a voice that sounded rusty to her ears.

"Hello, Constance," he answered after a brief pause.

Silence followed as neither seemed sure of what to say next.

Godwin regained his composure first. "Is all well at Bordweal?" he asked. Then, with a hint of sharpness, "All is well with Aldwin?"

"Oh, yes," she assured him. "Everything is fine." Another pause. "Cynwyse sends her greetings and her love," she added.

He smiled, saying, "Give her my regards as well, will you?"

"I shall," she answered. Then, before another awkward pause could form between them, she said, "Godwin, I've come to ask after the Jews. Ivetta came to Bordweal yesterday, seeking my help. What madness possesses the folk of Hexham? Why do they accuse the Jews of murder?"

A tired look crossed his face, but he relaxed a little, too. "Had I known her plans, I would have warned her against traveling, even the short distance to Bordweal." He shook his head. "After yesterday, there are many I do not trust, and I consider it dangerous for any Jew to travel about just now. But come, sit by the fire with me, Constance," he said, pulling over a chair. "You and Ivetta are close, I know. You must be very concerned." Moving to a small table that held crockery cups and a flask, he poured out a measure of wine for each of them. "I will tell you the whole tale."

Godwin first told her how Gwyn had discovered Alfred's body on Monday, then he described the wounds.

Before he could go further, Constance asked him to go over the injuries again. After, she told him of the additions to the story reported by Thecla: the crown of thorns and the cross found near the body.

"No," he said with a weary sigh. "No such things were found, but I can well imagine how they were added to the tale. I believe that Alfred's true wounds, and the fact that he was killed on Good Friday, planted in the minds of some the idea that the Jews killed him, after the manner of Christ. The rumor spread, leading to the arrest of the Jews, and the story of the so-called crucifixion grew no doubt with each telling."

He leaned over to pick up a small block of wood and a knife, and Constance felt her nervous tension begin to ease. She watched as he started to peel away curls from the still-crude figure. At first, she could not make out the subject of his carving, then recognized the curved staff and realized it was to be a shepherd. She said, "Aldwin is not to be parted from his knights and horses. How he loves them."

"This, too, is for my godson," Godwin said, turning the unfinished shepherd in his hands. "A flock of sheep to tend will accompany him. I want Aldwin to play at more than soldiery and knightly sports."

As he carved, he went on to describe the search of the nearby woodlands. "I think we may be looking for someone gone mad or else a thief. Whichever, our murderer may be hiding in the woods, and there's always a chance my knights will find him, though we've had no luck so far." More to himself, he added, "I'll send them out one more day. After that, we'll go about the hunt in a different way. Even brigands have to come out of the woods. We'll check with the outlying manors, towns, and villages for any word of a stranger.

"I sent Wulfstan to Corbridge," he continued, telling Constance of Alfred's travel plans. "But he could find no one who had seen the boy, though the pilgrims were recalled readily enough. He never reached the home of his kin either. When the boy didn't show, they assumed his trip was canceled for some reason or another. And no one recalled seeing a stranger arrive on Good Friday, only the party of pilgrims."

Godwin described his own search of Hexham, and the last known whereabouts of Alfred. "We must turn up a suspect soon," he said, putting aside the shepherd and rising to his feet. "Finding Alfred's murderer is crucial for the Jews. Many will go on doubting their innocence if the guilty man is not found." He reached for an iron poker and prodded the wood burning in the hearth, sending up bright sparks and flames. Adding more from a nearby stack, the fire roared as the new wood caught.

He came back and sat heavily in the chair. Constance could sense that he was deeply troubled, his usual confidence frayed, although this would be apparent only to someone who knew him well. The last of her anxiety vanished as she turned her mind entirely to helping Godwin and their friends. She asked about the miracle at St. Andrews and its meaning as proclaimed by Brother Elias. "How does it fit with Alfred's murder and the arrest of the Jews?"

Godwin shook his head. "I don't know what to make of that business. It's absurd of course." He waved a dismissive hand, then recounted his meeting with Prior Morel and Brother Elias earlier that day. "I don't sense any malice on the canon's part. . . . Actually, I don't know what to make of the man," he admitted. "How and why he came to have this vision informing him of the miracle's meaning, I cannot guess, but nearly the whole town was at the church. Perhaps someone who has it in for the Jews seized upon the opportunity to further advance their guilt. The idea that Alfred was communicating his approval of the arrest could have been whispered in the canon's ear. But Brother Elias clearly thought it was God speaking," Godwin finished dryly.

He watched Constance, curious about her reaction, but she only looked puzzled, and he said, "If you meet the brother, you'll understand why I make the suggestion. He seems . . . impressionable . . . fragile somehow. A likely sort for visions, but vulnerable to those who might take advantage. . . ." He trailed off, thinking of Brother Elias's disarming innocence. Had he been naive? Should he have looked harder for signs of ill will? Godwin considered himself a good judge of character, yet there had been a few occasions when he was taken in by an honest-looking face.

Constance was thinking about Alfred's miracle. "I suppose it's not unusual for such a claim to be made. Saints communicate their will frequently, or so people say. Once, when I still lived in Wells, monks stole the relics of a saint housed in a nearby priory cathedral.

The brothers came late at night, stole into the holy crypt and took the bones of the saint. When the bishop discovered what the monks had done, he was furious, for many pilgrims stopped coming to the cathedral to go to the monastery instead. Much revenue was lost. When confronted, the monks claimed it was the will of the saint to be stolen, a sacred theft they called it; for no saint would allow the theft of its own bones against its will. A miracle occurred at the monastery shortly after the arrival of the relics, and all took this as a sign that the saint was content in his new home."

"Yes," said Godwin, "I've heard of such thefts as well, but always thought them conniving acts on the part of monks out to increase their monastery's prestige and income. At Canterbury, I hear, watch chambers have been built near the shrine containing Thomas à Becket's remains. Monks keep vigil day and night for fear he might be stolen, so much do nearby monasteries covet those bones."

"Then you do not believe that saints communicate their will through miracles and visions?" she asked.

"A true saint, perhaps," he answered. "But our Alfred is no saint, only a boy foully murdered. Besides, miracles and visions have no say in the secular courts." Godwin stared into the fire. "And yet we are taught that visions and revelations are the final arbiter of truth, and is not justice a search for the truth?"

"You believe without a doubt that the Jews are innocent?" Constance asked.

"Yes," he said without hesitation. "Nothing I have learned so far points to their involvement. They withdrew to their homes the whole of Holy Week, and no witness has come forward speaking to the contrary. They are as likely to have killed Alfred as the weaver. Nor is there any reason why the Jews would want to see the boy dead. But most important, I know them too well. They are incapable of such violence."

"If you accept their innocence, as do I," said Constance, "then you have no choice but to conclude that Brother Elias's vision is false."

"Yes," he agreed, admiring how cleanly she cut to the heart of the matter, never one to become mired in troubling questions and nagging doubts.

Constance herself was contemplating all that Godwin had told her, trying to sort it out, but her mind kept coming back to the bizarre circumstances of Alfred's death. It seemed to her that something vital was being overlooked. She shook her head in frustration.

"What are you thinking?" Godwin asked. "Have you noticed something I have neglected?" His voice sounded strained. "So much time has been spent ensuring the safety of the Jews. I haven't been able to concentrate properly, and I fear this will be to the murderer's advantage."

"No," she assured him. "I was only considering the ritual-like slaying of poor Alfred. Why would someone kill that way?"

"Insanity," Godwin answered simply. "Or perhaps it was not intended, merely coincidence." Constance looked doubtful, but Godwin described his theory that Alfred may have been robbed while traveling alone to Corbridge. "He may have missed the rendezvous with the pilgrims and set out alone. Someone, a thief, say, strangled him for the few pence his father gave him, for they were not found on his body. His cloak is missing, too. Perhaps the boy struggled and was stabbed. Then the murderer, who was heading north, took the body to the south fields to throw us off his trail. No one recalls a stranger arriving in Corbridge on Good Friday so perhaps he veered away from the town to head somewhere else." After a pause he added, "Yet I don't believe our murderer is hiding in the woods between here and Corbridge. I sent my men to search there, too, and no signs were turned up. As for the murder taking place on Good Friday, that could have been pure chance."

Constance pondered his scenario. "What of the punctures in Alfred's palms?" she asked. "Why would a bandit mutilate him so? And if the boy was murdered on the road to Corbridge, why take the body to the south fields, risking exposure? There are many places in the woods along the road north of the river where a body could be hidden. A thieving murderer would no doubt want his evil work to remain hidden for as long as possible, giving him more time to escape your writ."

"Yes, I've thought of that. It's difficult to make sense of. Placing Alfred in the south fields suggests he was meant to be discovered immediately."

"Indeed," Constance agreed. "It's a wonder he was not found on Good Friday, but three days later." She looked at Godwin's carving. "Animals graze there year-round. Strange a shepherd did not find Alfred sooner. Perhaps the boy was placed there later than you think."

"It's possible," Godwin agreed. "Though experience tells me Alfred had been lying in the open since Good Friday. The bitter cold no doubt kept those who mind the animals from the common pasturage."

They were silent for a time, considering. Then Constance suggested, "Perhaps we should put aside for a moment your theory of a bandit attacking Alfred on his way to Corbridge. The bare facts say he was seized somewhere near the Shambles, then murdered and placed in the south fields with the intent that he would be found immediately."

"Very well," said Godwin. "But what motive have we? Robbery still? Despite my present disgust with many of the burgesses, I cannot fathom any killing a small boy for his cloak and pennies. Those who dwell in the Shambles, where Alfred was last seen, are poor, yet decent folk, and mostly elderly."

"You are right, I think," Constance said slowly, rising from her chair to pace the floor. "We are not seeking a common thief, for it seems unlikely one would be so brutal with the body and murder for so little."

"Who would want to murder a young boy of this town?" Godwin wondered. "I keep coming back to the same question: What reason could someone have for doing away with Alfred? He was an only son—no brothers competing with him for an inheritance. I suppose it's possible there is a cousin or some distant kin lurking in the wings who killed for the boy's patrimony." But Godwin sounded doubtful, adding, "The brewer's business is brisk enough, but surely not worth murdering for. And Ada's not so old she couldn't produce another heir."

Constance agreed that murder for the sake of Alfred's inheritance seemed unlikely. "Besides, it leaves us asking once again why the murderer killed by way of imitating Christ's crucifixion." She stopped her pacing to look at Godwin, asking, "You don't deny this was the intent?"

"Nay, I would not deny it," he said.

"It seems to me, Godwin," she said, resuming her pacing, "the so-called crucifixion of Alfred is the key to uncovering the identity of the murderer." She spun on her heel to face him as he sat watching her from his chair. "If we can reason why Alfred was killed this way, we might have a chance of discovering who murdered him."

Godwin smiled faintly, hearing how she included herself in the hunt for the murderer. How good it is, he realized, to be sharing his thoughts with her again. "Yes, I follow what you say," he said. "The question is, then, why would someone crucify a child, or murder in such a way to make it look like a crucifixion?"

The question hung between them as neither could hazard a guess. Finally, Godwin said, "A person deranged, with no reason save their insanity, is still the only answer that comes to mind."

"Yes," agreed Constance. "Certainly, we are dealing

with an insane person, but one with a purpose, perhaps? What could someone gain by making Alfred's death look like Christ's crucifixion?"

After another long pause, Godwin said slowly, "I can understand why some have looked to the Jews. Many Christians believe that they harbor a deep hatred of Christ and secretly display their contempt and malice. I heard a tale from the royal justices where the Jews of a small town in the south were once accused of stealing a blessed Host and desecrating it. The story goes they secretly nailed it to a wall and stabbed it, in a reenactment of the Passion. According to the townspeople, the Host bled profusely, by holy miracle. The Jews were found out when the blood of the Host flowed through the streets."

"What happened to them?" asked Constance, horrified.

"They were arrested and the royal justices called in to judge their guilt. The case was dismissed and the burgesses fined for false imprisonment."

"Then all ended well for the Jews?"

"Alas, no. The people were not satisfied with the verdict, and a parish priest who enshrined the bleeding Host like the relics of a saint kept the accusation alive. Pilgrims came from all over to see it bleed and work miracles. People visit the bleeding Host to this day. The townspeople kept the Jews under constant threat, and after one was found murdered, the rest moved away."

Constance considered the frightening implications of the story. "How do these tales get started, Godwin?" she asked. "What sorts of minds give birth to them?"

"People who hold great hostility toward Jews, or fear them terribly, then read events to fit their way of thinking. Such as what happened here yesterday."

"I've heard terrible tales of Jewish massacres and banishment, but I never knew that people here harbored such hostilities," she said.

"It's like a plague, I think, spreading swiftly by way of fear and ignorance. And the farther it spreads, the more emboldened people become, egged on by larger numbers."

"Godwin," Constance said sharply, a new thought taking shape in her mind, "we've assumed so far that the arrest of the Jews was a chance event, governed by the bizarre circumstances of Alfred's murder. But is it possible that the Jews have been purposefully made to look guilty of the crime?"

Godwin stared at her. "You think that blame is being deliberately cast upon the Jews?"

"Yes!" she cried. "You suggested as much yourself when you said that someone at the church yesterday, anxious to make the Jews suffer, may have whispered in Brother Elias's ear."

"Yes," Godwin said slowly. "It makes sense. Someone could have orchestrated it all. First the murder, made to look like a crucifixion, then a rumor whispered here and there. It would only be a matter of working up the townsfolk. The miracle was a lucky break, an opportunity not wasted, perhaps."

Constance's mind raced forward. "If the Jews are being set up to take the blame, it would mean that Alfred was not the true target, only a means to an end. The murderer wants the Jews dead, for if they are convicted, they will surely hang."

They stared at each other, both minds wrestling with the implications. Slowly, Godwin said, "The question is, then, who would gain from the death of Hexham's Jews?"

SEVEN ☥

W ednesday morning dawned clear and cold, bringing with it a late hard frost that blanketed the
ground with a frothy dusting of ice. The cool-weather
crops of peas and greens that had been planted out earlier in the month lay limp and blackened upon the
ground, unable to withstand the unseasonable cold.
Yet the bitter northeast wind had subsided a bit, and
the bright sun on the eastern horizon promised warmth
by late morning.

Mounted on her palfrey, Constance was making for
Middleton, a manor and village about a four hours'
journey north from Bordweal. Aidan's parents were
currently in residence there, and Constance went with
the hope of enlisting their aid in her effort to help the
Jews of Hexham.

She and Godwin had talked long into the afternoon
the day before, and when the time had come for her to
leave the Moot Hall, he had insisted on seeing her
home. Constance invited him to stay on for evening
supper—to the delight of both Cuthbert and Cynwyse.

Her terrier was extremely fond of Godwin. The two
had a ritual greeting that neither had forgotten, despite
not having seen one another for so long. As soon as

Cuthbert heard Godwin's voice in the hall, he lunged from his basket in the kitchen, charging for the bailiff. When the distance between them closed, Cuthbert launched himself into the air, like a soaring ball of black fur, to land in the outstretched arms of the bailiff. "Hello, old boy!" he said warmly, hugging the dog to his chest.

Cynwyse, too, was very pleased by Godwin's unexpected visit. "Bless my bread, it's good to see ye!" she had cried, giving him a hearty hug. Then, shaking his shoulders, she scolded, "Too long it's been since ye were at Bordweal! Been neglectin' us all, have ye! It matters not that yer bailiff, ye should mind yer kin!"

Constance had winced at the words.

Cynwyse, always forthright, was especially outspoken with her former charges, Godwin and Aidan. She was taken in as an orphan by the earl and raised in his household at Dunbar. She was cook when the cousins arrived, and quickly became their surrogate mother in a household that was new and strange to the boys.

"With you, Cynwyse, I will always be twelve years old!" Godwin said, laughing. Then, as Aldwin gave him a shy greeting, "Your words are true enough, though. I must make amends to you all."

"And you shall always be welcome, Godwin," she assured him.

After the meal, they had settled on a strategy for helping the Jews. Godwin felt certain that they would not hang for the murder; there was no evidence to convict them. No, the greatest threat came, they agreed, not from the law, but from the townspeople; for if they persisted in the belief that the Jews killed Alfred, then the lives of Isaac, Jacob, and Samuel and their families would be continually at risk, their livelihoods ruined, and they would be forced to leave Hexham.

Thus, they had decided on a dual course of action. Godwin would continue to search for the murderer, as was his duty as bailiff, by trying to uncover who it was that conspired to cast the blame on the Jews. Constance would follow a different route, using her family connections to hasten the arrival of the royal justices to Hexhamshire. Once these justices examined the facts of the case, they would surely rule out the complicity of the Jews, helping to affirm their innocence in the minds of the townspeople. Not a flawless plan, they knew. It was difficult to predict how much lasting influence the justices might have. Still, they were vital, for felony accusations against Jews are matters for the royal court; never do they fall within the jurisdiction of private franchises, like the archbishop's, even though they might dwell within them.

Jews were considered part of the crown's "property" or "demesne," and it used to be that cases involving them were heard by the regular royal justices. However, back in Richard I's reign, as the population of Jews increased in England, special justices were appointed to hear their cases, in order to keep the courts moving more efficiently, and thus more lucratively. Called Justices of the Jews, they dealt most often with suits involving loan defaults and fraud. Felonies were well within their purview; however, a murder accusation involving a Christian boy was beyond their usual scope. The crown's regular justices would likely serve. But Godwin knew it could be months before the royal justices turned their attention to this small corner of northern England, despite the potential notoriety of the case.

At the end of John's reign, in the aftermath of war and the forging of the Great Charter, the normal organs of justice had broken down and were only now beginning to function as they had. Last year, the itinerant justices had finally been sent on a general eyre to hear all pleas, the first since 1208. Slowly, the crown was providing the justice demanded in the Charter, but the

Jews could suffer no delay. Constance's hope was that her father-in-law might use his powerful connections at the royal court of regents to hasten justice to Hexham.

Setting out just after daybreak, she went accompanied by Hereberht, Hamo, and two robust squires, Giles and Tilly. She was a bit embarrassed by the entourage, but Godwin had insisted she travel well protected, still concerned that a murderer stalked the woods. With her mare Aurora trotting spiritedly beneath her, she rode out ahead of the small retinue, elated by the unexpected journey, despite its serious nature. The brisk morning air and wild landscape exhilarated her senses. She rode with a purpose—something she had not experienced in a very long while.

As the party wended its way up through the hills above Bordweal, oak and birch thickened, obscuring the sun to create pockets of damp icy air that made the riders shiver in their cloaks. Constance pulled hers closer, feeling the stiff slip of parchment sown to the inside by Cynwyse: a talisman inscribed with the names of the magi, according to the cook, a powerful inscription that would ward off all evil. Seeing they were almost atop the last rise above the river valley, Constance spurred her mount to a canter, eager to gain some distance. Once clear of the Tyne boundary, they would bear northeast across more gently rising ground until they reached the high ridge where Hadrian's great wall imposed itself upon the land. Then, turning easterly from the wastes of the Border Fells, they would make for the ancient Roman road that rode the Northern Causeway. Straight and true, the highway would take them on a direct course to their destination. Constance hoped to reach Middleton Manor before late afternoon.

As the noontime hour approached, the party found a grassy hollow not far from the road where they could stop to eat a meal prepared by Cynwyse. As the squires spread blankets upon the ground, Constance unpacked the food, laughing when she saw the vast quantity provided by the cook, enough for a three-day march: she unwrapped peppered pork chops, still warm from the stew pot, thick slices of cheese and loaves of fresh bread, hard-boiled eggs, and spiced meatballs rolled in parsley. For desert they had wedges of pear pie, pastries filled with sweetened custard, and a rice pudding garnished with apple pieces and toasted almonds.

They ate enthusiastically, for no one had broken their fast before setting out, and the fresh air had given them hearty appetites. Once sated, they languished in the grass for a time, sluggish with food and the warmth of the sun. The steward, however, stood apart on the rim of the hollow where he had taken his meal in order to keep a closer eye on the road and surrounding landscape. Hereberht would never be caught in an ambush, Constance thought with a rueful smile as she packed away the surprisingly few leftovers. Yet she felt safer for his cautious nature. She glanced over at Hamo, who lay on the grass wrapped snugly in his cape, snoring peacefully.

When they set out again, it did not take long to reach the Causeway, and once upon it, they passed many travelers, for the road served as a main trade artery connecting north and south. Constance began to think of how she might best phrase her request on behalf of the Jews. She was sure she could count on the help of her father-in-law, Lord Eilan, but first she would have to get past Galiena, her mother-in-law.

Constance had married into a powerful family. Aidan had descended from two distinguished Saxon dynasties, the Gospatrics and the Gosforths. The Gospatric clan had blood links to the royal lines of both Wessex and Scotland, and was among the few native noble families of Northumbria that had retained power after the Conquest. The Gosforth clan had managed as well, holding to their barony in County Durham. Aidan's mother, Galiena, was the daughter of Earl Gospatric, Lord of Dunbar and March, and Sergeant of Beanley. The titles had passed to her brother, Patric, yet Galiena's dower from her father had been generous, providing her with considerable property in Northumbria. It was wed to the lands of her husband, Eilan, second son of Baron Gosforth, and together they comprised a powerful knot of private power in the north country.

Aidan's parents, especially Galiena, had been adamantly opposed to his marrying Constance. Her lineage, they felt, was far too undistinguished, and worse, Norman, to mingle with the great Saxon houses to which they belonged. Constance had once been betrothed to a man of Norman stock and of middling noble rank, like herself. When he died in a hunting accident, her father had looked to his younger brother, but nothing formal had been arranged. Then she met Aidan at the tournament. After that, little could keep the two apart, and both families feared the couple would flee to Wales and marry if thwarted in England. Each side had finally relented, had come to accept, even welcome, the marriage. Save Galiena, who offered resistance to the last. Thus, the relationship between mother and daughter-in-law was marked by tension from the outset.

Galiena, Constance suspected, would not be sympathetic to her cause. Indeed, she would probably be outraged by Constance's involvement. She might even try to block attempts to help the Jews, and Constance decided that the less her mother-in-law knew about the matter the better. She only hoped she could manage some time alone with Lord Eilan.

They were now approaching the turnoff to Middleton Manor. As Constance and her party climbed down the great highway to a smaller tract, they were surrounded by the manor's vast farmlands; land worked by villeins who labored on their lord's demesne in exchange for tenure of plots. Many were out gleaning stones from recently tilled fields, and Constance watched as a young boy spotted her party and, putting down his bucket of stones, sprinted for the manor to announce the arrival of visitors. Galiena strictly followed the rules of hospitality, and Constance knew it would not be long before a greeting party arrived to meet and escort them to their host and hostess.

So it was that the steward of Middleton Manor rode out to accompany them the remainder of the way. Lord Eilan and his lady were waiting outside as Constance and her companions drew up to the manor, not stone like most, but a traditional English timber frame structure with great posts, tie beams and wind braces. Constance loved it for its antique beauty and welcoming warmth. Yet, while the expression on Lord Eilan's face was equally warm and welcoming, the same could not be said for her mother-in-law. Galiena stood beside her husband, looking breathless and perturbed, as if she had hastily donned her finery (her silken wimple was askew) only to find that the caliber of her visitor did not warrant such regalia. She glowered, girdled in a rich purple gown shaped to her figure, as present fashion dictated. But the look was not flattering to her mother-in-law, whose thick waist and abundant flesh were crudely accentuated. A coat ample in cut and trimmed in fur lay heavily across her shoulders, and her broad flat feet were wedged into elaborately embroidered shoes, pointed at the toes.

"Constance!" Galiena cried shrilly. "What a surprise this is!"

"Lord Eilan, Lady Galiena," greeted Constance, dismounting. "How good it is to see you both."

Lord Eilan gave his daughter-in-law a warm embrace and kiss on the cheek before turning to meet the rest of her party, giving instructions for stabling the horses and stowing gear.

"I *do* wish you had sent word before coming, dear!" Galiena cried petulantly. "We could have made proper preparations to receive you!"

"I'm only here for the night, lady. Please don't go to any trouble on my account. It was a sudden decision. It's been far too long since we've visited, has it not?"

Constance *wanted* to be on closer terms with Galiena, and at each new encounter, vowed to make every effort to bridge the gap between them. Yet, invariably, before the end of each visit, Constance would be silently furious with the woman, incensed by her backhanded slights and jibes. She would go away asking herself why she bothered to make the effort, as vain and insufferable as her mother-in-law could be. Eventually, though, as the unpleasant memories of each visit faded, so would Constance's irritation. She would tell herself she had misinterpreted Galiena, or was being thin-skinned. By the next visit, Constance was always ready to try again.

Galiena led her up the stairway to the vestibule where wraps and outerwear were stored. "How terribly thin you are!" she exclaimed as Constance shed her cloak. "And so pale. I must send you home with a reddener for your cheeks, dear. It will bring some life to that pretty face."

"I'm anxious to tell you of Aldwin's latest accomplishments, lady," said Constance, trying to deflect the conversation to a topic that held more promise.

"I was *so* disappointed when I saw you hadn't brought my grandson," she complained. "We see him so seldom, dear, I'm sure he wouldn't even know us after all this time!"

Constance felt her smile stiffen. Groaning inwardly, she thought, This is going to be a very long evening.

Later, after supper, as they sat in the great Hall sipping wine, Constance got her moment alone with Lord

Eilan, and she had Hereberht to thank for it. Her mother-in-law was grilling the steward on the most efficient way to run a manor.

"What!" Galiena gasped. "You've commuted all labor services owed by tenants to money rents?"

"Of course," Hereberht said smoothly. "It's the way things are done now, at least among those who want to realize the full potential of their assets."

Galiena looked stricken, suddenly fearful she was not realizing the full potential of hers. "But how do you manage? How do you acquire your supplies and services?" she demanded.

"Why, we pay for them," the steward answered indulgently. "It's much more efficient. One doesn't have to keep track of all those customary obligations—who owes three bundles of thorn three times a year or which tenant must carry four cartloads of corn during harvest. Everyone pays a flat rent for their plots of arable land, and sells their produce at market. We purchase our supplies at a fair price like everyone else."

Galiena looked skeptical at this novel means of running an estate, one that flew in the face of tradition. She liked to see her tenants and villeins humbly delivering up their owed foodstuffs and services, to see them toiling for her as their forebears had toiled for her own ancestors. These were customs that reinforced the social order, and she was loath to tamper with them. *Purchase* foods and services while tenants in turn paid cash for rents? Why, it almost put everyone on an equal footing! How intolerable! Still, if new ways are more profitable. . . . "How do you know it works out to your mistress's advantage, Hereberht?" she asked, suddenly suspicious that he might be on the side of the lower born.

Hereberht took no offense, patiently explaining, "You see, Lady Galiena, agricultural profits are climbing. When tenants and villeins sell their produce directly at market, they stand to make a better profit. They are also motivated to produce more. And, with more produce available at the markets, prices are more competitive. The manor and everyone else purchasing at market benefits. More important, I can increase rents at a reasonable, yet steady rate. Customary dues are fixed, money rents are not."

Galiena leaped from her seat, grabbing Hereberht's arm. She had seen the light and was eager to convert. She led him from the room, posthaste, and Constance smiled, watching them go. Presumably, Middleton's steward was to be instructed forthwith in Hereberht's superior methods.

Lord Eilan and Constance sat quietly together, enjoying the peace that followed Galiena's abrupt departure. She knew she should ask her favor quickly, lest her mother-in-law suddenly return, yet found herself wanting to prolong this quiet interlude with her father-in-law.

They had been much alike, father and son. Lord Eilan radiated the same calm composure that put companions at ease. But where Aidan was retiring, mostly preferring his studies to the battlefield, Lord Eilan was born to lead, commanding an unshakable loyalty among his vast retinue of knights and men-at-arms. He was known throughout England, Scotland, and Wales, and kings and princes sought his support and advice.

Like a Saxon warrior of an age gone by, he was tall and fair, stalwartly built with a thick, flaxen beard streaked with gray, and bright eyes that missed nothing.

"I'm glad you've come, Constance, " he said after a few more minutes had passed. "It's good to see you traveling about again. This past year—it's not been an easy one for you."

"No," she agreed. "Nor for you, I fear."

They sat in silence once more, Constance thinking about the year just passed. Difficult indeed, but with the worst behind perhaps. "I've come to ask a favor of you, lord."

Eilan nodded, as if he had known there was more to her coming than a simple visit. Constance told him of the Jews' dilemma. He said nothing while she told the tale, and sat for a time mulling it over when she had finished. At length, he said, "It would be best not to mention this to Galiena, Constance. She cares little for Jews; as a matter of fact, it is a subject I avoid, so passionate are her feelings." He looked uncomfortable, and Constance feared he would refuse her request. "However," he continued, "I do not share those feelings, and will help as I can."

He paused, considering. "I'll get a message to the royal justices immediately—some are in the north, as luck would have it. As you know, the justices completed a general eyre only last year. Yet, some in the north are defying the verdicts, and the justices have been sent to bring these men to heel. Fortunately, two are in my debt for some lengthy hospitality I provided. That is useful to us! They will go to Hexham at my request. I am sure of it."

The remainder of the evening passed pleasantly. Constance felt that she had accomplished something useful on behalf of her friends, and her mood lifted. She minded not when later Galiena insisted upon a tour of her vast wardrobe. When they all retired early to their bedchambers in preparation for the party's sunrise departure, Constance lay in bed wondering how Godwin had fared that day. Then she fell into a deep, peaceful sleep, not waking until dawn.

EIGHT ✠

Godwin awoke early Thursday morning with a start, roused by a dream, or a nightmare perhaps; he could not say which at first, for the dream-images that stirred him fled swiftly, as if borne away on wings, leaving in their wake only vague and unsettling memories.

He sat up groggily, propped on elbows, fearful that if he stayed prone he would succumb to sleep once more and fall prey to the same disturbing dream-images.

It had had something to do with a terrible, winged creature, he slowly recalled. He had been pinned beneath its great shadow as it flew overhead, blotting out the sun before wheeling off. He had stood frozen, his only defense, staring after the evil shade, terrified it would circle back for another pass.

He tried to dismiss the disturbing image, but could not rid himself of a lingering disorientation, a feeling compounded by the sudden realization that he did not know where he was. The beams overhead looked strange, and the bed he lay in was definitely not his own. Even the pearly dawn light shining weakly on his face was somehow wrong in its direction and angle. Then memory caught up to his wakened state, supplying the answer: of course, he was in the loft of the Moot Hall.

As drowsiness receded, memory of yesterday's events came into clearer focus. He had stayed in town last night rather than going home, lest another disturbance flare up. Besides, he had been so weary by day's end that even the short ride home to Dilston Hall seemed too arduous to undertake.

Godwin and his men had spent the entire day on a wild-goose chase. In the morning, word arrived from a distant manor that a trespasser had been chased from an abandoned shed. Thinking this might be the felon sought by the bailiff, the hue and cry was raised. Godwin dispatched several men to run down the intruder, but they were given the slip. Then another sighting was reported and the hunt was on again, this time led by Godwin himself. But the brigand was wily, and the search went on for most of the afternoon. Finally, just as Godwin was about to call off the chase, a scout spotted the quarry as he lay on his belly lapping water from a brook. He was taken without resistance.

But the man who had led Godwin's worthy knights through field and wood, from one end of the shire and back again, turned out to be a mere boy, age ten. His name was Corby, and they soon learned from him that he had run away from his home late Sunday after losing some of the flock he tended for his family. Rather than face his father's ire, he had fled. When asked why he feared the bailiff's men, he said he thought they had been sent by his father to track him down.

Godwin had been furious at a whole day wasted chasing down an errant child when a murderer was on the loose. Yet, he was sorry for the boy, too, and had escorted him home personally on his big gray gelding. The bailiff wanted a careful look at the father who could strike such terror in his own son's heart. But Corby's anxiety dissolved almost immediately, and he showed not the slightest concern over returning home.

Godwin suspected he'd had his fill of living rough, and was more than ready to return to his family, whatever punishment awaited him.

The boy informed Godwin that he lived in a small toft above Haydon Bridge. As they made their way along the narrow woodland tract that Corby pointed out as the quickest route, Godwin asked him, "Were you not afraid, Corby, wandering the woods by yourself these past few days?"

"Aye, lord, I was, but I was fearin' more the back of my da's hand!" he answered cheerfully. Any fears he might have had were only dim memories, leaving hardly an impression, or so it seemed to Godwin. Corby's attention was consumed by the great horse beneath him, Godwin's Saedraca, and he was clearly delighted to be going home by such grand means.

"Did you meet anyone as you wandered about?" asked Godwin.

"Only a beggar," the boy readily answered, leaning forward in the saddle to stroke Saedraca's mane. "He it was that showed me the old shed."

Godwin's interest quickened. Beggars were common enough and seldom posed a threat, still, every possibility had to be explored. "Did this beggar seem dangerous, or threatening to you?"

"Nay, what?" Corby said, surprised by the suggestion. "I never thought that, lord. Mild as a May morn, that one, and kind, too, sharin' his food with me though he had little. I was happy for the company and sorry to see him move on."

Godwin looked at Corby. He wore sturdy homespun—a baggy woolen tunic fitted over a coarse shirt and belted at the waist. Leather breeches covered long, lanky legs, while upon his feet were skin boots secured by thongs. The beggar was obviously no thief, or Corby's rugged attire would not have been passed up. Yet, despite his apparent harmlessness, the man would have to be found, for no suspect could be overlooked. Besides, in his wanderings he may have observed something that could prove useful.

"Did he give you his name, Corby, or say where he was heading?"

"Nay, he said neither. I asked him, but he told me travelers meetin' in the wild or upon the road did not offer such information. If I wanted to live the wandering life, he said, I would have to learn its proper ways."

"Ways you need not trouble with, Corby," Godwin assured the boy. "Can you describe him for me? Was there anything about him that would mark him out in a crowd?"

"He was old—as old as you, lord," Corby said, turning to inspect Godwin, who smiled, amused that his thirty-five years made him "old." "He seemed smaller than you, though," the boy continued. "And he had a great scar running across his forehead. I wanted to know how it got there, but didn't dare ask for fear I'd break another rule." The boy twisted in the saddle to look at the bailiff again. "Did he do something wrong, lord? Is he the man you're hunting?"

"I wouldn't mind talking to him, that's all," Godwin answered, trying to keep his tone casual. He didn't want Corby clamming up, becoming wary of incriminating someone who had shown him kindness. "Did you see him last at the shed?"

"Yes," he answered, sounding cautious now.

"What day and hour did he depart? Can you recall?"

The boy hesitated, shifting in the saddle. "Daybreak on Tuesday, lord."

"Did you notice the direction he went?"

When Corby didn't answer, Godwin added, "I only want to speak with him. If he's done nothing wrong, he has nothing to fear from me."

Reluctantly, Corby said, "He looked to be heading southeast."

Toward more heavily populated towns, no doubt, thought Godwin. Alms were more plentiful in such places. He might be making for Durham. The city lay in that general direction, and shelters for the sick and poor were numerous there.

"Did the beggar tell you where he came from? A town he'd been to recently?"

"No," Corby answered, and with a finality that told Godwin no more information would be forthcoming.

The bailiff let the matter go, asking Corby if he wanted to take Saedraca's reins, and the boy's former gaiety was soon back. "How did he get his name, lord?" he asked, holding the reins reverently, keys to power he thought never to possess. He tentatively took up some slack, eager to command the might beneath him. But Saedraca gave a great snort and tossed his head. He was not a horse to be reined in needlessly, and the startled boy came close to losing his grip.

Godwin's powerful arms were there to steady him, and he laughed, saying, "It is said that his line descends from Saedraca the great—the sea dragon legend speaks of." At Corby's questioning glance, Godwin continued, "Saedraca was a great warrior dragon who defeated all his foes dwelling in the oceans. He came to land seeking greater challenges, and there he met the mare Meagol, whose name means 'mighty.' She captured his heart and he took her for his mate. It is said that in their offspring the power of land and sea are forever joined."

When they reached Corby's home, tucked beside a meadow opening before them in the woodland, his parents were so relieved to see their son that Godwin ceased to be concerned about an excessively harsh father. The errant sheep had turned up during the boy's absence as well, making for a happy ending all around.

Godwin smiled, recalling the reunion, then pushed himself from the makeshift couch in the loft, turning his thoughts to work at hand. He had much to do. Around midday, he would see Isaac, Jacob, and Samuel back to their homes and families. Plenty of protection would be provided, possible now that he had recalled his men from the search of the forests. Some of these would be sent to outlying towns and villages as Godwin broadened the scope of his search. He himself would tackle the possibility that someone, most likely a resident of Hexham, was attempting to cast guilt for the murder onto the Jews. Constance was due back from Middleton today as well, and he planned to ride to Bordweal in the afternoon to hear Lord Eilan's response to her request concerning the royal justices.

Suddenly, the floor beneath his feet shuddered, and the ladder leading up to the loft groaned alarmingly, bearing a weight that tested its limits. Bosa's large, round face appeared through the opening in the floor. "Morning, lord," he said, offering his shy smile. "The men have assembled."

"Good morning to you, Bosa," Godwin said, returning the smile. No matter the worries that occupied him, there was something about his deputy that always lightened his mood. "Tell them I'll be down in half a moment." Then, as Bosa's head began to disappear beneath the floorboards, he added, "Could you fetch me a loaf from the baker, Bosa? I'm near starved, it's been so long since I've eaten."

Godwin held a brief meeting with his men, listened to their assessments, then handed out assignments. Wulfstan and William the Welshman he sent southeast toward Durham to look for the beggar. He gave them Corby's rough description of the man. The great scar upon his forehead, he told them, should make him easier to locate. He instructed others to relieve those on guard in the Jewish quarter and the Keep, while the rest were sent to fan out into the countryside, making for distant manors and hamlets, seeking reports of any strangers or news of trouble.

When they had all gone, he sat munching thoughtfully on his bread. Then he noticed Bosa standing nearby, trying to be unobtrusive—a difficult feat for a man his size. Godwin realized he was waiting for an assignment. "We need to keep to our rounds, Bosa," he said. "I'll leave that to you. Look in on Saedraca for me, too. See that he has fresh water and feed. When you've come back, post yourself outside the Moot Hall. Try to keep away any who have nothing urgent to complain of, will you? I need some time to think."

As the door closed behind Bosa, Godwin finally turned his mind to the question he and Constance had previously raised. Who might have killed Alfred with the intent of casting the blame upon the Jews? Why would someone want to see the Jews arrested and quite likely executed? What was there to gain?

His crusading experience led him first to ponder the possibility that a religious fanatic was at work. In times of heightened religious fervor, as when a crusade was called, or during the season of Lent, Jews, he knew, sometimes came under attack. Zealots asked why Christians should seek enemies in the East when "infidels" lived right here among them. History had recorded numerous massacres of Jews by crusaders on route to the Holy Land. Thirty years ago, Godwin grimly recalled, York was the scene of one of the worst, prompted, some say, by Richard the Lion-Hearted's call to recapture Jerusalem.

One hundred and fifty Jews fled to the castle keep when the York residents suddenly turned on their Jewish community. Besieged by a violent mob, the sheriff's protection of the Jews melted away, and they were abandoned to their enemies. Many committed suicide in the hallowed tradition of their forebears, and were still honored as martyrs. Others were burned alive. A sad remnant survived, promising conversion to

Christianity, only to be slaughtered as they emerged from the castle.

The Church condemned such terrible acts of violence, yet Godwin always sensed a mixed message from ecclesiastical leadership concerning Jews. On the one hand, Christians were taught that Jews should be preserved as living symbols of Christ's Passion, to be converted not annihilated. On the other hand, the pope was constantly haranguing Christians on the danger of associating with Jews, and while persecution was officially denounced, it was often tacitly accepted, as bishops looked the other way when atrocities were committed.

Perhaps, Godwin thought, he should be seeking a religious zealot, a former crusader even. The murder took place on Good Friday, the holiest day of the Christian year. Perhaps this most sacred of days incited someone to act on their hatred of Jews.

But why kill an innocent Christian to persecute Jews? Why not go after the despised enemy directly? Was the murderer trying to throw off suspicion—muddying the trail that leads to his door? It was possible, he supposed. If a Jew was killed and the murderer discovered, the penalty would be the same as for killing a Christian—murder is murder in the eyes of the law. Perhaps this zealot desperately wanted to strike out at the Jews, but was afraid of being detected and so devised an indirect way of getting to his enemy.

Godwin shook his head. No, the scenario just did not ring true. Only a fanatically devout Christian would act on a desire to see the Jews dead, but surely such a person would not act by killing an innocent Christian, thus incurring eternal damnation. It was too extreme and contradictory—even for a fanatic! Besides, attacks motivated by religious passion were usually spontaneous, not coldly calculated, as this murder appeared.

He sat drumming his fingers, trying to think of other

possibilities. Maybe Lioba was onto something when she said that many harbor jealousy toward the Jews. Perhaps someone who resented their prosperity in Hexham was incriminating them as a way to destroy their lives and wealth.

But this raised the same objection: Why kill an innocent child to get at the Jews? It was such an extreme way to vent jealousy. If the Jews were the intended target, why not go after them directly?

Godwin racked his mind for an answer to the puzzle, staring across the length of the Moot Hall. His eyes came to rest on the *archa*, the chest where the Jews kept their bonds, the record of all debts owed to them. Godwin was on his feet immediately. Crossing the floor to the chest, he wondered if the motive could be right here in front of him, within the *archa*. Could someone be attempting to escape their debt by getting rid of the lenders?

It was possible, he realized, unclasping a ring of keys from his belt. If Isaac, Jacob, or Samuel turned up dead, murdered by someone trying to escape debt, it would not be long before those indebted to the Jews were scrutinized, leading straight to the murderer. Alfred's death could have been a diversion after all, obscuring the way to a desperate individual, overwhelmed by debt. It was an evil motive to contemplate—killing a child and implicating the Jews as a way to escape indebtedness. Godwin could not imagine anyone in Hexham even remotely capable of such wickedness. Yet, it was the first motive that made any sense to him.

As bailiff, Godwin kept one key to the *archa* while Jacob held the other. Opening the chest, he gathered up the folded parchments, taking them back to his desk. The first bonds he scanned were not portentous, recording loans of only small sums: three shillings borrowed by Gerald the scribe against a bowl of mazer wood; Ebba, the fuller's wife, had pledged two silver buckles for a loan of two shillings. Godwin leafed through more of the bonds, finding that most recorded similar small loans.

St. Andrews seemed to be the largest debtor, which came as no surprise to Godwin, for it was common knowledge that the priory borrowed regularly from the Jews. Indeed, the small Jewish community was largely supported through its business with the priory. A multitude of church items had been pawned and redeemed over a span of several years. Ornaments, altar cloths, silver bowls, and platters—any movable property seemed fair game for pawning. He even found a bond that pledged a relic of St. Wilfrid, one of his arms encased in silver and gold. Godwin wondered grimly how the fastidious Isaac felt about storing that pledge in his home.

He came next to a separate sheaf of documents tied in a neat bundle with cord. As Godwin took these out and scanned their contents, his interest quickened, and he slowed his reading. The bundle represented a substantial number of loans made to a knight of the shire, Sir Havelok. Godwin frowned at the name. The same knight who had hired Alfred to run errands. . . .

It appeared that Sir Havelok had not been fortunate in his financial dealings. Many of his loans had gone delinquent and had been paid by the priory in exchange for all the knight's lands and possessions. He was given lifelong room and board at St. Andrews, plus an income, in addition to the payment of his debts. Not an uncommon arrangement, and one that could be most beneficial to the corrodian, for it brought permanent security, provided the monastic house flourished. Yet it was an arrangement usually made by elderly folk with no heirs, overwhelmed by the formidable task of running a household in their declining years. It was difficult for many to part with a patrimony, and Godwin himself would find it very hard to give up his primary residence at Dilston, where his ancestors had long dwelled. As he looked through more of the bonds, Godwin found a substantial number of loans were still outstanding, taken against a horse and various pieces of armor—mail mittens, a helmet and a shield.

He read the detailed descriptions with interest, noting that Havelok's war gear was dated. The pawned helmet was bowl-shaped with a flat nose guard instead of the improved, and more fashionable, square-topped helm that covers the entire face. Mail mittens had protected his hands rather than mail gloves.

Godwin reminded himself that he knew little of the knight. His former lands were far from Hexham, and he wondered why Havelok had chosen St. Andrews to live out his days. Surely there was a monastery closer to his own manse, one his family had patronized. Was he here to hide his shame over the loss of his patrimony, unwilling to face the reproaches of friends and family? Perhaps, Godwin speculated, he became so embittered over his circumstances, blaming the Jews, that he conceived a way to exact revenge. It would take a bitter and ruthless man indeed to kill a child out of vengeance for the Jews. He decided to pay Sir Havelok a visit immediately.

Godwin gathered up the bonds and replaced them in the chest. He was reaching for his cloak when he heard a commotion outside the door. It swung open to reveal Bosa's back, which obscured the doorway so completely that hardly a chink of light was let in. A voice on the other side of his deputy exclaimed, "Will someone *please* remove this oak tree from my path!"

Fulk de Oilly. Godwin recognized the voice at once, and he sighed, wondering with annoyance why the archbishop had sent his chief man to Hexham. "Let him enter, Bosa," he called out.

His deputy obediently stepped aside. Fulk apparently held no grudge, for he eyed Bosa appreciatively as he strode past into the Hall, looking the deputy up and down. Taking in his immensity and guileless expression, he said merrily, "I'll wager I can find you better service, boy—a more profitable lord to serve . . . Bosa is it?" Fulk gave Godwin a roguish grin. "A strapping lad like you shouldn't be locked away in this godforsaken corner of England! Why, I bet I could get you into royal service, Bosa! You'd be invaluable at a siege—no need for battering rams and siege engines with you on our side!" He laughed heartily. "What do you say, boy? Are you game?"

Bosa looked panic-stricken, and Godwin realized that Bosa had not comprehended the full meaning of Fulk's words, nor his bantering tone. He heard only the suggestion that he serve another lord. Fulk, laughing merrily, seemed delighted by his distress.

Godwin said quickly, "Bosa is *my* man, Fulk. He's paid homage to me, and I'll not release him from my service—I value him too much."

Relief washed over Bosa's face, and Godwin sent him outside to resume his post.

After he had gone, Godwin turned to Fulk, saying, "Keep away from that one, Fulk. He's a special case and I'll not have you tormenting him."

Fulk shrugged and walked over to the wine, helping himself. "Still the mother hen, are you, Godwin, clucking after your chicks?" He raised the brimming cup to his lips. His eyes danced as he stared at Godwin across the rim. After drinking down the wine with relish, he said, "Is that why you took the job of bailiff? To be the good shepherd, protecting your flock from the cruelties of the wider world?"

Godwin ignored the words, having learned to disregard this man's taunts. Responding only fueled his bantering and increased the pleasure he derived from it. He had dealt with Fulk on several occasions and did not trust him whatsoever. Yet, despite this and almost against his will, Godwin found he rather liked the man.

A year or two past thirty, Fulk was elegantly handsome with a lean, lithesome body. His eyes were dark and inscrutable, save for the hint of mirth they revealed, reflecting his amusement with the world at large. He moved lightly with natural grace and boundless self-assurance, equally at ease among lowborn ruffians and the highest officials of the crown.

Some would put him in the ranks of the "new" men, or men "raised from the dust" as they were sometimes called, for they served both king and barons, though not a drop of noble blood coursed through their veins. Efficient and pragmatic, ceremony and custom were instantly dismissed by Fulk if hindering his objectives. He had risen to the top through sheer will and talent. University trained, Godwin knew him to be smart, ambitious, and not a little ruthless. The Church and crown were employing many such talented men these days, finding them more able administrators than the pampered, spoiled men of the noble class.

On those occasions when the archbishop suspected his bailiff was not enforcing his will strenuously enough, Fulk was usually dispatched to set Godwin on the proper path. Yet, while he was bound to carry out his lord's commands, the bailiff found that Fulk was often willing to compromise, if he could, or offer Godwin a more agreeable alternative. He excelled at bringing order, though it frequently came at the cost of someone's principles. "What brings you to Hexham, Fulk?" Godwin asked.

Fulk refilled his cup with another generous draught. "I'm here to deliver orders from your lord, the archbishop," he answered pleasantly. "I'm also commanded to stay and see they're carried out." He turned to look at Godwin, a smile playing around his mouth as he waited for the anticipated outburst.

Godwin did not give him the satisfaction, only stared at Fulk through narrowed eyes. Something was afoot. The archbishop's chief man did not normally deliver directives. They were sent by courier, and it was left to Godwin to carry them out. "What are these orders?" he asked.

Fulk took a seat in Godwin's chair and propped his travel-stained boots upon the desk. "Word of the arrest of the Jews has reached the archbishop's ears—"

"They have not been arrested," Godwin broke in. "They are in the Keep for their own protection."

"Yes, yes, we know the tale," Fulk said, waving a hand at Godwin. "Word of the boy's murder was carried to us by your man, and then a courier arrived late Tuesday from Prior Morel updating us on the situation. The archbishop is quite fascinated by this miracle—"

"By God's eyeballs!" roared Godwin. "Morel had no right!"

"He has every right, Godwin," Fulk said calmly. "More than that, it's his duty. He must keep the archbishop abreast of all matters pertaining to St. Andrews."

"He has no business reporting on matters concerning *my* jurisdiction," Godwin argued.

"The miracle happened in his church," Fulk pointed out. "And quite a show it was, or so we heard—"

"What is the will of the archbishop, Fulk?" Godwin interrupted again. "I pray he has sent more besides you to help me track down the murderer."

"He has no men to spare. Besides, it's likely you have your murderers." Before Godwin could interrupt, Fulk said quickly, "Your lord has sent me to ensure that the Jews remain imprisoned. Morel has told us of your reluctance to hold them, and unlike you, the archbishop is not convinced of their innocence. He feels that the circumstances of the murder—the ritual slaying and the miracle—betoken the guilt of the Jews."

Godwin struggled to control his anger. Through gritted

teeth he said, "You are saying, based on a second-hand report by a meddling prior, that I am commanded to charge the Jews with murder?"

Fulk's legs dropped to the floor, and he leaned toward Godwin, saying, "The archbishop bids you to consider their guilt, and orders they be kept in prison while you work to prove it. He is wondering, Godwin, why you have dismissed so quickly the possibility that they are responsible." The question hung in the air like a sordid accusation.

"Because I *know* these people," Godwin exploded. "They are not capable."

Fulk stared at Godwin, a peculiar expression on his face. "If the archbishop heard you, he would say you have become altogether too friendly with these Jews, that your judgment has been impaired." At the look on Godwin's face, Fulk said quickly, "Ease your temper, Godwin! You look as you did when you threw me from this Hall—I wore those bruises for weeks! I am not the archbishop and care not who you befriend. But I am obligated to carry out his bidding, and he orders you to keep the Jews imprisoned."

"If I am not mistaken," Godwin said evenly, taking another tack, "evidence of guilt is required to hold a person for a crime."

"But you have not even looked for evidence against the Jews, or even considered them as likely suspects, or so the archbishop has heard," Fulk protested. "Why are so many in this town convinced of their guilt? Surely there is something to the charge, for why else would so many believe?"

Godwin was seething. Most of his ire was directed at Morel, who had obviously provided the archbishop with a thorough report. He said, "The townsfolk's beliefs are not guided by proof and reason, Fulk. Besides, do you think it matters to me that many consider the Jews guilty? Guilt and innocence are not determined by the opinions of the majority, which in this case are governed by malicious rumors and gossip. The Jews have not been considered suspects, nor has anyone, because I have no evidence that points to them or anyone else. If it happens that some comes to light that implicates the Jews, they will be investigated like anyone else. I know how to set aside my personal feelings and carry out my duties as bailiff, though the archbishop obviously thinks I lack the ability." Godwin's tone was bitter.

Fulk came from behind the desk to stand before him. "The archbishop has faith in your ability, else you would not hold this post, no matter how powerful your patron uncle. Only he is used to employing a more ruthless kind—like myself." He flashed his devilish grin. "Your generous ways at his expense rankle him at times, yet he thinks highly of you, Godwin—I have heard him say as much. He is stingy with praise, that one, so take heart. Consider that he is far away, hearing of these events secondhand. News of this murder is spreading across the countryside, and he is under pressure to see the matter resolved without delay. His reputation is at stake." Fulk spread his hands beseechingly. "See the situation through his eyes, Godwin. A Christian boy has been murdered, possibly by a Jew, in the archbishop's own liberty. It is a grave affront that must be met with swift, harsh justice. If not, his reputation will suffer. He could be ruined."

"I don't care about his political ambitions!" Godwin shouted. "Or his damned reputation! I only care that the proper person is punished for this crime!" He threw up his arms, calling to the rafters, "Is that not my duty? Why am I being blocked at every turn?"

"I have not said you cannot do your job, Godwin, only you must keep the Jews in custody while you carry on your inquiry and be more attentive to the prospect of their guilt."

"But why not let them return to their homes while I prove their innocence?"

"The archbishop fears they will flee, and it would reflect poorly on him if they should escape his grasp. He's convinced of their guilt, Godwin, and is sure that evidence will turn up to prove it. There had been other cases like this in England, you know, several where Jews have been found guilty." Weighing his words carefully, Fulk added, "And besides, the archbishop doesn't approve of Jews dwelling in his liberty, as the former archbishop did. I believe he sees this as his opportunity to be rid of them."

Another thought struck Godwin, and he said, "He has no authority over the Jews, though they dwell in his liberty. He cannot administer justice where they are concerned. It is a matter for royal authority."

"Yes, of this he is fully aware, but *you* have every right to keep the Jews imprisoned if they pose a threat. Still, the archbishop has taken the precaution of consulting the regent, who is now in York, and he, too, bids you to keep the Jews in custody."

Godwin sagged at this news, feeling that all were conspiring against him. Fulk continued, speaking more to himself, "In fact, the archbishop is negotiating with the regent for jurisdiction over Hexham's Jews, though I cannot think why it's important to him. . . . The regent might well give it to him. He is anxious for support in the north and is handing out favors right and left to secure it."

Godwin's mind raced. It was imperative, he realized, that he find the murderer and quickly, lest the situation escalate beyond his control. "Fulk," he said, "I told you before that I have no evidence yet that points to a guilty party. That was not quite true. Just before you arrived, I found something that might prove damning for a certain individual."

Godwin first told Fulk of the theory he and Constance had reasoned: that the Jews were being set up to take the blame for the murder. Fulk looked at once intrigued and skeptical, and Godwin went on to describe his search through the *archa* and his discovery of Sir Havelok's debts. "Think of it—this man is in debt beyond hope, and his lands and possessions have been lost. He must be terribly bitter. Perhaps, with nothing else to lose, he conceived a way to get rid of the Jews. With them gone, he has his revenge *and* is clear of debt—"

Before Godwin had finished, Fulk was shaking his dark head. "It won't wash, Godwin. One can't simply kill a Jew to escape debt. If it were that simple, England would be littered with dead Jews." At Godwin's puzzled look, Fulk continued, "You see, debts owed by Christians to Jews come into the king's hands on the death or forfeiture of Jewish creditors. That is why Jews are considered part of the royal demesne—if a Jewish lender dies, or cannot pay his taxes, or is convicted of a felony, the crown confiscates his bonds and collects on the debts. It has proved immensely lucrative—the crown protects the Jews and their livelihood of money-lending, and when the king needs cash, he squeezes them. If the Jews can't pay, their bonds are confiscated and the money is demanded instead from the borrowers. It's like an indirect tax, really. Most people do not know that when they borrow from Jews they are really borrowing from the king. Nor is the crown obligated to the terms of the bonds—once in the king's hands, the borrower can be forced to pay immediately. If your Sir Havelok was looking for a way out of debt, the last thing he would do is kill his Jewish lender—the crown is a far worse creditor to have on your back!"

Fulk snapped his fingers suddenly, saying, "That's it, Godwin! That's why the archbishop wants jurisdiction over Hexham's Jews—he wants their bonds! Sly bastard—even I hadn't thought of that." With no response from Godwin, Fulk explained, "Don't you see, if the archbishop obtains custody of your Jews, and if they hang for the murder, he'll get their bonds. You've been through the *archa*, Godwin, how much would you say there is in outstanding debt?"

Godwin shrugged. "Most debts are trifling. But when taken together and added to the sums owed by the priory and Havelok, I suppose it's a fair amount indeed."

"That's it then," said Fulk. "He's set his sights on those bonds. There'll be no stopping him—"

"He won't get his greedy hands on the bonds because the Jews are not going to hang!" Godwin said this with more confidence than he felt. "Back to Havelok, Fulk. Maybe he has some scheme in mind— like offering military service to the crown in lieu of repayment on the bonds. Or perhaps he's setting up the Jews simply to get his revenge."

"Mmm . . . it's possible I suppose," Fulk admitted. "One can never tell." He took a few steps toward the door, saying, "Let's go along and visit this Sir Havelok, shall we? Size him up, see if he looks capable."

"I can see to Havelok myself, Fulk, but there's another matter we should discuss." Godwin told him of Constance's errand to the north, and their plans of bringing the royal justices to Hexham. "I haven't heard yet whether she was successful, but if she was, ought we to proceed with the justices?"

Fulk considered for a moment. "If the justices come to Hexham," he said, "their journey will have been in vain, I think. As I said, it's likely the archbishop will secure jurisdiction over Hexham's Jews, and the crown will have no say in the case." Fulk looked thoughtfully at Godwin, seeming to weigh the matter in his mind. "You're convinced the Jews did not murder the boy, Godwin?"

"Nothing so far has led me to think they had a role

in Alfred's death, nor is there any reason why the Jews would want him dead," he answered. "Yes, I'm sure of their innocence."

"And you're set on proving it? It would be easier, you know, to declare them guilty—no one would gainsay you. Most are certain of their guilt and care not about evidence. The verdict would please many, especially the lord you serve."

"I won't do it, Fulk," Godwin said evenly.

The two men stared at each other. "I know," Fulk said, heaving a sigh. "Why must it always be the hard way with you, Godwin?" Then, more briskly, "Very well, here is my advice. Call off the royal justices, for their presence will only anger the archbishop, and you need him on your side, else the Jews are lost. Then, you must direct every effort to finding your murderer—time is short, I fear. The archbishop will see this matter resolved with or without you. And the Jews must remain behind lock and key in the meantime. If the archbishop hears you have released them, matters will be taken from your hands." He walked a few paces toward Godwin, saying, "For now, I will leave you to deal with this. I have another errand to attend, but when I return, Godwin, this murder must be resolved. I cannot put off the archbishop very long. Word will come here concerning the matter of jurisdiction. Watch for your lord's messenger, and send for me if you have need."

"Where can I find you then?"

He flashed his wicked grin. "I'll be at the home of a certain baron who is presently overseas. His young wife is quite lonely and seeks my company." Moving toward the door he said, sweetly innocent, "Her offer of hospitality is quite irresistible, and I go in hopes of providing her the comfort she desires." Fulk's dark eyes danced once more. "You can find me at Warden Manor, just west of here."

Godwin shook his head. Women were attracted to Fulk, though he wasn't sure why. His dark looks, perhaps, or maybe it was the smile, which could broaden into a resplendent beam so disarming that Godwin had once seen a woman take a flustered step backward when awarded it. He said, "You play a dangerous game, Fulk. I know this baron well. He's prone to unexpected arrivals, and his temper rages like the wildest gale. Watch your back, else I fear the next time we meet I'll be pulling a dagger from it."

Fulk only grinned, and Godwin saw him out. Then he made ready to visit Sir Havelok. First, though, he would have to go to the Keep and relay Fulk's orders to Isaac, Jacob, and Samuel—a task he dreaded. Jacob would be especially bitter, he knew, over the news that they would not be returning home today. Their wives would have to be told as well. He would also need to keep knights posted at both the Keep and in the Jewish quarter. Damn the archbishop for not sending more men!

Later, he would have to go to Bordweal. Alas, Constance's journey had been made in vain it would seem; the royal justices offered no way out for the Jews now. As he headed toward the door, he tried to shake off the heavy foreboding that was beginning to grip him. It had been difficult enough struggling against the townspeople on behalf of the Jews. Now his own lord was joining their ranks, and Godwin was not at all sure he could stave off the assault. Just as he reached for the door, it opened suddenly, and Godwin stepped back to make way for Bosa. His good-natured deputy looked troubled. Trailing him was Grendel. "Lord Godwin," said Bosa. "Grendel here says he saw young Alfred go into Isaac's house on Good Friday."

Nine ✦

Constance and her party made good time on their journey back from Middleton, having left by daybreak. Galiena was put out by the early morning departure, as she preferred to sleep late. Yet it was her duty to stand beside her lord and bid their guests farewell, and she had huddled begrudgingly on the stoop, squinty-eyed and grouchy, wrapped in a voluminous purple robe. When Constance reached the end of the lane and turned to wave a final farewell, only Lord Eilan remained, arm raised in a parting salute. Even from a distance, his noble figure was conspicuous, enhanced by the backdrop of the fine Saxon manor.

Having stopped only once for a brief rest, they approached the hills atop the Tyne by late morning. As they descended the short distance to Bordweal, Constance was cheered by the sight of the familiar valley and by her own small manor tucked amid its forested hills. Across the river, Hexham sat regally upon her dais, the tower of the church proudly prominent. A mist hung heavy over river and haughs, so that the town almost seemed aloft—a heavenly city amidst the clouds.

Surveying the countryside, she marveled that it could be April. Another hard frost had come in the predawn hours, and although the sun was shining brightly again, the air was very cold, made harsher by the biting gusts that swept up the valley from time to time. Yesterday's brief respite of pleasant warmth, it seemed, had only been a taste of the coming spring. The party arrived at the manor with numbed fingers and reddened noses, despite gloves and thick scarves swathing their faces.

"Please see that Aurora and your own mount are watered and fed immediately," Constance told Hamo as she dismounted in the manor yard. "We'll be on to Hexham shortly." She had decided to take her news straight to the Moot Hall rather than wait for Godwin to come to Bordweal, eager to share the tidings of her success and equally anxious to hear how he had fared with his own task.

"Once the horses have been tended, Hereberht, why don't you bring the boys to the kitchen for some wine." The three sat miserably hunched in their saddles in a hopeless attempt to evade the frigid air. "We can all warm ourselves before the hearth."

Hereberht pursed his lips, irritated no doubt by the impropriety of squires and stable boy mingling with their mistress over mulled wine in the manor kitchen. But he acknowledged her instructions with a crisp nod, then led the party down the lane past the garden's wattle enclosure to the stables.

Constance ascended to the main entrance, taking care not to slip on the frost that still clung to the shaded steps. No one was about, and the absence of human activity imparted an unusual serenity to the countryside. At the landing, she turned to admire the rare, silent world. The bright sun on the open fields had transformed the frost to a light mist that hovered over the earth in a thin band like a gossamer veil. Ice-encased grasses and fallen leaves that had escaped the sun's melting brilliance glinted like jewels strewn about the landscape. Then another bitter wind blew up, and

Constance regretfully turned to go inside, hastening to close the heavy door against the cold.

Tenants and servants had found indoor tasks to attend, no doubt, thought Constance as she relished the warmth of a lively fire burning in the Hall's hearth, the first sign of life at Bordweal she had yet to encounter. She debated going directly upstairs to the private chambers in search of her son, or making straight for the kitchen. Opting for the latter, she threaded her way through the tangle of trestle tables that filled the room, heading for the kinked passage that led through the pantry to the kitchen. Constance had continued her husband's tradition of taking the noon repast in the Hall with the entire household, servants and all, so that many benches and tables were needed to accommodate everyone. When meals were finished, the trestles were folded and pushed out of the way against the walls along with the benches.

As she reached the passageway, made with many turnings to keep the cooking smoke from the Hall, she heard the chatter of voices in the kitchen. Drawing nearer, she could distinguish her son's chirpy babbling from Sidroc's slow, measured intonations, but above all, Cynwyse's exuberant voice stood out as she gladdened her listeners with one of her stories.

"So I fixed her up with a bit of mandrake and the proper words," Constance heard her say. "And she went away merry as a maypole dance. Curse my bread if she wasn't back inside a week, lookin' to find a way to put things as they were! 'Nay what!' I says. 'First ye come to me for a charm to get him interested again, now ye want it undone? There be only one way to cure his appetite now,' I told her. 'No charm have I that can reverse mandrake. Powerful plant, that! You got your wish, now ye must sleep with it!'"

Constance entered the kitchen as the group chuckled over the dilemma of Cynwyse's sufferer. They looked surprised to see their mistress returned so early, perhaps a bit embarrassed, too, to be found standing with backs to the fire and hands wrapped around steaming cups. Cynwyse was vigorously grinding spices with pestle and mortar as she amused her listeners, while Aldwin's nanny, Hilda, sitting on a stool near the cook, kept a watchful eye on her charge. When her son caught sight of Constance, he whooped and made a straight course for her skirts. Cuthbert followed in his wake, tail wagging hard as he pranced forward to greet her. The staff parted to make way for them, and as Constance lifted her son high over her head, she felt a surge of happiness to be back amongst her family. Leave Bordweal permanently? She wondered if she could.

Cynwyse hurried forward. "Welcome back, lady!" she cried. Clucking loudly, she drew Constance to the hearth. "Ach! Cold as ice are ye! Come close to the fire, lady. Make way everyone!" she ordered, shooing people from her path.

A cup of warm wine was pressed into her hands, and Constance pulled her rocker closer to the fire, wondering as she sat down if she would ever again be warm. Aldwin clambered onto her lap, and as she maneuvered to keep her wine from slopping, he slid down again to chase Cuthbert into the pantry, Hilda close on his heels. She heard his squeals of delight in the Hall, and thought about poor old Cuthbert. It was getting difficult to put in a full day's rest.

She sat back contentedly and sipped at her wine, watching the servants melt away as they moved to go about their business. They were anxious no doubt to avoid Hereberht, who could not be far away. Constance noticed a few sidelong glances in her direction as they filed out of the kitchen and she wondered at the meaning. Concerned, she asked Cynwyse when they had all gone, "Has there been any more trouble for the Jews? Has Godwin sent word?"

"Nay," the cook assured her. "No word of trouble, nor news from Lord Godwin. He's been sore occupied, or so I've heard." Cynwyse described Wednesday's massive hunt, all for a truant boy.

"Poor lad," said Constance. "What a fright to have all the knights of the shire on your heels!" Then, recalling the furtive glances of the servants, she asked, "I was wondering about the staff, Cynwyse. Why do some look at me so strangely?"

The cook pulled a face. "Pay them no mind, lady!" she answered, waving her pestle dismissively. "Workin' hard at the rumor mill are they, grinding out their useless gossip." She went back to her pounding, saying, "'Tis Thecla behind it all, spreadin' her tales and eggin' folk on." Cynwyse shook her head in disgust. "If there was a charm to silence a tongue, I'd use it on that one!"

"Are they still going on about the murder?" Constance asked. "Or has new grist been added?" Cynwyse did not answer immediately, and Constance watched as she carefully poured her pungent dust from the mortar into a sheepskin pouch. Pounding and sorting spices was tedious work, and many times she had suggested that Cynwyse buy them ready prepared. But she always demurred, suspicious of the convenience, convinced that the quality would be lacking.

A beleaguered Cuthbert wandered back into the kitchen, liberated from the affections of Aldwin for the time being. He made straight for his basket, giving her a long-suffering glance as he passed by the rocker. Then he dug into the scrap of blanket that lined his wicker bed, front paws working. It was the start of a laborious process he always undertook to fashion himself a comfortable nest. Next, he tugged at the blanket with his teeth, positioning it just so. Finally, after turning several tight circles to locate just the right position, he plopped down with a sigh.

Constance glanced up, curious as to why Cynwyse

had not answered her question. "What are they saying?" she asked, a slight frown on her brow.

"I won't be repeatin' rubbish. Nor will anyone, I reckon, now I've had my say. Folks here better tread their toes straight or they'll be answerin' to St. Peter!"

Constance was truly alarmed now. Cynwyse was not usually reluctant to repeat "rubbish" though she might condemn it. "For the love of Mary, Cynwyse, tell me what they are saying!"

"I won't and that's that!" she declared. "Mind what I say or take it up with—"

She broke off as Hereberht came in with Hamo, Giles, and Tilly following at a discreet distance, as he preferred. Constance stood to retrieve the vessel of wine warming in the coals, then poured them each a generous measure. The boys did not idle over their drinks, however, and seemed anxious to be free of the steward's rigid watchfulness. Within a few minutes, they were thanking her and hurrying from the kitchen. As Hereberht turned to follow, Constance said, "Stay a moment, will you? Cynwyse was about to tell me of some gossip." She gave the cook a stern glance. "You ought to hear it as well."

Cynwyse shot her mistress a defiant look, but relented, heaving an exasperated sigh. Opting for bluntness now, she said, "Word's got out that ye be aiding the Jews, lady. Some are sore unhappy about it, saying ye ought not to show them such high favor."

Constance was surprised, then realized that she should have expected such a reaction from some. "Is that all they say, Cynwyse?"

The cook hesitated. "Well . . . one or two folk, and mind you it's just one or two—they say ye dishonor their dead lord, who gave his life fighting the infidel. Ye help those every bit as wicked as our enemies in the Holy Land when ye ought to be settin' a proper example for your son, their future lord, who must one day avenge his father as a crusader—"

"No!" cried Constance, startling both cook and steward. "Never will that happen," she said. "No more pointless deaths will there be."

There was an awkward pause. Cynwyse cast a nervous glance at Hereberht, who wore a deep frown. Constance saw that they did not understand. How could they? "There is nothing I can do about gossip," she said, suddenly very weary. "Save let all know that I condemn such evil tongue-wagging. That is for you to take up, Hereberht," she said, facing the steward. "Idle talk is one matter, harmless for the most part, but these tales they are spreading can be dangerous for the Jews. See that it stops. I know it's a difficult task to ask of you, but you must do what you can."

As the steward took his leave, Cynwyse followed him to the passageway, standing poised with her ear cocked, listening. Satisfied that no one lurked nearby, she went back to her mistress, saying, "Ye ought to guard that tongue more closely, lady," she warned. "Ye never know who's about to overhear, and it's no good adding fuel to their fire. Some might be grieved and vexed by yer words. You saw Hereberht—you near shocked his ears off!"

Constance waved an impatient hand, saying, "I care not what people think of me, Cynwyse." But walking to the window and gazing out at her deserted garden, Constance felt betrayed. She had come to think of those who served at Bordweal as a family of sorts, and it hurt to know that some spoke of her so wickedly.

As if discerning her thoughts, Cynwyse said, "Remember, mistress, it's only a few who carry on so— those bent on stirrin' up strife. Most adore ye and never speak ill. They may not speak up for ye as they should, but it takes a tough hide to stand up to certain knaves around here. Ye must give them that."

Constance turned from the window to give Cynwyse,

her staunchest supporter, a faint smile. When she had first arrived at Bordweal, there had been some unsettling opposition among the servants toward their new mistress. They had mistrusted her like they would any foreigner, yet Constance had slowly earned their respect, due largely to Cynwyse's unwavering support. The cook, like her kitchen, was the core of the household, and most of the servants, Constance knew, followed her lead eventually.

"You're right, of course, Cynwyse. And I'm ashamed to be carrying on when there are more vital matters to attend. Besides, this whole affair with the Jews will be over soon." Constance described for the cook her meeting with Lord Eilan and his willingness to help. "The royal justices could be here any day, Cynwyse! I'm off to Hexham to tell Godwin!"

Once in town, Constance found the Moot Hall deserted and locked up tight. Looking around the Market Square she could find no one, not even young Eilaf, who could tell her where she might find the bailiff. Disappointed, she decided to try back later, going in the meantime to the priory, for she had not yet had the opportunity to kneel at Alfred's grave to offer up a prayer. But before going to St. Andrews, she decided to stop and give Ivetta and the others her good news.

But she was disappointed again when she reached the Jewish quarter; for the Jews were not in their homes, a fact that troubled her. Constance knew that Godwin had planned to release the men from the Keep around midday. Surely, they should be home by now. And where were the women and children? Had they gone to the Keep to accompany the men? Or could they be at Isaac's, deep in prayer within the synagogue? She stared up at the shuttered stone house, listening for signs of life. But there were none, and the place had a deserted air about it, her knocks echoing through empty space.

"You won't find anyone at home," called a man's voice, just as Constance was about to knock once more.

Turning, she saw two of Godwin's knights posted across the lane at the bend in the road. Their positioning allowed them to detect approaches from either direction.

She crossed the street, recognizing both men. One was called Burchard, the other Waldeve, a former man of her husband's, now in Godwin's service. She greeted the men, asking, "What news have you of the Jews? I expected to find them in their homes."

"They're in the Keep, lady," Burchard answered. He would say no more, and neither knew the bailiff's whereabouts.

Constance hesitated. Should she go to the Keep? Godwin might be there, but if not, the guards would be equally noncommittal and think her meddling in affairs that did not concern her. No, she decided, resuming her course for the priory, it would be best to wait and hear any news from Godwin. Besides, it was likely a simple matter of prolonging the release for the sake of prudence. She smiled as she considered the depth of Godwin's concern, realizing, too, that there were many things about this man she admired.

When she reached the priory's gatehouse, Constance was greeted by Brother Michael, who waved her on cheerfully when she had stated the purpose of her visit, adding, "Join the throng, lady!"

A throng indeed, she was surprised to find. The courtyard outside the west doors of the church was packed with people. Had she overlooked a feast day, she wondered, quickly calculating the date in her head. No, Hexham honored no saint on this day. Looking around for a familiar face to inquire after the meaning,

Constance realized that she did not recognize most in the crowd. She also noticed that many bore sad afflictions and ailments. One little girl with crippled legs sat in a wheeled cart, low to the ground, propelling herself forward by thrusting hands encased in leather mittens against the ground. Constance marveled at her speed, watching as the girl shot through the crowd, arms working furiously.

Then she caught sight of Brother John hastening across the courtyard. "Brother Cellarer," she called.

He turned at the hail, and recognizing Constance, veered off in her direction, panting with the exertion of hurrying so portly a physique. "Greetings, Lady Constance," he wheezed. "And it's not Brother Cellarer any longer, I'm sad to report." He struggled to regain his wind, and at Constance's look of polite inquiry, plowed on breathlessly, "I've been demoted by the prior— errand running is my occupation these days!"

"Yes, I've heard that the new prior is making some changes."

The canon lowered his voice. "Not all are for the good, lady!" His eyes darted furtively, and he bent forward, a conspirator whispering a plot: "I mention this only because you are one of this house's greatest benefactors. It is your right and duty to know how the priory's affairs are managed."

Constance quickly perceived the brother's meaning: he wanted St. Andrews's influential patrons to intercede on behalf of the canons and stem the flow of change that was wreaking havoc on their comfortable lives. But she had no desire to be drawn in, and thinking of the crippled girl in the wagon, thought it somehow appropriate that the canons were being shaken from their complacency. "Perhaps, in the end, the changes will bring about a better house, one that serves a larger community," she said, gesturing to the crowd. "Already you seem to be drawing from the distant countryside—there are many faces here I do not recognize."

Brother John looked around, a mournful look on his pudgy face. "Yes, it used to be so quiet here . . . ," he said wistfully. "As befits a house of God," he hastily added. Constance saw no sympathy in his eyes as he surveyed the pitiful cases assembled in the church's courtyard. "We never had to bother with pilgrims and penitents before," he lamented. "Hexham's long been off the pilgrim trail, you know. And no one ever wanted Mass said, save on Sunday. We canons had the peace and solitude to dispatch our duties." He heaved a great sigh. "Now it's Mass every day, eight offices of prayer a day, and this endless stream of pilgrims! Oh for the days of Prior Eadwy!"

Prior Eadwy, Constance remembered, was a reclusive, saintly old canon who had taken the office of prior only after it had been practically forced upon him. He had soon returned, however, to his tiny abode in the wilderness, living on a diet of pignuts, wild marjoram, and streamside cresses. He had been a most unsuitable choice for prior, for Eadwy detested all things worldly or having to do with the administration of the monastic house. The canons, happy to oblige him, had been left to run the priory without him. Prior Morel was apparently dealing with the consequences.

"Ah well," said Brother John, "with pilgrims returning to St. Andrews, revenues are up, though we humble canons are run off our feet! But the prior should be pleased, and perhaps now he'll ease up on us poor, simple servants of God."

Of course! thought Constance, suddenly understanding the nature of the gathering. Word of Alfred's miracle must have spread to the countryside. These people have come with the hope of being healed. They have gathered to pay homage to a little boy seemingly graced by God, to ask for another miracle. Thinking how Alfred's first miracle was interpreted, she wondered anxiously what a second would mean for the Jews. Increasing fame over Alfred, she reasoned, could only mean more trouble. "I've come to say a prayer for Alfred, Brother. Has he been laid to rest in the church-yard?"

"Oh no, lady," he said with a reproachful smile, as if she had made a tactless remark. "He's in the chapel still, in a tomb that befits his special holiness." Constance looked over to the crowd hovering by the west doors, and Brother John, following her gaze, offered, "Shall I escort you to his side, lady?"

"Well . . . I ought to wait my turn."

Brother John paid no heed, and grasping her arm, led her to the church. Nor was there any call for Constance to feel contrite over preferential treatment. As she entered the church, she saw that most were not awaiting a visit with Alfred, but were gathered around a little table holding clay vials stoppered with bits of cloth. A canon was selling them for one pence each. How curious, she thought as she passed into the cathedral's dim light.

Brother John accompanied her to the north transept of the cathedral where the tiny chapel was located, then bowed a good-day to hastily resume his errands. Several brothers were posted outside the half-walls of the chapel, letting only one person enter at a time. As she went in, Constance was surprised by the grandeur of the tomb that faced her. Alfred was encased in a great stone sarcophagus, ancient by the looks of the carvings on its sides and lid. Against it lay many gifts. Much of these were humble offerings, foodstuffs mainly. Other items were of a more symbolic nature: crutches, presumably given by the crippled man, healed and doubtless thankful; and pieces of wood carved to look like various parts of the body—a foot, an ear, and an eyeball. Constance assumed they were left by people praying to be cured of various afflictions corresponding to these parts of the body—a deformity of the foot, deafness, and blindness, she guessed. Other gifts were more substantial, including items of silver and gold, and on the stone floor was a wooden bowl half filled with silver pennies. She took two from the leather pouch fastened to her belt and added them to the collection.

She knelt before Alfred, bowing her head in prayer. As she raised her head, she saw an unfamiliar canon removing a cloth that had been draped over the tomb. Constance followed him out of the chapel, noting how reverently he carried the cloth. She passed another supplicant coming forward, a man squinting and grimacing with pain. He cradled a small carved head in his arms, and Constance wondered what ailment afflicted him—a severe headache maybe?

As she started for the west doors, she saw the canon with the cloth disappear down the stairwell leading to the crypt. Curious, she followed.

The stairs were steep and unevenly hewn from massive blocks of stone. Constance descended carefully, going slow so that her eyes could adjust to the increasing gloom. There were no torches or lamps to light the way, only a distant source of illumination that cast a feeble glow within the twisting passageway. She went with arms outstretched, as if blind, becoming increasingly uncomfortable in the suffocating space. She was about to turn back when she noticed the light growing brighter. Rounding a turn, she found herself in a cramped room that housed a well at its center. The canon who had borne the cloth from Alfred's tomb was drawing water, and he looked up, startled, when Constance appeared. Jumping backward with a cry, he let go the bucket, sending it clattering back down the well. He stood timorously against the far wall, clutching at his heart.

"Forgive me, Brother," she said quickly. "I did not mean to startle you." She stepped forward, drawn by concern, for the canon was deathly pale and looked on the verge of swooning.

But he relaxed as she spoke, a ghost of a smile brushing his lips. Dropping his hand from his chest, he said, "Ask no forgiveness, lady. It is my own foolishness that frightens me . . . and my loathing of this place," he said, looking nervously around the dank chamber. "For a moment I thought you a long-dead Saxon princess come to exact a penalty for disturbing her rest!"

Constance smiled and introduced herself, saying, "No Saxon am I, Brother, but a Norman. Nor a princess, only Constance of Wells, Lady of Bordweal."

"I am called Brother Elias," he said, humbly inclining his head.

Constance's interest quickened. So here was the brother who had proclaimed the meaning of Alfred's miracle.

"Did you come here by misfortune, lady? Shall I lead you back?"

"Actually, Brother, I noticed you bringing the cloth here and wondered at your business. I hope I have not acted irreverently. . . ."

"Not at all, not at all," he assured her. "I'll show you if you like." Brother Elias led Constance to the well where he retrieved the bucket, filled with water. He took it to a stone basin. She saw that Alfred's cloth had been placed inside, and he poured the water over it, filling the basin.

Constance was puzzled. All this fuss over rinsing out a cloth? But she said nothing, waiting for the canon to explain. Perhaps it was some strange ritual, like one of the many Cynwyse performed.

"This water is now holy," he said solemnly, spreading his hands over the basin. "It has been consecrated by Alfred and now holds the power to cure."

Constance finally understood. This cloth must be the same one that Alfred had been lying on when the crippled man touched it and was cured. It was being treated as a relic. She noticed a pile of clay vials near the basin. The canons must be selling the holy water to the pilgrims.

She recalled the grand tomb, the offerings—Alfred was being treated like a saint! "Brother Elias," she said, "is not the priory acting hastily? The boy's not been dead a week, after all. How can you be certain Alfred's been singled out as one of God's favorites?"

"We are not certain, lady," he admitted. "But the portents are favorable, and evidence of sanctity is mounting."

"To what evidence do you refer? Surely, one miracle does not make a saint," she objected.

"No," he answered slowly, his eyes drifting to the wall of the chamber. "Miracles do not make a saint, but they are proof of sanctity . . . expressions of God's holy favor. Alfred's holiness derives from his martyrdom. . . ."

"Martyrdom!" cried Constance. "How can you say he died a martyr's death, Brother? We know not who murdered him!"

Her sharp tone brought the canon's attention back to her. He stared, confused. "Why, because of the miracle . . ."

Constance was becoming confused herself, the canon's answers making no sense. She said carefully, "Brother, forgive my ignorance, but how do saints and martyrs go together?" At his shocked expression, she added hastily, "I know of the early martyrs, of course. St. Peter and the rest," she gestured vaguely. "They gave their lives for the faith in the days when Christians lived among pagans. But we can have no martyrs in our midst now, for all in the West, save the Jews, are Christian. There is no more need to die for the faith."

"You are right, lady. The days when Christians died at the hands of their persecutors in the name of Christ are long past." Brother Elias talked earnestly now as though instructing a novice. "When the Christian faith spread to encompass all," he said, stretching his arms wide, "many came to be venerated as saints by another means—the way you are probably more familiar with—by leading lives of exceptional piety and deprivation—a martyrdom of the senses, if you like. Others became revered as saints because they proved exceptionally potent leaders—popes, bishops, and abbots. But still, there are these two roads to sanctity—piety and martyrdom. And while martyrdom is the rarer of the two, it still occurs—recall Thomas à Becket."

Yes, Constance thought, Thomas à Becket died protecting the rights of the Church from an encroaching king, or so the monks of Canterbury claimed. "Then martyrs do not always die at the hands of pagans or non-Christians?" Constance asked, recalling that four knights of King Henry II had killed Becket.

"It is rare to become a Christian martyr at the hands of another Christian," Brother Elias answered. "And of course, not every murder is a martyrdom. Yet it was well known that the dispute between Thomas and the king centered on the rights of the Church. When he was murdered, it was clear he had given his life for the Church. The miracles afterward proved he died a martyr's death."

Constance was not accustomed to pondering the finer points of Christian doctrine. She had been educated by an astute parish priest, yet gospel study had not been a topic he favored. More attention had been devoted to pagan Roman poets. She still did not grasp the connection between Alfred's miracle and martyrdom, and at her perplexed look, Brother Elias continued helpfully. "So you see, lady, if it comes to pass that Alfred is venerated as a saint, it will prove he died a martyr. It is the only way to explain his sanctity, for I've not heard that he lived an exceptionally pious life or showed signs of divine favor . . ."

Constance recalled Alfred romping about the streets of Hexham and squirming through Sunday Masses. "No . . ." she said. "But we do not yet know the circumstances of his death," she objected. "He was just a child, very likely killed by someone for reasons having nothing to do with his faith. Only when we know who killed Alfred can we say anything about the manner of his death—" The image of Alfred's "crucifixion" abruptly formed in her mind, causing her to falter.

Brother Elias looked embarrassed, as if Constance were missing an obvious point, and he was loath to point up her ignorance. "But you see, lady," he said, "if Alfred becomes a saint, and he did not achieve his holiness through the manner of his life, his sanctity *must* be attributed to the manner of his death. There is no other way to account for it. It will prove he died at the hands of someone who threatened his faith, killed him because he was a Christian. . . ." The canon looked down at his hands, suddenly unwilling to say more.

But Brother Elias did not have to explain further. Constance had finally followed the thread of his argument to its inevitable conclusion. If Alfred becomes a saint, then all will believe he died a martyr's death, in the name of his faith. And they will accuse the Jews, now the only enemy of the faith in the West. Could the royal justices dispute the conclusion? Would they even try? She thought it unlikely. "We must pray that Alfred does not become a saint," she said. "Pray, Brother, that there are no more miracles."

Without warning, Prior Morel appeared. So deep were they in their thoughts that Constance and the canon jumped back when his looming figure emerged from the dark passage. He looked from one to the other, frowning severely, as if he had stumbled upon an illicit tryst. Then, as if in dramatic accompaniment to his ominous presence, a deep rumble sounded from above and the earth trembled. Had a storm come? Constance wondered.

She straightened, feeling embarrassed. Brother Elias hastily stepped forward, blurting out, "Lord Prior, this is Lady Constance. She was asking after Alfred's altar cloth, and I was explaining its miraculous powers. . . ."

Morel's expression warmed somewhat at learning her name. Bowing slightly, he said formally, "I am Prior Morel, lady. It pleases me to finally make your acquaintance. Your gifts to this house have been very generous, and I hope to make this priory worthy of your continued patronage."

Constance inclined her head. "Welcome to Hexham, Prior Morel. I, too, am pleased to finally make your acquaintance." It seemed absurd to her, exchanging civilities in the oppressive crypt with the forbidding prior, especially on the heels of her disturbing conversation with Brother Elias. She felt an overwhelming desire to escape. "Please excuse me, Prior Morel, Brother Elias. I really must go." She quickly made for the passageway, the prior following her hasty departure with a frown, rankled no doubt by her abruptness. But Constance cared not, and as she turned the corner to head back up the dark corridor, she could hear Morel scolding his canon.

"Brother Elias, you incompetent fool! Do you know how many are waiting at the church doors to purchase their vials of holy water?"

Constance did not hear the canon's reply, only a soft murmur. She was hurrying for the stairway now, anxious to be away from the dreadful crypt, anxious to find Godwin. But as she rounded another corner, her outstretched arms met with pliant flesh. She jumped backward with a cry. Then she heard the familiar labored breathing of Brother John and sagged against the tunnel wall in relief. "Brother, you nearly frightened the life out of me!"

"Lady Constance, is that you?" the canon panted. "Is the prior within? I must fetch him! There's been another miracle!"

Ten ✠

"Show me again, Grendel, where you were standing when you saw Alfred enter Isaac's house," Godwin said. The two men were standing in Jewry Lane, on the stoop fronting Grendel's house, where it was possible to see well along in both directions from the tenement's location at the bend in the road.

"Right 'ere on the step, like I told ye before. Cum out 'ere every mornin', I do, fer a sniff of air and a look 'round while I wait on me porridge. Ask the wife, she'll tell ye the same." He gave Godwin a sideways glance. "Then I sees 'im, Alfred. Trottin' down the lane, makin' straight for that Jew's house. Let in after a knock or two 'e was, and I never saw the lad alive agin," he ended darkly.

Godwin stood on the step looking toward Jacob's house. From Lioba's corner shop, he could hear the rhythmic clang of hammer beating metal. "What hour of the day would this be, Grendel?"

"Just before Tierce," he answered readily. "Hard-workin' folk are we—up 'fore the sun and busy as bees on the moor by time she's showin' 'er face. I work a few hours, then stop around Tierce for a bite. That's when I saw 'im, just before I had me porridge."

"You labored on Good Friday then?"

"Course not," Grendel said, drawing himself up, offended. "We follow the rules same as any decent Christian. But always there's a chore needs doin'. No slugabeds on feast days are we, like some."

"How can you be sure it was Alfred? There are many boys his age in town."

"'Twas Alfred all right," he growled. "No mistake about that. Know every soul in this town, I do. I saw the lad go into that Jew's house, clear as day." He stomped one foot on the step, either to emphasize his statement, or because he was cold.

Godwin grimly considered this new and potentially devastating development. It had been a huge advantage for the Jews that no witness could place Alfred near them on Good Friday, for the testimony of a witness carried great weight in the eyes of the law, provided the person giving it was a reliable and respected member of the community. Grendel, though unsavory to Godwin's way of thinking, met the criteria for a credible witness, as many of his friends would no doubt swear.

They were respected and quite industrious, Grendel and his wife, Verca. While the man did not own any one trade in particular, he did well enough, or so it appeared to Godwin, hiring out his labor, and there seemed no end to what he could turn his hand to: thatching roofs, working as a mill hand, curing herring, and grooming horses. He hauled for hire with the cart his wife had brought to him years ago as part of her dower. Though ancient now, the wagon was meticulously maintained and a familiar sight around town with its brightly colored panels.

The priory bought Grendel's services more than anyone, and Godwin had seen him doing everything from lighting lamps to cleaning the stable to harvesting apples from the precinct orchard. His wife was his equal in hiring herself out. She did spinning, selling her thread to the weaver, and was scullion, washerwoman, and seamstress for the canons. On occasion, probably when the couple had the capital to purchase malt, they brewed up ale and sold it from a rented market stall. But Godwin found it on the bitter side for his taste, preferring the rich, sweet brew made by Gamel and Ada.

Godwin looked again to Isaac's house, then back at Grendel. It seemed unlikely that Alfred would have come this way to reach his rendezvous destination on Good Friday, for the route from his home to the vintner's shop was not close to Jewry Lane. If the boy came this way, he had a purpose. But Godwin was certain that the boy did not go into any Jew's house. He had just spoken with Judith, Ivetta, and Mirabella, and they had insisted once again that no visitors came during Holy Week, including Alfred.

"He is lying!" Ivetta had cried angrily when Godwin reported Grendel's account to the contrary. "The boy went to Isaac's often, that is true enough, but not last week, not on Friday."

"What business did Alfred have with Isaac?" Godwin had asked her.

"He came often on behalf of the knight at St. Andrews," she answered. "The man frets constantly over his pawned goods, fearing they are not properly cared for, that his horse is not groomed often enough. Alfred was sent to vouch for their security."

Godwin had then given the women the next bit of bad news: Fulk's directive from the archbishop ordering that Isaac, Jacob, and Samuel be kept imprisoned until the murder was solved. The women were, of course, terribly disappointed. All morning they had been eagerly preparing for the arrival of their husbands, readying the homes and cooking favorite dishes.

Ivetta, after a moment of solemn reflection, said, "When the townsfolk hear of this, Lord Godwin, they will be bolder than ever in their abuse. Even now they find ways to insult and mistreat us. Some hurl rocks from afar, despite your men outside. What might they do when they hear the archbishop believes us guilty?" she asked. "I fear for our children."

"Remain inside and you will be kept from harm," Godwin promised, though inwardly he worried about another raid. His knights outside were really just deterrents, reminders to people that he was prepared to meet aggression with force. But his men could not withstand a serious assault. Would people dare to attempt one? A week ago he would have laughed at the notion.

"If we are all to be prisoners, why not remain together?" Judith had suggested. "If we go to the Keep and remain there with our husbands, we should be safe enough."

So it was decided that the women and children would join the men in the Keep. Godwin was both relieved and troubled by the decision, but could think of no better alternative. He had left the women to pack some belongings while he went down the street to question Grendel. Once finished, he would come back and escort them to their husbands.

Godwin emerged from his recollections to find an obstinate-looking Grendel staring defiantly at him. Regarding the man, Godwin thought how easy it would be to check his story, for the knight would surely remember if he had sent Alfred to Jacob's house on Good Friday—provided Havelok was willing to speak the truth, and provided Godwin could get to the priory to question him. It seemed that one obstacle after another was being thrust in his path.

He did not believe that the Jews were lying, though, and besides, something in Grendel's tale was suspicious. Godwin said sharply, "Here it is Thursday, Grendel, and you're only now coming forward with vital testimony? Why didn't you report this to me on Monday?"

Grendel puffed out his chest, saying, "It slipped me mind is all—went clean out. The boy was a-goin' there often . . . shameful how his folks gave 'im leave. But no concern of mine is that, though I knew trouble'd cum of it. Anywise, last night, all of a sudden, it cum back to me." He knocked the side of his head with his large paw of a hand in a ridiculous gesture. "Aye! I remembers seein' the poor lad a goin' into Isaac's house on Good Friday."

He was thoroughly unconvincing. Godwin studied him, weighing matters while Grendel squirmed and pulled at his lower lip. His story was unlikely, but would that matter to the archbishop? Godwin was deeply worried about the chances of a fair assessment of the evidence now that his lord was personally involved in the case and inclined to find the Jews guilty. Would the archbishop and his court take pains over veracity so long as a witness mouthed the words they wanted to hear? Godwin was not at all sure, feeling that his best strategy lay in getting Grendel to renounce his story. He said, "If Alfred was there often, as you say, how can you be sure it was Good Friday? Might you have mixed up the days? Perhaps it was the Friday before? Think carefully and be certain, Grendel. This is no light matter," Godwin warned sternly. "Lives are at stake, and not just those of the Jews, but any who would give false testimony." Perhaps if he impressed upon him the seriousness of lying under oath, he might get him to reconsider his account; for it is a grave offense under English law, punishable by death in some cases.

But Grendel would have none of it, only jutted out his chin and folded his arms tightly over his broad chest. "I know what me eyes saw, Bailiff, and ye cannot make me say otherwise though ye favor them." He jerked his head toward the homes of the Jews, then lowered his voice to a vulgar hiss, saying, "If ye knew more 'bout their doings, maybe ye wouldn't be so quick to defend 'em."

Godwin eyed his "witness," finding the man more repugnant than usual. Grendel's eyes were pooled with hatred and contempt, and Godwin fought the urge to look away. The man's swarthy looks and heavy stature, his greasy hair and grimy, gnarled hands, now balled into giant fists, called to mind an evil, dwarfish creature Godwin remembered from a frightening tale told to him as a child. He recalled little of the story now, only the menacing troll-like man who preyed on helpless, infant creatures—squirrels, rabbits, birds, children.

Sharply, he said, "Speak plainly, Grendel, and say what's on your mind. I have no time for your dark hints."

Grendel's arms remained folded, stout legs spread wide, knees locked. "Very well, *lord*," he sneered. "I'll tell ye what me and most folk in this town know about yer Jews. Sorcerers they are for one, in league with Satan. The gospel says it, plain as day—spawn of the devil it names Jews. Heard 'em meself, I 'ave, summoning their dark master, wailing away up in that Isaac's house. He's the ringleader, ye know." Grendel started talking faster, spittle gathering at the corners of his mouth. "They plot with Satan fer our ruin, fer the ruin of all Christendom. And 'ere's the topper. They need the body of a Christian child each year fer sum ritual. Poor Alfred, 'e be chosen this year. It's only by God's good grace that little ones 'aven't gone missing from 'ere 'fore now. But I knew there'd be trouble one day. God, He be punishin' folks fer lettin' the Jews live 'ere, fer minglin' with them, like they were the same as any Christian." He stopped his ranting to stare accusingly at the bailiff, as though Godwin were the biggest offender of all.

Godwin stared back impassively, though the depth of Grendel's loathing for the Jews shocked him considerably. Here was a man, he realized, who longed for their destruction, motivated by fear and ignorance. Was there any reasoning with a person so driven? He gave it a try, saying, "The wailing, as you call it, Grendel, is only the prayers they sing in the synagogue. Our rituals and chants at Mass, our processions in the streets, these are equally strange to them."

He suddenly remembered a conversation he once had with Jacob on the topic of Christian ritual. Jacob had asked him to make clear the meaning of Holy Communion and the Eucharist. Godwin had fumbled about for a way to explain the sacrament, doing a poor job of it, for he had never bothered much with the philosophical underpinnings of his faith. Bread and wine were transformed into the body and blood of Christ. How? He hadn't a clue. Why? Well, so that Christians could consume their Lord—be joined with their Savior. Jacob had scarcely been able to conceal his revulsion, and Godwin had realized how bizarre Christian practices must seem to an outsider.

Grendel was staring at the bailiff now through narrowed, seething eyes. Contempt twisted his mouth. "Ye would defend those who killed Christ?" he spat out.

"Grendel," Godwin calmly replied. "Recall the sermons we have heard all our lives. Have we not been taught that God sent Christ to pay for man's sins by sacrificing His life? Was it not ordained? It had naught to do with Jews and Gentiles, but with the sinful nature of mankind. This is the message of the Gospels. If you seek to blame someone for the death of Christ, then all mankind since Adam and Eve must be included."

But Grendel was not listening now; he stood rigid, mouth clamped shut, and Godwin saw that reasoning was useless. He would understand according to his nature. What could turn a man from such poisonous thinking, he wondered. Then another thought suddenly occurred to him. "Call Verca out here, Grendel. I have some questions for her as well."

Grendel hesitated, started to protest, then shrugged and poked his head in the doorway to call his wife. She quickly appeared, and Godwin suspected she had been listening to the conversation from close by. She glanced nervously from her husband to the bailiff, her calloused hands gripping a cloth rag.

Godwin said, "Grendel has just been telling me that he saw Alfred enter Isaac's house just before Tierce on Good Friday. Did you see the boy as well, Verca?"

"Ach, no," she said. "I was inside, cooking the porridge."

"And you didn't come out until it was time to call your husband to the table?"

"Aye, just so."

"You always serve at Tierce?"

"Aye," she agreed, nodding, "or thereabouts, depending on when he gets himself home." More relaxed now, she added, "Grendel, he puts in a few hours' work, then has a bite. No work was there on Friday, but he went along to the priory to help prepare for the Good Friday—" She stopped abruptly, seeing too late the warning look from her husband.

"She answered yer question, Bailiff," Grendel snarled. "She was at work in 'er kitchen when I saw the boy, nor was anyone else about. What does it matter to ye? The word of one Christian is enough."

Godwin left Grendel to escort the Jewish women and children to the Keep, instructing his men on Jewry Lane to continue guarding their homes. It was a happy reunion, despite the circumstances, and Godwin was loath to check the rare moment of pleasure. Yet he was feeling pressed to get on with business, and quickly repeated to the men Fulk's message from the archbishop, including the news that the archbishop intended to gain jurisdiction over Hexham's Jews.

Jacob took the decree hardest, but instead of blustering with rage, as Godwin had expected, he received the tidings as a final blow. Dropping heavily onto a bench, he said, "We shall be hanged. No hope is there now, if the archbishop has willed us dead."

Isaac and Samuel said nothing, inclined neither to deny nor affirm Jacob's grim assessment. Godwin was deeply disturbed by his friend's despondent turn and said, with a confidence he did not fully possess, "The archbishop has made no pronouncements of guilt or innocence, Jacob. That is for me to judge, and I am certain of your innocence. But I must find the guilty man to prove it. Give me time and the chance to win your freedom."

Jacob glanced up at Godwin, his expression bleak. "You are one man and the archbishop is power itself. If he declares our guilt, no one can refute him."

"He is a man beholden to the law, like any other," Godwin countered.

Then, before Jacob could respond, Isaac said, "Enough, Jacob. Your words help not, only hinder." He turned to Godwin. "You cannot disobey the commands of your lord. We will stay until you find the one guilty of murdering the boy."

Samuel perked up hopefully, asking, "Tell us, lord, have you any idea where to look? Have you come upon a sign or clue?"

Godwin told them how Constance and he thought it likely that the murderer had intentionally set out to cast blame for the crime upon the Jews. Then he described his suspicions concerning Sir Havelok. They looked surprised, doubtful even, but allowed that the knight was indeed bitter over his indebtedness to Jews.

Godwin left the Keep to finally pay his visit to Sir

Havelok. But as he crossed the Market Square to head up Gate Street, he felt a tugging at his arm and looked around to see one of Lioba's apprentices. His mistress needed the bailiff's ear, he said. Would he come?

Godwin followed the boy, somewhat wearily, to Lioba's shop. "You had better come inside," she said when he arrived, glancing down Jewry Lane. Godwin turned to see Grendel back on his front stoop, staring at them through baleful eyes. Lioba led him in, and he followed her across the sweltering shop, past the roaring furnace where her apprentices labored and out a rear door that opened onto a small courtyard. Here she tended a kitchen garden in summer, now barren and lifeless. Yet the soil was rich and dark, promising that any seed or slip planted here would be rewarded with vigorous life and bountiful fruit. Godwin resisted the urge to stoop and sink his hands into the soil. He wanted to fill them with the crumbly black loam, let it run out between his fingers. Instead, he followed Lioba across the courtyard and into her private dwelling.

"Does this concern Grendel's testimony, Lioba?" he asked, guessing that word of his account was spreading about town.

"It does," she said, gesturing to a bench. "I want you to hear the *whole* tale." She took a seat opposite, saying, "For one, his memory was stirred, though I'd say addled, by a few tankards of ale taken last night at the tavern. I heard it from my boys, who were there, too. They also heard Grendel and others complaining that the Jews were going to get away clean, for you seemed reluctant to hold them to the crime. Grendel's memory was suddenly jogged and out came this story 'bout seeing Alfred at Isaac's house on Good Friday."

"You think he made it up then?" Godwin asked.

"Does the pope sit on a throne?" she snorted. "Course he did! He's a bitter, hateful man. He'd say anything to bring the Jews to harm. You can't believe a word he says."

"I do not believe his story either, Lioba," Godwin said. "And under any other circumstances, I would not be concerned, for his account sorely lacks the ring of truth. But nothing is usual about this murder, and Grendel will be credible enough for many." Godwin told of the archbishop's personal interest in the case. "Many will stand surety for Grendel, lending credence to his tale. This is a serious setback for our friends, I fear. We must prove Grendel a liar, or better, find the murderer!"

"But the Jews *always* keep to themselves during Holy Week," she insisted, "especially on Good Friday and the holy days following. They wouldn't risk bringing trouble on their heads by seeing a Christian in their home on Good Friday, even in a peaceful town like Hexham."

Godwin nodded wearily. "We must have proof though, Lioba, a witness." He looked at her, sitting across from him, worry shadowing her kindly face. "Were you about shortly before Tierce on Good Friday? Can you bear witness to the fact that the Jews received no visitors that morning?"

"That I cannot do," she said, her eyes shifting regretfully downward.

With a sigh, Godwin followed her gaze, noticing for the first time the tile mosaic that occupied the center of the floor, its edges shading indistinctly to packed earth. The furniture, he realized, and everything else in the small room, seemed reverently oriented around it, setting it off, giving the composition a place of honor.

The mosaic was a relic of a time long past, a reminder that before the Normans, before the Saxons, another people had ruled this land: the great warrior race of Romans. It was an idyllic landscape decorated with shepherds, goats, fauns. A tiny temple with garlanded columns sat at the center amidst a copse of trees. Each element was portrayed with such exquisite detail that Godwin thought they must be symbolic portrayals, allegories for ideals vital to that long-dead civilization. He wondered what they might signify, how a Roman would read the picture.

He looked around at the humble structure now shielding the ancient work of art. A Roman villa stood here once, he guessed, like those still found in remote parts of the country, deserted and dilapidated, yet potent reminders of Roman greatness. Perhaps an officer once dwelled in it, a captain of a legion, a soldier like himself. Did he return home each day, Godwin wondered, to gaze upon the mosaic, finding peace in the soothing pastoral scene? Did it lighten burdens carried from battles fought, wars waged? Godwin thought it would be fine to have such a diversion in his own home, a restful place to visit when the world pressed too close, when memories plagued.

"It's a peaceful place isn't it?" Lioba said, echoing his thoughts. "I can almost see myself there at times, sitting beneath one of those trees, or on the steps of that wee temple. Paradise it looks to me. Never mind that it's pagan."

Godwin strode briskly from the priory gatehouse to a wing of guest rooms situated on the east side of the cloister. He had wakened Brother Michael from a peaceful slumber at his post to ask after Havelok's whereabouts. The canon had been made nervous by the mere mention of the knight's name, but had suggested Godwin try his private chamber, describing its location. Havelok, Brother Michael informed him, constantly roamed the priory grounds, terrifying the canons with his barks and scowls, but with the noon hour approaching, he would likely be found in his room, impatiently awaiting his midday meal.

As Godwin passed by the church courtyard, he saw more people gathered than was usual, but did not stop to investigate now that he was so close to confronting the knight. Havelok's room was at the farthest end of the wing. Godwin rapped twice upon the door and heard an irate exclamation within.

"If my meal is not too early, then it is late!" an angry voice cried as the door was yanked wide. Brought up short by the sight of Godwin, the expletive died on the man's lips, and he stood motionless, gaping, hand frozen upon the latch.

Godwin was equally surprised, though his face did not betray it. Havelok looked not at all as he had imagined. Expecting a haughty, lord-like figure, proud and arrogant, here instead was an ungainly, unlikely looking knight, awkward and unpolished at first glance. Godwin glanced beyond to see if another lurked within the shadows of the room, but there was no one else.

He guessed Havelok to be around thirty. His face was homely, made more so by a cantankerous frown. Godwin could see deep lines where his brows drew perpetually down. Around his mouth was a rigid cleft seldom stretched by merriment. Frizzled brown hair was distributed unevenly in patches on his head and face. He was shorter even than Wulfstan, with a thick waist and stout legs, propped like logs on broad, flat feet.

No, Sir Havelok was altogether different from the man Godwin had invented in his mind. But he gave it barely a passing thought, for his attention was seized by the knight's eyes, which were not in sync with one another: one glinted at Godwin unflinchingly beneath a glowering brow while the other strayed off on a different line of sight, as if looking at some mysterious object in the distance.

"My pardon, Lord Godwin," the knight said, his voice gruff. He offered an awkward bow, saying, "I thought you were my servant, bringing supper too late."

"No matter," Godwin said, deciding to focus on the eye that glared back, though it was difficult to ignore the other. It was like being with two men: one stern and severe, who aggressively met his gaze; and an absent other, a visionary perhaps, pondering life's mysteries, benignly oblivious to the trivia of day-to-day existence. "You know me then?" Godwin asked. "Have we met?"

"No, lord, but I have seen you about town and know your reputation. I am called Havelok." The clumsy bow was offered once more. "I should have announced my presence sooner. My pardon. I am in retreat here at the priory."

Retreat from what? Godwin wondered as the one eye stared expectantly, waiting for the purpose of his call. "I've come to ask about Alfred. He ran errands for you, I'm told?"

The stern Havelok looked bewildered, and momentarily the two personalities merged. "Alfred?" he asked uncertainly. Then comprehension dawned and the two went their separate ways again. He said shortly, "Oh, the boy. Yes, he did tasks for me. Evil business his murder. Now I must find another."

An awkward silence followed before Havelok remembered proper form. Hurriedly, he stepped back, almost tripping in his haste, and gestured for Godwin to come inside.

It was only one room, yet spacious. The knight stiffly led Godwin to a table and benches placed beneath a carved wooden cross affixed to the wall. As he took the offered seat, Godwin cast his eyes about the room. The chamber was bare of adornments, however, aside from the crucifix, and little could be learned about the man from his dwelling. There were no hangings on the walls, or carpets on the floor, no trinkets or treasures set out to admire. Had he lost everything, save his war gear, Godwin wondered. The canons of St. Andrews must own more than he.

Havelok had apparently been oiling his armor. It was strewn about the floor, and there were rags and a pot of oil laid down near his mail greaves. A hauberk and gambeson were neatly laid upon a large chest, their polishing and cleaning complete. In a corner, a sword stood propped, and Godwin went over to admire its old-fashioned fishtail pommel. "A treasure this one," he said. "May I handle it?" The knight spared a curt nod, and Godwin hefted the blade. "A well-ground sword," he said admiringly, parrying once before carefully replacing it.

Havelok's grim eye softened. "Faerwundor it is called," he said.

Godwin took his seat again while the knight stood by awkwardly. "Can you tell me, Havelok, when you last saw Alfred?"

The knight hesitated a moment, then shrugged. "Who can say? He came most every day to do my bidding. One day last week he told me he was going on a journey, that he would return in a week or so. I was angry, him leaving me in the lurch like that. I thought him gone until I heard the rabble buzzing." Havelok waved a hand toward the door. "Those who call themselves canons," he sneered. "They said the boy was murdered on Good Friday."

"Can you reckon back and tell me when he last came here?" Godwin asked. "Did you see him on Good Friday? Take some time to work it out if you must."

A queer look came into the hard eye while the other roved aloof. "Why does it matter?" he asked. "You have his murderer, or so I've heard. The filthy Jews have struck again. Curse that race, the scourge of Christians!"

Godwin said nothing, only waited for the knight to answer his question.

Havelok began to prowl about the room. "I tell you, I cannot say with any certainty. Every day is like another." He stopped his pacing. "But now I think on it, I'm sure he did not come on Good Friday. I spent the day of our Lord's Passion alone in prayer within the church."

Godwin said, "I'm told you sent the boy often to the house of Isaac the Jew, to check on some pawned goods. Can you recall the last time you sent Alfred on such an errand?"

He hesitated a moment, then said, "I sent him there often, yes. I do not trust the Jews with my goods. It is disgraceful how they have become England's bankers, is it not? Yet that is the way of things now. All must turn to them when the need arises."

Godwin again made no reply. He sensed that Havelok was trying to downplay his dealings with the Jews, unaware, perhaps, that Godwin knew of his financial predicament. He was probably hoping to pass off his removal to St. Andrews as voluntary, an impulse to lead a quasi-religious life. It was common enough among burned-out warriors with wounds and scars aplenty. Yet uncommon for someone as young as Havelok.

"Yes, I sent the boy to the Jew's house often," the knight repeated. "Yet I cannot say which day was the last time. He had standing orders, you see, to regularly check on my horse and gear. I doubt he went as often as I wanted, though. Always trying to dodge work, that one." Havelok glanced sharply at Godwin. "Why these questions? No fault of mine is it that the boy was murdered by the Jews!"

"He did not go to the home of Isaac during Holy Week," Godwin said. "I have learned that the Jews receive no Christian visitors during this time, nor do they stir from their homes."

"A clever trick then, murdering the boy." When

Godwin said nothing, Havelok burst out, "They are lying, of course. Either the boy went to Isaac's as I requested—and it mattered not to me that it was Holy Week *or* Good Friday—or the Jews stalked him in the streets to carry out their evil deed. One way or the other, you have the murderers."

"You say you did not leave the priory grounds on Good Friday?" Godwin asked. "And had no visitors? I believe Alfred passed this way on his way to a rendezvous. You never saw him?"

The commanding eye looked uncertain for a moment, then widened as it perceived the bailiff's meaning. His face went red as a beet. "You think I had something to do with the boy's death?" he sputtered.

Godwin replied evenly, "I think the boy was murdered in town on Good Friday by someone he knew, and it is my job to learn where he went and who he saw. So I ask, did you see the boy on the morning of Good Friday?"

"Nay! I arose early and prayed in the church until my noon meal. I spoke with no one. Many can attest to this, no doubt, for the church was swarming with Christians—pretenders who ignore their faith the rest of the year." The one eye stared hard at Godwin, perturbed and confused. "Why do you look elsewhere when the stinking Jews are within your grasp. It is obvious they are guilty! Look how the boy was murdered! What other evidence do you need?"

Godwin abruptly changed the direction of his questioning, saying, "Tell me of your kin, Havelok. You are far from home, are you not?" Instinctively, he began with kinship ties when he wanted to know a person better. Family roots offered a place to start, a context. He knew nothing of Havelok's past. Even his name was unfamiliar, putting him at a disadvantage.

"My family is not noble," the knight said angrily, "if that is what you are trying to uncover."

"I do not judge nobility by blood," Godwin replied, "but by actions."

"Easy words for a man born into wealth and power," he replied bitterly.

"Perhaps," Godwin agreed.

Silence followed, and the bailiff thought Havelok might refuse to speak of his family, but finally he took a seat opposite, saying, "My kin dwell south of here, down Copely way." He fell quiet once more. Then, staring across the barren room, he continued, "My father was freeborn, but had no interest in tilling soil. He had a natural talent with horses and arms, and as a young man offered his skills to the nearby lord of Balliol.

"He tended this man's war horses and gear and trained his son in their handling. One day, my father saved the son from a deadly accident. Lord Balliol was most grateful, for he dearly loved his son and rewarded my father by giving him his own arms and a horse. The son and my father were fast friends, and they set out to be apprentices of the tourney, to seek competition in far-flung places like France and Germany. They went from tourney to tourney, winning praise and wealth. They returned triumphant, laden with horses, armor, and silver gained from prizes and ransoms.

"Lord Balliol was very proud, and he knighted my father, granting him a nearby fief. He betrothed him also to a local lady of high regard, not noble, but generously dowered.

"My father knighted me when I was twenty-two, girding his sword about my waist himself, for no churchman would have that honor. He was old and feeble, but still it was difficult for him to give up his arms. He was loath to part with them, for they were the same given all those years ago by Lord Balliol. Difficult it was for him to give up the tourney, too. Indeed, he seemed unable to quit them. He lost much wealth as he grew older, unable to avoid capture from worthier opponents. The ransoms were difficult to pay, often-times, yet he never gave up his first armor." Havelok indicated the various pieces strewn about his room.

Godwin could not help but admire the father Havelok described. A likable adventurer, he sounded, a self-made man, talented and capable. He looked at Havelok. How much of these qualities did the son inherit? His present situation indicated that his life had diverged radically from his father's. "And did you follow your father's ways? Take up his sword and enter Balliol's service?"

"I did," he answered, fixed eye glinting proudly. "I was not as skilled as he, but I burned to be a warrior. I had my fief and armor, a good horse, and some silver. I headed for the tourney to learn the ways of knights."

Godwin was beginning to sense the direction of the tale, knowing as he did its ending. "And how did you fare in the tourney?" he asked, not sure he wanted to hear the answer.

Havelok said nothing at first, then he shrugged and said, "I did not fare so well. At my first, I was captured for ransom. Much silver went to my freeing. At another, I was broadsided with a lance—lifted clean out my saddle. The force of the blow did this." He reached a hand to his errant eye, gently fingering it. "I wore a patch for a time, but hated the darkness. Light still comes through, you see. Shapes and figures, too."

Godwin said, "Sometimes I think England's warriors suffer more at tournaments than at the hands of our enemies. I side with the Church in this matter, and with our dead King Henry, thinking they should be banned."

"I disagree," said Havelok. "The tournament is the training ground for knights. How would we prepare for battle without them? No, the problem lies in how they are conducted. In my father's day, a tourney was a simple test of skill and bravery. No bated weapons, no rules and judges as there are today. Pah!" he spat out, lips curling. "It's all pomp and ceremony now. Men fretting about how finely they are outfitted, how well they dance and carry on a conversation with a lady. There are more feasts than jousts. Heralds and minstrels scurry about, wanting to know your lineage and blazon."

Godwin felt a surge of pity for the man, envisioning Havelok at a typical tournament. Awkward, homely, and outfitted in his old-fashioned armor, he must have been the butt of many jokes.

He himself despised tournaments and the behavior they fostered—the ostentation, the hangers-on. But most of all he hated their violence. Despite the rules and blunted weapons, tournaments still took many lives. Only four years ago, the Earl of Essex, a good man, was trampled to death when his line broke up and he was unseated. And the violence inevitably spilled over into the surrounding countryside. Godwin had seen crops trampled, villages plundered, women raped.

"It became difficult for me to attend tournaments, nor was I made welcome," Havelok was saying. "I could not afford fine clothes, and I knew not how to court a lady, to sing and dance and carve my meat just so." He looked at Godwin, perplexed. "What have these things to do with knighthood?" he asked.

Godwin did not know. He had no interest or patience with such pursuits and had never bothered to contemplate their significance. But he did so now, for it seemed important to offer the knight an answer. "Have you seen real battle, Havelok?"

He shook his head regretfully.

"Count yourself lucky then, I say, for it is not a noble pursuit. Lords and knights make tournaments seem like fairy tales, full of finery and acts of chivalry because true war is without such things, yet warriors still want these in their lives. Their livelihood is war, a brutal business, and they desire to make it more heroic."

Havelok said, "At my last tournament, I was captured once again. To pay my ransom, I was forced to mortgage my lands and goods. All that was left to me is gone; the mark made by my father has been erased by the son."

Godwin could not think how to reply. Anything he might say seemed trivial in the face of such misfortune. Havelok had only wanted to follow in his father's steps, but was cheated by changing times and evil luck.

He must have sensed Godwin's pity, for he said, "I mind it not, though. A true knight is poor and unencumbered, free from worldly ties, a simple soldier of Christ. I own only my life and am willing to hand it up at any moment for the sake of Christendom. I am a rich man so long as I wear the badge of knighthood." Havelok gestured to his sword.

A polished speech, often rehearsed. It only increased Godwin's pity.

At that moment, they heard a commotion outside. Godwin went to the door and opened it to see canons scurrying past, robes flapping in the wind, a migration of large, ill-shaped blackbirds. He reached out to catch the sleeve of one, pulling the canon up short. "Why the hurry, Brother?"

"The church!" he cried, tearing free of Godwin's grip. "We must get to the church!" Off he ran, hiking up his habit while calling over a shoulder, "There's been another miracle!"

"Not again!" cried Godwin. Turning to the knight, he said, "I must go, but I will return."

Havelok remained motionless, heedless of the canon's dramatic announcement. "Why? I think we have no more business together."

At that moment, his sword clattered to the floor, and the two men cast startled glances at the ringing blade. A portent. "Faerwundor says otherwise," Godwin said.

ELEVEN ✝

Constance had run for the mouth of the crypt while Brother John, panting off in the opposite direction, hastened to summon Prior Morel to the scene of yet another miracle.

As she'd rushed up the stone stairway to locate the source of the priory's latest drama, her attention was seized by an awesome sight directly in front of her: the west portal to the church was completely blocked by an avalanche of stone. A massive heap of hewn blocks lay interspersed with broken statuary. A thick cloud of dust hovered over the wreckage.

The posts and lintel had apparently collapsed, bringing down the massive stone and facade of carved figures that sat fixed above. Constance prayed that no one had been beneath when the deadly rock came tumbling down, but in her mind she saw the crowd of eager penitents, awaiting their turn to buy a vial of Alfred's holy water.

Before her stood several stunned canons. She recognized the two who had been standing guard at the chapel where Alfred's body lay, Brother Thomas and Brother Paul. Then, as the dust over the rubble began to settle, she saw large shafts of daylight streaming into the cathedral from the courtyard, and the shocked faces of people gathered at the awesome fissures, talking excitedly and pointing at the ruin.

Prior Morel emerged from the stairway behind her, Brother Elias close on his heels. He stopped short beside Constance, sucking in his breath when he took in the colossal destruction. "Brother John!" he bellowed. "Pray tell how this disaster constitutes a miracle! God's wrath descended on a clutch of witless canons, more like!"

Brother John had not yet come forth from the crypt, doubtless still puffing his way back along the winding passageway. Brother Thomas, galvanized by the prior from his dazed wonder, ventured to explain the miraculous event, crying, "But it was a miracle, Lord Prior! I witnessed it myself!"

Morel glared expectantly at the canon, who continued eagerly, "I was standing watch at the chapel with Brother Paul. There was a man inside kneeling at Alfred's tomb. I did not know him. Someone from the countryside perhaps." He waved his hand vaguely. "We heard the sound of coins clinking and looked to see him filling his pockets with Alfred's silver!" Breathless or appalled, Brother Thomas stopped his narrative to gulp down some air. "We took after him, of course, and he led us on a chase through the church before making for the west doors. Quick as a hare, that one, and we feared he might get away by losing himself in the crowd gathered outside. Suddenly, there was a fearsome noise, a rending crack that came from the west portal." The canon paused again, his eyes growing large as he recalled the extraordinary event. "Everyone in the doorway scattered, yet the thief ran on, and as he passed beneath, the entrance collapsed, crushing him. It was a marvelous sight, Lord Prior, like the mouth of God gulping down a sinner!" Brother Thomas's voice was filled with wonder. "Is not Alfred's divine vengeance terrible to behold? It was a miracle indeed—a twofold one, for it is a miracle that only the thief was taken and no one else."

Constance stared sadly at the huge pile of rubble, thinking of the poor man, thief or no, who lay crushed beneath it all. A miracle? It seemed more like a desperate act of thievery combined with ill luck. A quick death it must have been, though, she realized gratefully.

Most did not share her view, however, for Constance could hear joyous shouts from the courtyard: "Another miracle! Another miracle!" Remembering her conversation in the crypt with Brother Elias, a heavy dread descended as she contemplated the likely consequences of a second miracle for the Jews. The hope and optimism she had carried back from Middleton were slipping away like faithless friends.

She had better find Godwin, she thought, glancing around for the nearest way out of the church. Looking over at Prior Morel, she saw that he still stood transfixed, staring at the wreckage. She felt a twinge of sorrow for the man. A real setback this was to his efforts at restoring St. Andrews. Repairs would indeed be costly. She watched him shake himself from his trance-like survey of the damage, and as he turned toward her, Constance saw that his face was not angry or despairing, as she had expected, but lit with pleasure. Not a setback at all for a devout man of God, she realized, but a wondrous demonstration of His power on earth.

Prior Morel, followed by Constance and the canons, headed for the transept, while Brother John emerged from the crypt in time to bring up the rear. The prior unlocked the north transept door with a large iron key that hung from his belt, and they all hurried around the church to the courtyard to see how the situation looked from the outside.

Constance immediately glimpsed Godwin amidst a

gathering of men. As she hastened across the courtyard, she could hear him giving orders, instructing them to quickly fetch levers and pry bars. "Constance!" he cried, shocked to see her in the midst of the mayhem.

"I came to the priory when I could not find you," she said. Then, looking at the immense pile of stone, "I heard you calling for levers. Is there a chance the poor man still lives?"

"No, I think he must be dead," he answered, his expression grim. "Still, it's possible he was caught in a pocket somehow. We will work as quickly as we may, lest by a miracle he still lives."

Townsmen came running with as many pry bars as could be mustered and set to work on moving the great blocks of stone. Godwin cleared the courtyard of onlookers, fearing that a rolling block might injure others. Prior Morel, encircled by his black brood, stood aloof, watching from a safe distance.

Godwin supervised the removal of fallen debris. It was heavy work and slow going, and Constance, standing out of the way, grew cold in the biting air, yet felt compelled to stay and see the outcome. As she waited, she felt a disturbing sensation at her back, a strange pricking, and turned to see a dark figure of a man dressed for battle standing in the distant shadows of the monastery. He turned and walked away when he saw her looking at him.

Finally, the men came to the last layer of rubble. As they loosed a block, they found the unfortunate thief. He lay crushed beneath the large statue of Christ that only a few hours ago had hovered menacingly above the lintel.

The scene above the west portal was one that Constance had always found disturbing, and she was not sorry to see it destroyed, though she felt a fleeting stab of guilt for permitting herself such an impious thought.

It had been a representation of Christ as Divine

Judge, with the judgment in progress, a set of scales at Christ's feet weighing souls. The angry demeanor upon His colossal face suggested that our Lord was not all pleased with the results of the reckoning. The eternal souls were depicted as naked, terror-stricken men and women, pitiful to behold as enraged angels summoned them to account for their sins. Dreading judgment and its outcome, they wept and wailed while terrible demons taunted and roared nearby. One demon was but a giant mouth to hell where souls were dragged headfirst into Satan's fiery furnace.

The ghastly images always brought a shudder to Constance as she entered the church, causing her to wonder why such a frightening spectacle need be placed at its entrance. She knew, of course, that it was meant to compel Christians to properly observe their faith, or face eternal damnation. But it seemed to her that the same could be achieved through less intimidating means. Why not place Christ the Shepherd above the entrance, benevolently smiling upon His flock, welcoming and encouraging followers? Perhaps, when the priory turned to repairs, she could offer her suggestions along with a gift to aid in the restoration of the west front.

When the forbidding statue of Christ was lifted from the man, it was clear that he was dead, his skull crushed beyond recognition. A swift death indeed, Constance thought as they all gathered around the body. He wore tattered clothes and rags wound around his feet.

Prior Morel broke the solemn stillness with a booming exclamation, "The punishments of God are inescapable and just are His judgments. The saints in heaven sit at His feet, meting out divine verdicts without mercy."

Ignoring the gloomy exhortation, Godwin said, "Prior, I want the church inspected by you and the brothers before another soul enters. Too long has it been neglected in its maintenance." He scanned the exterior. "Who knows where else danger might be lurking, waiting to take or maim another life."

Many of the canons peered nervously at their church. Constance, too, scrutinized it anxiously, thinking of her recent journey into the crypt. She suddenly recalled the dark, narrow passage, twisting like a rodent's tunnel toward its den. She paled at the thought of the quantity of stone bearing down on that place. Being trapped there was unbearable to contemplate, and she vowed never to return.

Prior Morel drew himself up, glaring at Godwin. But he said nothing, only turned on his heel, black robe snapping as he stalked toward his private chambers. Brother Elias hesitated, but doubtless thought it wiser to stay with his master and scurried to catch up.

Godwin stared thoughtfully after them. Then, turning to face the canons, he said, "Some of you must see to this poor man. Lay him in a casket, but do not bury him. We need to find his name. He did not live in town, that much we have learned. We can only hope that someone will come looking for a missing kinfolk. Alas, I cannot spare any men to inquire in the countryside.

"The rest of you do as I have asked and make a thorough inspection of the church. I mean business when I say that no one will enter until I deem it safe." He looked sternly at the canons, who nervously shuffled their feet and ruffled robes. "It would also be prudent, brothers, to check the other buildings of the monastery. I would hate to see all of you crushed in your sleep because the dorter roof had been neglected."

"But lord," Brother John whined, "what are we to tell the pilgrims? They will surely come in droves when word of a second miracle gets out. All will want to see Alfred. We cannot turn them away."

"You might consider giving the boy a proper burial in the churchyard, Brother," Godwin offered dryly.

The canon looked scandalized. "Oh, I think that

shall never come to pass now, lord. Alfred is bound for a burial at the high altar, no less, for his holiness cannot be doubted now." The canons nearby nodded and mumbled agreement. "Two miracles he has worked within days of his death. Imagine the miracles to come! Alfred's fame will be celebrated throughout England. St. Andrews is destined for greatness!" Brother John's loathing of increased visitors to the church, Constance noted dryly, was evidently overcome by thoughts of fame and fortune.

"If it does not come down around your ears first!" was Godwin's response. "I'll return tomorrow with some men to help you clear the courtyard of this mess and to seal the west entrance. You can tell me then what your inspection has revealed. After that, we will take up the issue of pilgrims."

Brother John and many of the canons looked doubtful, but the force and firmness of Godwin's speech kept them from voicing any objections. All moved to go about their business. Constance did not envy those who must care for the dead man's remains, and she was grateful to finally turn from the grisly sight. She was sore wearied with care and cold and wanted only to be gone from the priory.

Godwin put an arm over her shoulder, leading her to the gatehouse. "I'll see you back to Bordweal," he said quietly. "We can share our news along the way. I have much to tell you."

A large crowd was gathered at the gates, people eager to view the sight where a second miracle had occurred. Godwin did not address them, though they waited anxiously for an announcement when they saw him approaching. He paused only to give instructions to Brother Michael. "I want no one coming through, Brother. Keep your gates barred. I don't care if the pope himself begs entry. No one is to go near the church until I know it's safe."

Brother Michael nodded briskly, heavy jowls aquiver. Constance and Godwin left him to deal with the clamoring crowd, making their way down Gate Street to the Moot Hall where Godwin needed to counsel with any of his men who may have returned from their appointed tasks. However, they found only Bosa, Eilaf, and Hamo inside, absorbed once again in their board game, oblivious to the hum and buzz outside the Moot Hall. So fiercely was Bosa concentrating that he did not hear Constance and Godwin enter. He lunged from his seat when he saw his lord, spilling the game. As Eilaf, Hamo, and Constance bent to retrieve its pieces, Godwin asked him, "Do you have news for me, Bosa? Have any of the men returned from the countryside?"

"Aye," his deputy answered. "Some have, lord, but with nothing to report."

Godwin heaved a tired sigh, and was about to suggest to Constance that they go and fetch the horses and return to Bordweal when Eilaf said, "Will you hang the Jews, uncle?"

"No, Eilaf," he answered firmly. "The Jews will not be hanged. They are innocent."

"Everyone says they killed Alfred."

"You must not heed them. They are wrong."

Eilaf's blue eyes grew less troubled, trusting in his lord and kin, and Godwin said, "Now come, it is growing late! Let us get Constance home to Bordweal."

They left the Moot Hall, securing it for the night, for Godwin, Bosa, and Eilaf would go on to Dilston Hall after seeing Constance to her manor. As they walked toward the stable on Gilesgate, the boys trailing, Godwin began to tell Constance of the day's events, beginning with Fulk's arrival and his message from the archbishop. Something in her expression prompted him to ask, "You know Fulk? You have had dealings with him?"

"Yes, I know Fulk," was all she would say at first. Then, "But the archbishop has no authority over the Jews. Is that not why I went to Middleton? To summon the royal justices? And it's likely they will come, Godwin," she told him, though with much less enthusiasm than she felt earlier that day.

Godwin explained how the archbishop was maneuvering for jurisdiction and Fulk's theory as to why. "Alas, Constance," he said, "I fear your journey to Middleton was made in vain."

She nodded slowly, saying, "Yes, it seems so. It is regretful because Lord Eilan is willing to intercede."

"We must call it off by sending a messenger to him at first light," Godwin said, explaining that any meddling by the royal justices might irk the archbishop, something they could not afford. "Besides, I think it very likely that the regent has already granted him jurisdiction."

"I wonder how much help the royal justices could have offered," Constance said, "now that a second miracle has taken place." Godwin looked at her, puzzled, and she described her conversation with Brother Elias concerning the emerging sanctity of Alfred. "If it comes to pass that he is revered as a martyr-saint, no one will believe the Jews are innocent."

"That was no miracle today!" Godwin objected. "Nor, I suspect, was the first miracle genuine." Somewhere in his head, a warning bell sounded, faintly, elusively, yet distinct, and Godwin was silent a moment trying to track it down.

"*You* and *I* may not believe they are miracles, but what if most do? The Jews will be under constant threat, and we will have no power to help them, for how does one dispute the divine, or argue against miracles?"

"It cannot be done, which is why these have no place in the king's court."

"But we are dealing with the archbishop's now. Will not a church court see the miracles as evidence?"

They reached the stable, pausing before it. "Yes . . . ," Godwin said slowly. "I suppose they will." The miracles, he realized with an unpleasant start, added to Grendel's testimony, would surely be sufficient evidence for the archbishop—more than enough—to condemn the Jews. With mounting alarm, he described Grendel's account to Constance, then his own assessment of the man and his motives. "He hates Jews enough to give false testimony, I have no doubt."

"Enough to murder?" Constance asked.

"I wondered that myself. But it seems too . . . devious a murder for Grendel. Still, it's a possibility that ought to be investigated. Nor is he the only enemy the Jews have in Hexham." Godwin went on to tell her of his discovery in the *archa*, describing Sir Havelok's indebtedness and Alfred's connection to him as an errand-runner.

Eagerly, she asked, "Could Havelok be the one who killed Alfred? It seems a perfect fit. If he has been deprived of his property and livelihood, perhaps he's seeking vengeance for his losses?"

Godwin was silent for a moment. He had not assessed his impressions of Havelok. "Those were my thoughts as well," he answered slowly. "I was questioning him when the west wall collapsed. He maintains that he did not see Alfred on Good Friday. I've yet to verify his story, but he claims he was in the church all morning, though I suspect he had the opportunity to slip away unnoticed for a time. He could have nabbed the boy, murdered him, then hidden the body away until nightfall." But Godwin sounded doubtful, adding, "He is difficult to judge. Capable of violence, certainly . . . but something tells me he is not Alfred's murderer."

Constance thought the connection between the knight, the Jews, and Alfred too strong to be coincidence. "Are you certain? He sounds like just the man we seek, Godwin. Was there nothing about him that made you doubt?"

"He is bitter and angry," Godwin conceded. "But so are many, yet they do not turn to murder." Something else struck him. "All that Havelok has left is his honor and faith. Would he sacrifice both for his hatred of Jews?"

"Honor and faith can be deceptive notions," Constance answered, a trace of bitterness in her voice. "They mean different things to different people."

"True enough," Godwin admitted, remembering how his own beliefs had conflicted with those of his fellow crusaders. "But surely every Christian, including Havelok, would see the murder of an innocent child as sinful and dishonorable."

"Not every," she replied.

Hamo went inside the stable to fetch Aurora and his own horse, while Godwin, Eilaf, and Bosa began saddling theirs. Constance strolled down to the bridge, listening to the swiftly flowing river, thinking about the murder. It was carefully planned and carried out to incriminate the Jews. But why? Until they could answer this, she feared they would never find the killer.

As they rode from Hexham into the darkening night, crossing the river at High Ford, Constance and Godwin were quiet, each deep in their own thoughts. Bosa, Eilaf, and Hamo rode well behind, talking in hushed tones. The sky was clear and bright with stars, the air very cold, exhaled in great white plumes by the horses as they trotted briskly along, anxious for their home stalls.

They had the road to themselves as dusk gave way to evening, and the sounds of the night were mostly their own: the steady footfalls of the horses, the tinkle of bells on Aurora's harness, hung there by Cynwyse to ward off evil, the boys' low-pitched murmurs. Occasionally, Constance heard the hoot of an owl in the distance. It must be almost Compline, she realized, wondering if any canon would brave the church to ring in the hour.

She was considering what they ought to do next, but her mind kept coming back to the knight. She found everything about Havelok suspicious and expressed as much to Godwin.

He said nothing, and Constance looked over to see him staring dejectedly at the road ahead. "Do not give up, Godwin," she said quietly. "We can save the Jews, I know. We *must*."

"Can we?" Godwin asked, the confidence shown Eilaf gone. "Prior Morel is at this very moment dispatching a letter to the archbishop, informing him of the latest miracle, and Grendel's testimony, too. It will only be a matter of days before another messenger arrives, ordering me to condemn the Jews."

Constance could think of no reply, and Godwin went on despondently, "And what have I accomplished in the days following the discovery of Alfred? Nothing. I wonder if I'm fit to keep law in Hexham."

"I know of no one more capable than you!" Constance protested. When he continued to stare off into the darkness, she added, "When I first learned that you had become bailiff, I was surprised. I thought the post beneath you, not worthy of your status. I realize now that such offices have suffered in their reputation, for they are often monopolized by corrupt men and lords who have taken advantage of the recent chaos and war in our country. Most seek power for personal gain, caring not about justice and good rule.

"If justice is ever to reign again, as it did in the days of King Henry, it will only do so through men like you, Godwin. Worthy leaders must serve when royalty fails. And worthy you are, never doubt that."

Her speech brought a faint smile to his lips. "Your

words are kind, Constance, and mean much to me—more than you know. Yet the truth cannot be denied. The noose is tightening around the necks of the Jews, and I am no closer to saving them. Does that not say that I am the wrong man for this job?"

"No! You are more than capable! More important you are committed to proving them innocent! It is not over yet, Godwin."

"Good intentions will not save our friends, and time is running out. Soon the Jews will pay the price for my failings."

Constance pulled sharply on her reins, stopping in the middle of the road. Behind, the boys broke off their soft speech. "This talk leads nowhere, Godwin!" Her voice was low, but intense. "You have made progress. You know of two men with possible motives for killing Alfred. Now we must keep working to uncover more. Time is short, as you say! Let us not waste a moment with fruitless discourse. Besides, what other choice have we, but to persist?"

"No other," he agreed.

He grew thoughtful again, though Constance sensed the heavy gloom was lifting.

"I will send a man to Copely in the morning," he said, sounding more like himself. "I want to find out if the story Havelok has given is accurate and what his kinfolk have to say of him. If he has lied, or has kept something back, then I will pay our knight another visit. I must also learn the whereabouts of both the knight and Grendel on Good Friday.

"In the morning," he said, briskly now, "I'll meet with my men to learn what today's scouring of the country-side has turned up. Who knows?" he said, giving Constance a smile, "perhaps one of my knights has already uncovered something vital."

TWELVE ✠

G odwin rode into Hexham the next morning just after dawn. He was anxious to get to work, though his night's rest had brought him little in the way of refreshment. He had lain awake for hours going over every bit of information he had gleaned in the past week. Something was eluding him, a larger pattern that he could not quite grasp; he was too near, he realized, not seeing the contours of the constellation, though he perceived its existence. The key to unlocking the mystery of Alfred's death, he was sure, lay in discerning the pattern and order of events surrounding the murder. He needed to uncover more, as Constance had said, needed to reveal other stars, brighter ones that would light his way.

But first he needed food, and once Saedraca was stabled he headed to the baker's shop. As he crossed the Market Square, Godwin passed between two old ladies, backs bowed over walking sticks. Oh, God, he groaned inwardly, giving them a weak smile. He knew what Cynwyse would say: he who walks between two old women early in the morning shall have bad luck the rest of the day.

When he arrived at the Moot Hall with fresh wafers,

dripping with honey and crisp from the oven, the morning's unlucky harbinger seemed already at work. There awaiting Godwin was one of the archbishop's messengers. He had ridden hard from York, taking little rest, it appeared, for his clothes were mud splattered, his expression weary. Yet he also wore the smug, self-important look common among young courtiers. They were an unsavory lot, oftentimes, poised upon the lowest rung of power's ladder, willing to do most anything to reach its summit.

Just as Fulk had predicted, the archbishop had obtained jurisdiction over the Jews and had dispatched this messenger, posthaste, to inform his bailiff. The royal justices were now officially barred from interfering where the Jews were concerned.

Godwin resisted the urge to tear up the writ and toss the messenger out on his ear. Instead, he nodded dismissively and told the young man there was no reply. He had no intention of relaying the news of the second miracle to his lord. The archbishop would hear about it soon enough from Prior Morel.

"My lord," the messenger said in a tone that conveyed more boredom than deference. "The archbishop requests an accounting of all debts owed to the Jews. I'm to take the list with me when I journey back to York."

"By God's eyeballs!" Godwin bellowed, sending an astonished messenger backward several paces. "A murderer is on the loose and he wants me to tally accounts! That greedy, insufferable—"

Just then, some of Godwin's knights filed into the Moot Hall, turning wary eyes on the object of their lord's discontent, hands reaching casually to the hilts of their swords.

Godwin reined in his outrage. It was not the messenger's fault, after all. But his voice was quietly menacing when he said, "Tell the archbishop that, regretfully, I cannot submit to his request as I am preoccupied with a murder investigation."

The messenger nodded quickly, then hastily took his leave.

When the door had closed behind him, Godwin turned to survey his men. He saw that Wulfstan and William the Welshman were not among them and took this as a hopeful sign. It was the only one, as it turned out, for none of his assembled knights had anything useful to report. No strangers were wandering abroad, nor had they come across any accounts of unusual happenings. All was quiet, save for the clamor concerning Alfred's murder and miracle. The news of a second miracle will be fodder for the fire! Godwin thought dourly.

Once again, he assigned two men, Oswey and Atla, to guard the Jewish quarter while Eoban, Chadd, Beorn, and Anlaf were sent to relieve those on duty at the Keep. Then he instructed Burchard to travel to Copely. "Find out anything you can about our knight, Sir Havelok," he said. "Speak to his kin and Lord Balliol. Go to the local priest as well. Often they are willing to reveal things kin will not." Godwin gave the knight some silver for travel and his seal on a scrap of parchment, lest someone question his knight's errand.

Finally, he sent Waldeve to Bordweal to give Constance the archbishop's latest message. From there, he was instructed to go to Middleton, requesting that Lord Eilan withdraw his summons of the royal justices. He gave his knight a hastily written note to be delivered to Lord Eilan describing the situation in Hexham.

"The rest of you come with me to the priory church," Godwin said. "You've heard, no doubt, about yesterday's calamity—or miracle," he added dryly, "depending on your point of view."

* * *

When Godwin and his small company arrived at the priory gatehouse, they encountered a flustered gatekeeper. "Lord Godwin," Brother Michael cried. "It's no fault of mine," he stammered. "The prior pronounced our church trusty—"

But before the distraught canon could finish, Godwin stormed past the gatehouse to come to an abrupt halt in the courtyard, his knights drawing up behind. The clanking of their mail hauberks and swords could be heard even above the din created by the mob gathered in front of the priory church. Many turned to stare at the armed retinue, giving them dark looks and muttering under their breath.

Godwin was astonished by what he saw: a long line was streaming into the church at the west end, passing within an opening that had been tunneled through the stone debris. As he watched, he saw many bend to reverently touch the tumbled rock, or rub it with bits of cloth that were then tucked away in their clothing or scrips. The line streamed back out of the church at the north transept door.

Who were all these people? he wondered. Where had they come from? Godwin recognized only a few of the faces.

As he stared, he saw Brother John exiting from the north door with a burlap sack tied securely at its neck. It must have been very heavy, for both his hands were couched beneath the load, causing him to waddle forward like a corpulent duck. When he saw Godwin, he faltered, looking nervously left and right and back over his shoulder.

Godwin strode up and relieved the unprotesting canon of his burden. The bag clinked noisily as the silver pennies within were jostled.

"An impressive haul of booty, Brother," Godwin said, weighing the bag of coin appreciatively. "Bound for your lord, are you?"

Brother John nodded, then braced himself for the coming gale, squinting his eyes shut.

But the bailiff only said, very quietly, "Allow me to deliver this for you."

The relieved canon hustled off, and Godwin turned to his men, saying, "I want everyone cleared from the courtyard. The whole west side of the church could collapse at any time." Godwin looked at the people waiting to go in, knowing that if they were hindered, he could well have a riot on his hands. "Inspect the north portal, Brandon," he instructed the knight. "Ensure that the passage is safe, then route these pilgrims in that way. The rest of you go back to town and gather some men. Then collect any carts and tools you can find and set to work on clearing the courtyard of this mess. I'll return when I've finished with the prior."

As Godwin approached Morel's private chamber, not far from Havelok's, he saw the door was slightly ajar. Brother Elias was seated before the great desk, emphatically nodding his head.

"I want those partitions down at once!" Morel was demanding. "This is appalling, Brother Elias, simply appalling! A dortor divided into private apartments! Canons segregated, sleeping in isolation! It is heinous, evil! A perversion of the sacred Rule!"

"Actually, it is not unheard of, Lord Prior," Brother Elias ventured. "Some monasteries provide private sleeping chambers so that canons may pray through the night without disturbing—"

"Pray?" Prior Morel choked. "You think this dissolute collection of worthless canons prays!?" The prior took a deep breath, struggling to master his rage. Lowering his voice, he said, "Early this morning, Brother Elias, before Prime, I saw a young woman creeping from the dortor by way of the night stairs. The wanton canons of St. Andrews do not seek privacy in their bedchambers to pray, Brother, but to wallow in befouled nests of licentiousness!"

Brother Elias's cheeks were as red as cherries as he sprang quickly from his chair to carry out the prior's command. Eyes set firmly on the ground, he did not see Godwin standing nearby as he passed out of the chamber.

Under other circumstances, Godwin would have found the exchange amusing. But not now. He knocked once upon the door, entered, then strode in and dropped the sack of coin heavily on the prior's desk.

Morel's outrage seemed to evaporate at the sight of the bailiff. He did not acknowledge the sack, only motioned to the chair just vacated by Brother Elias.

"Ah, Lord Godwin," he said pleasantly. "How good of you to return. I was just about to send a message."

"Oh?" Godwin replied evenly. "I am pleased to spare you the trouble then."

"The church and priory are sound. That is my message. I conducted the inspection of the buildings myself, though I knew it to be a waste of time." He gave Godwin a smug look. "That vile thief was taken yesterday, not because of a decrepit building, but by an act of God." He clenched a bony hand into a fist and banged it hard on the desk, making the coins jingle in their sack.

"Nevertheless, I have the utmost respect for you, Lord Godwin, and your office. I know you are motivated, if not misguided, by concerns for those who worship in our house of God. Thus, I have carried out your request and have found all well." The prior looked expectantly at Godwin, as if waiting for a show of gratitude for his indulgence. "I must say," he added when Godwin did not reply. "It proved to be a useful endeavor, for my scrutiny turned up certain . . . irregularities among the canons that might have continued uncorrected." He tapped a long finger on the desk, preoccupied by thoughts of his wayward flock. "It is usually the case that a prior or abbot lives aloof from his canons." He gestured to his private chamber. "As befits his status. I have always known this to be satisfactory. Yet at St. Andrews the arrangement seems to have fostered deviant behavior."

Godwin was not interested in the prior's trials with the canons of St. Andrews. "I would like to have a look at the church myself, Prior," he said. "You would not object?"

Morel's jaw clenched, but he tightly inclined his head.

"And there is the matter of the west entrance," Godwin said, gazing steadily at the prior. "It is not safe to allow people through that way. The rest of the wall could give way at any moment. It is reckless of you to put lives at risk."

Morel's eyes flashed, and the two men locked eyes in a confrontation of wills that lasted until the prior suddenly shook his head and laughed softly, saying, "Lord Godwin, anyone would think that you are prior here, not me." He stood up and came around to lean against the front of his desk, one hand toying with a heavy ring he wore upon his left hand. "I have been patient thus far, yet you are taxing my limits, I fear. I have deferred to your requests as graciously as I know how, but now I am forced to point out that you have no right to interfere with the running of this establishment. Long ago St. Wilfrid secured for St. Andrews the right of sanctuary, which extends for one mile around this church. The outer boundaries are properly marked. You have no authority within these bounds."

Godwin said nothing, only watched the prior twirl the ring on his finger. Morel saw him staring and held out his hand for Godwin to get a closer look. The ring was shaped like a tiny golden casket. It was a reliquary, he realized.

"It holds a nail paring from the finger of St. Peter himself," Morel said. "It is my most treasured possession."

Godwin looked dubiously at the elaborately encased fingernail clipping.

There was a knock on the door, and Brother Elias tentatively poked his head in to say that one of Godwin's knights had arrived with an urgent message for the bailiff. Godwin went to the door where William the Welshman stood breathlessly beside Brother Elias.

"Your knight may enter," invited Morel, moving discretely to a window.

Godwin swung the door wide, and William stepped in, saying, "Lord Godwin, I come with a message from Wulfstan. We have found the beggar! It was just as you said. The scar upon his face made him an easy find. What's more, he claims to have some knowledge of Alfred, though he refused to tell us all he knows. He says it is a delicate matter. He will speak only to you."

"Where is he now, William?" Godwin asked, his skin prickling. He had known, somehow, that the beggar would prove important in the matter of Alfred.

"Both he and Wulfstan are south of here, in Knitsley where we found the man. He's taken ill and traveling is hard going for him. Wulfstan took him to a nearby convent. They plan to lay up a day then set out tomorrow. I came ahead to bring the news."

"Good man," said Godwin, putting an arm on William's shoulder, guiding him back outside. Brother Elias stepped quickly aside. Godwin saw Havelok just beyond the doorway, walking slowly toward his quarters. "William," he said, lowering his voice, "get some rest, then take yourself back to Knitsley. Tell Wulfstan to come as soon as possible. And I want the both of you to keep a close watch on this man. I'll set out that way myself as soon as I'm able. Watch for me on the road!"

When William had gone, Godwin went back inside to finish his business with the prior, but he was preoccupied now and anxious to conclude their discussion. "Prior Morel," he said. "What you say about jurisdiction is true, yet we are both men of the archbishop and serve a common purpose—to guard the souls entrusted to our care. Let us work together to that end." When the prior nodded, Godwin continued. "Entry to the church from the west side must be barred until repairs are made. But if the north portal is safe, as you say, then I do not object to its use."

"That is acceptable," Morel answered, glancing at the sack of coin on his desk. "I've sent for the best masons in England to repair the entrance." His eyes suddenly shone. "It will be grand, Lord Godwin, much grander than before. I have plans for a new tower. A new bell shall be cast also to crown the rebirth of St. Andrews. St. Wilfrid will be proud when he gazes down from heaven at his beloved church, young Alfred at his side."

"Alfred is another issue I wish to take up with you, Prior," Godwin said. "I ask that you refrain from celebrating his so-called miracles, until I find his murderer. More and more are hailing him a saint, a Christian martyr killed by Jews. I need not tell you that such talk only increases the peril of Hexham's Jews."

"I would not dare to impede the hand of God, Lord Godwin."

"But surely you agree, Prior, that it's misleading to celebrate him as a saint, a martyr, when we do not yet know who killed him? And what of the pope? You cannot simply declare someone a saint. There are . . . procedures, are there not?" Godwin said vaguely, for he really was not sure how a saint was made.

"Alfred's death and his miracles speak plainly, and all save you have heeded their message." He gazed sadly at Godwin. "The Jews are threatened because

Alfred is seeking vindication. As for his sanctity, that is not something which is guided by procedure. It is a spontaneous wonder, a divine revelation that must be embraced when revealed, its coming proclaimed and celebrated among the community of Christians. Authority must acknowledge it, yes, but that comes later."

"Someone is seeking vengeance, yes, but I do not think it is Alfred," Godwin argued. Then, with a sigh, he said, "I know there is little you can do but welcome pilgrims when they come. But can you not curb this desire to brand Alfred a saint, until I get to the heart of this murder?"

"As I have said, I cannot hinder God's hand. His divine work is already in motion. As soon as the archbishop sends his approval, Alfred will be translated to the high altar of St. Andrews. He will be buried there, attended by a great celebration that befits his status as this priory's new martyr saint."

Godwin stalked out of Morel's chamber, disgusted by the prior's arrogant manner, his ceaseless platitudes. The man shouldered no responsibility, laying everything at the feet of God. How easy, how convenient, Godwin thought angrily, to attribute every action, every event to God's will, never having to accept the burden of accountability.

Back in the courtyard, he saw that the townsmen and his knights were making progress hauling away the blocks of stone. Brandon reported that the north entrance looked sound enough, and Godwin went around to have a look for himself.

It was difficult with so many gathered there, for people were now entering and exiting this way. Godwin scanned the portal and agreed that the doorway was safe, then he turned his eyes on the crowd.

The people jostled and elbowed each other in the cramped line, and those with injuries and afflictions seemed not to be faring well.

Godwin saw a blind woman pushed out of line to stand helpless, turned around in the unfamiliar surroundings. He took her arm and guided her through to the chapel as many shouted protests. When he had seen her in, he turned to begin an inspection of the church's interior, but a voice behind him shouted, "When will ye do yer duty, Bailiff, and hang those murderin' Jews?"

Godwin turned slowly, his eyes coolly surveying the large crowd of Christians wedged into the transept. He saw the same hostile look on each face. Several he recognized, wryly noting that they had not stepped into the church for a very long while. "Who is asking?" was his reply. When no one spoke, he said, "I will tell you all then. The Jews will never be hanged because they did not kill Alfred."

They erupted all at once, shouting at him, accusing him and the Jews of monstrous acts. One voice rang out over all others, calling the Jews a people of the devil, a grave threat to all Christians.

"Listen to what you say!" Godwin called out. "It is madness! You have only to open your eyes and look upon the Jews to see that they are not the creatures you describe!"

They only glared back, as Grendel had, seeing him in the ranks of their enemy. Godwin felt suddenly like an outcast with people he had always dwelled among. He turned his back on the hostile faces, becoming angry, wondering why he bothered to guard their safety. Yet he went all around the church, up and down the aisles and through the choir, looking for signs of damage or decay.

In the south transept, he found some serious degradation over the doorway leading to the cloister. He was just about to run down a canon to warn him of the danger when he heard a noise on the night stairs above him. It was Brother Elias, struggling with a portable partition wall. He looked in danger of tumbling down the stairway with his burden, and Godwin ran up the stairs to assist him.

"Brother Elias," Godwin cried. "Cannot another help you? This is too great a burden for one man."

Together they wrestled the partition down the steep stairs to prop it against a wall. Brother Elias was breathless with the exertion, and Godwin noticed that he looked especially pale and worn. "Are you well, Brother?" He urged the canon over to the stairs and helped him take a seat on a lower step.

"I am fine, Lord Godwin," he said, passing a hand over his face. "These last few days have been tiring is all."

Godwin looked closely at the canon. It seemed to him that there was more than fatigue clouding his delicate features. "What troubles you, Brother Elias?" he asked gently.

He looked up at Godwin, staring with anguished eyes, but said nothing.

"Come, Brother," Godwin encouraged. "You may speak freely. Perhaps I can help."

"I think not," the canon said sadly. "For it is a matter of faith." He looked up quickly. "I mean no insult, lord."

Godwin laughed softly. "In matters of faith, it is true, I have less experience than many. But could this be of some use?"

Brother Elias sat silent, mulling it over. Finally, he said, "You see, when Alfred was first found, and it was clear that he had been ritually slain, I had no doubt that the Jews were responsible. Then the first miracle came, followed by my . . . vision. . . . I was even more sure."

"And now?" asked Godwin. "You are not so certain?"

"No," he admitted, head hanging. "The signs speak clearly, and yet doubt grows in my heart. I fear what this may mean . . . that I have lost my faith," he confessed sadly.

Godwin sat down beside Brother Elias, saying, "No, Brother, I think not. In fact, I am sure of it, so take heart, for I am not certain of many things these days!" The canon only stared at his sandals, and Godwin went on, "It is human nature to question, to seek the truth. We live in a world where man's work is often more apparent than God's, and for this reason we must be wary and careful, trying to discern God's desire from man substituting his own. I do not think it was meant to be clear, for the test comes, perhaps, in distinguishing between the two."

Brother Elias was silent, and Godwin asked, "Do I make any sense to you, Brother?"

"Yes . . . I think so. You are saying that I doubt Alfred's sanctity because it is guided by man, not God?"

Godwin stared at Brother Elias.

Suddenly, there was a disturbance at the north entrance, and he stood to see Eoban burst through a crowd of angry pilgrims and penitents. He looked around wildly, and Godwin hailed him. He came running to the bailiff, crying, "Lord Godwin! The Keep is under siege!"

THIRTEEN

Ada carefully cracked open the door to her brewery, putting a wary eye to the opening. She looked relieved to see that it was Constance waiting on her stoop, a bundle of parcels in her arms, and threw the door wide to welcome her.

"Lady Constance," she said. "Please come in."

"Thank you, Ada. I hope my visit is not untimely." Constance was acutely aware of her own experiences with well-wishers after the death of her husband. A steady stream had journeyed to Bordweal when news of Aidan's death spread through the shire. Townspeople, tenants, local nobles, and landowners came to express their sympathy, and while she knew that most had only the kindest intentions, she had nevertheless grown weary of receiving them. Donning a stiff smile, she had nodded obligingly at the empty assurances and sentiments she could not share: There is no death more noble than a crusader's. How honored you must feel.

"Not at all, not at all," Ada was assuring her.

But her voice was hoarse with strain, and the changes she saw in this woman once lavishly endowed with might and vigor shocked Constance. She was but a hint of her former self, a pale, reflection with haunted eyes.

Ada led her to a snug sitting area in the corner of the brewery. As she took her seat, Constance cast her eyes around the room, noting that the place had a neglected feel to it, as if Ada and Gamel had halted production. No fires were lit beneath the vats of water, no casks stood ready to receive the freshly brewed ale.

"Cynwyse sends you her heartfelt sorrow. And these," Constance added, handing the bundle to Ada. It contained some baked goods, as well as a mixture of herbs Constance herself had become familiar with. They were a part of the cook's charm for curing grief. The herbs were to be mixed with tears, then poured into a running stream. The grief would be drawn out of the sufferer and carried far away.

Other items were included, their meaning mysterious to Constance: a bit of iron, the end of a candle burned on Easter Sunday, a clay vial of raindrops and a small flagon of wine that Cynwyse claimed essential for "sin-drinking."

Constance had been reluctant to bring these; for it made her uncomfortable to be the conveyer of goods whose properties and purpose she did not know or understand. "Perhaps you should take them to her yourself, Cynwyse," she had suggested, looking doubtfully at the odd collection. "You may need to make clear their purpose."

"Just ye do as I say, mistress, and take these along to Ada. She'll know what to make of them, don't ye worry."

"Please send the cook my thanks," Ada said. She unwrapped the bundle and looked at the assortment inside. To Constance's relief she did not look surprised or perplexed, seeming to understand the function of each item. Picking up the little pouch of herbs and handing it back to Constance, she said, "This I cannot take." Ada, as Constance had been, was unwilling to part with her grief.

Constance asked, "Is there anything I can do for

you, Ada . . . help you and Gamel in some way?"

"You are very kind, lady. But no, I do not think there is anything . . . unless you can keep those dratted canons from coming around."

"The canons of St. Andrews? What business have they here?"

"It's to do with Alfred," she explained wearily. "They've been coming to collect his goods—clothes, toys, everything." She heaved a sigh. "I protested, of course, for I have a nephew in the country who could sorely use those things. But they claimed them as holy relics. They're to be worshiped in the church alongside my boy."

"I was wondering, Ada," Constance said tentatively. "Do you believe that Alfred's become a saint?"

She was quiet for a moment, reflecting. "I'm not sure what I think, lady," she answered slowly. "I'd like to believe that he's behind the miracles, that he's been singled out by God. It would make me feel easier about losing him—like he had a greater purpose to serve than just being my boy. . . . Yet, I can't help remembering how he hated going to Mass, how he squirmed and chafed to be outside playing. I was lucky if I could get him to say a *paternoster* at bedtime. So to hear everyone talking about my little boy as if he was a saint. . . . well, it's going to take some getting used to."

Ada puzzled over the matter a little longer, then added, "Course I've never known anyone who went on to be a saint. But I would've thought there'd be hints along the way, as he was growing up, giving us an inkling of his destiny, like in the stories. You know, lady, like the story of St. Wilfrid?"

Constance nodded. She had heard the tale from Cynwyse. It was said that Wilfrid was sanctified in the womb, like Jeremiah, and at his birth, his future greatness was foretold by the Holy Spirit. As Wilfrid's mother struggled through her labor, surrounded by midwives, the house caught fire and burned like an inferno with flames licking at the heavens. Men ran everywhere, panic-stricken, trying to douse the fire, but to no avail. The midwives, however, emerged unscathed to announce the birth of Wilfrid, and the cottage bore no sign of burning, just as when Moses saw the burning bush with flames roaring yet consuming nothing. It had been the Holy Spirit, they realized, awestruck, in the form of fire, announcing Wilfrid's destiny as a holy bishop who would shine brightly upon all the churches of Christendom.

Constance had heard similar stories about Wessex saints as she was growing up. According to these, it was commonplace for saints to foretell their future glory through marvelous occurrences in their childhood. Most saints, too, had miraculous foreknowledge of their death. Yet if these things were so common, she wondered, why did not more people witness them? Constance never had, nor did she know anyone who had. She suspected that many miraculous stories were invented after the person had been made a saint, long past the time when any could recall the individual as a mere mortal.

Who knows what people will say of Alfred a hundred years from now? None of those who lived among him will be alive to say yea or nay, to confirm or deny the veracity of the stories.

"I mean to say, Lady Constance, Alfred was a rascal most of the time, a real handful—" She broke off to wipe a tear from her eye.

"It matters not, according to the canons," Constance said, remembering her brief "lesson" with Brother Elias. "Because they think he died a martyr."

Ada looked anxiously at Constance. "That's another part of this business that has me worried," she said. "I just can't believe the Jews would do that to my boy, murder him like that—" She choked back more tears.

"I'm so sorry, Ada," Constance said. "I've no business asking you to speak of this."

"Don't you worry, Lady Constance," she said, drying her face. "It helps to talk. Gamel, he doesn't say much. He's taken Alfred's death real hard . . . closed himself off. We haven't done any brewing all week. I'm lucky if I can stir him from bed in the morning."

Poor Gamel, Constance thought. She could not imagine what it would be like to lose a child, to lose Aldwin.

"No, I just can't believe the Jews had anything to do with it," Ada said again. "I think people have got it wrong. The town's divided on the matter, that's for certain." She turned a worried gaze on Constance. "It doesn't seem right luring all these pilgrims to Hexham when we don't know anything for sure. . . .Yet, what of these miracles? They point to something, don't they? And isn't it a sin *not* to believe? Oh, I don't know, lady!" She threw up her arms, exasperated. "It's church business. Who am I to have a say in matters so great."

Constance led Aurora through town, making her way to the Keep. She had more parcels to deliver, this time to the Jews. Cynwyse had packed up some foodstuffs to help ease their situation.

As she wended her way along the winter-rutted street, black clouds gathered overhead, obscuring what pale sunlight there had been. An icy sleet began to fall, angling sideways on a newly gusting wind. She huddled against her horse, wondering miserably when this foul weather would ever give way.

The town seemed oddly deserted. Most had anticipated the storm, she guessed, and were snug in their shops and homes. Yet these had a deserted quality as well, and she saw few with candles lit and hearths burning.

Perhaps everyone was at the church, joining those

flocking to Hexham from the countryside. Hereberht had told her that news of the second miracle was spreading like wildfire, drawing pilgrims from far beyond the borders of Hexhamshire. Several parties had halted at Bordweal earlier that morning, anxious to confirm that they were on a true course for St. Andrews.

Reaching the end of Hawk's Lane, Constance stopped to gaze at the forbidding structure squatting on the hill before her. She shuddered at the sight of the Keep, her dread of the place inspired in large part by the stories told of the fortress by Cynwyse.

Her cook was convinced that the Keep was haunted by Saxons who had been tortured to death within by Norman conquerors. Cynwyse had been distraught over Constance going there, for she was convinced that her Norman lineage would put her at dire risk. "The Saxons won't tolerate having ye there, mistress," she had cried. But Constance would not be swayed against her plan.

Then, as she was preparing to leave the manor, Waldeve arrived with Godwin's message from the archbishop—curse that man! She had sent the knight on to Middleton, but not before giving him her own message to deliver to Lord Eilan.

Cynwyse had settled for arming her mistress with all the protective charms and talismans she could muster. Constance went laden with rowan sticks, hawthorn catkins, balls of red thread, and mysterious-looking holed stones with saints' names scratched on their surface. Now, staring up at the Keep, Constance was inclined to believe that it was indeed frequented by phantoms, for it looked particularly ominous to her today.

The icy wind had settled suddenly, allowing the dark clouds it summoned to hover menacingly before they slowly descended upon Hexham. She watched as blowing sleet transformed into a dense fog that settled thickly over the ground and encircled the rise upon which the Keep sat hunched. It stood wreathed now in damp clouds, suspended against the dark sky like a hungry vulture.

Determined to shake off the awful dread the place inspired, Constance chastised herself for succumbing to the cook's tales. She strode purposefully to the base of the citadel, leading Aurora.

"Who goes there?" a voice called sharply from the mist.

"It is Lady Constance," she called, halting.

The knight Anlaf appeared in front of her, as if by sorcery, and Constance stepped back, startled. She had not known the voice was so near.

"Anlaf," she said, feeling foolish at her swiftly beating heart. "I've come to see the Jews. Can you help me find my way?"

He turned and led Constance up the steep climb to the gatehouse. She went quickly after him, anxious to be out of the blinding fog. They unloaded her packages, leaving the horse tied near the entrance to the gatehouse, then proceeded down the narrow passageway to the Keep's great oaken door. Anlaf looked overhead, signaling to the knight manning the portcullis chamber. "Hoy up there, Beorn," he called.

"Aye," the knight acknowledged, though Constance could only make out his shadowy outline as he leaned over the dark opening.

Anlaf pounded on the Keep's door with the hilt of his sword, calling out his name to the guard inside. It was opened by Chadd, another knight of her husband's who, after the death of his lord, had gone into service for Godwin. To Constance's relief, Chadd quickly closed and barred the door after her. She could hear Anlaf retreating back down the passageway to his post.

The Jews welcomed Constance, the women coming over to warmly embrace her as she handed them the bundles of food. They led her to the fire where she stood steaming as her fog-dampened garments began to dry. Constance then gave them the latest news, describing the arrival earlier that morning of the archbishop's messenger. They had already learned of the second miracle from the guards.

"It has always outraged the archbishop to have Jews dwelling in his liberty," Jacob said bitterly. "Now he has his chance to reverse matters, he wastes no time or opportunity."

"Is it unusual for Jews to dwell where Church lords hold sway?" Constance asked.

Isaac answered, saying, "There is nothing usual or unusual in the lives of Jews, Lady Constance, for these words imply predictability." He smiled faintly, his lined face serene. "For Jews, life is unpredictable, serving the whims of powerful men. We are possessions, servants of the crown, to be used as the king desires. Only in our law do we find stability and security."

"Was it always like this, Isaac? Were Jews ever free in England?" Constance asked.

"Our fortunes have varied through time," he answered. "Hatred and tolerance wax and wane. Who can say why?

"Long ago, Jews were sought out by kings and great men. Your first Norman king, William, invited Jews to dwell in England, for there were none here before, or so I have been taught. Jews often brought prosperity, oiling the wheels of trade and commerce with their capital and expertise and connections to the East. Jews were offered the protection of the crown, yet this privilege became the means to our oppression.

"The king is our guardian, yet this renders Jews his servants. We are subject to any demand, however arbitrary or onerous. We can be taxed into destitution, financing one foreign campaign after another." Isaac spoke calmly, without emotion. "The laws you are subject to are fixed by custom," he continued. "Not so for Jews. Like any other of his goods, they can be disposed of as the king sees fit. Yet he guards us with the dedication of a dragon astride his treasure. This is why lords of the Church often deny Jews residence in their liberty, for the crown keeps its power over them."

Constance considered his words. The English demand that their kings observe tradition and custom during their reign. The war against John was fought over that very principle; *Magna Carta* wrested from him to secure it. Some laws were more unjust than others, yet most were at least known and predictable, fixed in time.

How precarious life must be for Jews, she realized, never knowing what lay ahead. Their existence was like a candle, whose flame burns bright and steady in a quiet room, but sputters in a draft, and is finally extinguished by the cruel breath aimed at dousing its fire.

"Yet there are many Christians in Hexham who stand with us," Samuel said, smiling warmly at Constance. "It is not everywhere so grim."

"Yes, but there are many who stand against us," countered Jacob. "It remains to be seen who will win the day."

No one had a reply to Jacob's stark assessment, and they were all thoughtful for a time, quietly clustered around the fire.

Suddenly, a disturbing crash brought them to their feet. The Keep shuddered with such a force that Constance thought a wall must have given way. Ivetta ran to the children.

"The portcullis!" Chadd cried. "It's been lowered! The Keep is under attack!"

They could hear a disturbance in the gatehouse, yet the thick oaken door and portcullis now fortifying it muffled the noise. They stood stock-still, straining to hear.

Chadd was poised before the door, his sword drawn. "Move to the far side of the hall," he commanded, eyes on the door. "I do not think any will gain entry, not soon leastwise, but we cannot be sure. Let us pray that the portcullis chamber was secured in time!"

Jacob ran to one of the slit windows and peered outside. "There is a mist about us—I can see nothing," he cried. "I cannot say who attacks us or what their numbers may be."

"Move away, move away," Chadd shouted. "An arrow might come through!"

"It would be a lucky shot indeed to come through so narrow an opening," he called back, though he did not resist when Ivetta ran over to pull him from the window.

Jacob did not stay in the far corner of the Keep, however, where the others stood ringed around the children, but went to stand beside Chadd, who handed him his dagger.

Godwin had raced down Gate Street and through the Market Square, his sword raised high, his knights trailing. He was forced to slow his pace, though, for while he had tarried on the night stair with Brother Elias, an evil fog had descended upon Hexham, and he could not see beyond the tip of his outstretched blade.

He raised his hand to signal a halt as the company approached the end of Hawk's Lane, then assembled his men behind an ancient clump of holly, taking care not to alert anyone near the Keep to their presence.

Godwin peered around the hedge, and noticed that the fog was lifting a little. He cursed, for the cover would have given him an advantage. He could make out several shadowy figures clustered at the foot of the Keep's rise and more men above, outside the gatehouse entrance.

"Eoban," he called softly. "Can you tell me their

number, or who they might be?" Eoban had been posted outside the Keep with Anlaf, having been instructed to fetch Godwin at the first sign of trouble. And while he had been fairly confident that none would dare an assault, Godwin had nonetheless taken precautions to repel one. For this he was relieved, yet he knew also that he hadn't the manpower to beat off a sustained attack by a professional force. He only had ten knights, including the two who had been standing guard on Jewry Lane. His greatest hope for success lay in the impenetrability of the Keep itself.

"I cannot say whose force they are, or their number," Eoban was saying. "I was guarding the rear of the Keep when the storm blew in. I heard a great commotion and knew an attack had come when I heard the portcullis fall. I wanted to go back and stand with Anlaf," he said, staring miserably at the ground. "Instead, I went down the slope and circled back into town to summon you, as I was ordered."

Eoban was obviously greatly shamed for having forsaken his comrade. "You did well, Eoban," Godwin assured him. "If you had not alerted me, who knows how long it might have been before the hue and cry was raised." He looked around at the deserted lane. "Too late, perhaps. Besides, it's likely that Anlaf made it into the portcullis chamber with Beorn. They are safe enough there."

He sent Murdac and Owain to scout the fortress. "See if any besiegers are posted at the rear, then hasten back and report their numbers."

The knights soon returned to say that there were no other besiegers besides those at the foot of the hill and above at the gatehouse.

"We will charge the men at the bottom, first," Godwin told his men. "And trust that those above will not come to their aid, but rush inside the gatehouse to be trapped with the others who must be trying to breach the portcullis." Godwin was fairly certain this would be the case, for now that the fog was lifting he could make out certain individuals. This was no professional band, as he had feared at first; several townsmen he recognized—unskilled soldiers and no match for Godwin's battle-hardened men. "Eoban, watch our backs."

The knights drew up in tight formation, then pushed forward as one, wailing war cries and brandishing their swords and shields. As they closed in on their prey, Godwin saw terror in the eyes of the besiegers as they now understood the peril. They braced for the assault, though, bunching into a tight circle with rude weapons pointed outward.

Godwin looked up briefly to see those posted at the gatehouse run inside the passageway, forsaking their fellows. He called his men to a sudden halt, drawing them up to surround the motley group of would-be besiegers, seven or eight in number. He recognized more townsmen and some rustics from the countryside, but there were other faces he did not know. By the look of their weapons—pitchforks, axes, and scythes—they were local farmers and herdsmen.

"Throw down your weapons," Godwin shouted, "and your lives shall be spared."

None hesitated. They quickly dropped the crude weapons and held their arms high, turning frightened, beseeching eyes on Godwin.

"What is your number?" Godwin demanded. "Who leads you in this wicked plot?"

But the terrified men would say nothing, and Godwin turned from them in disgust to address his knight Osbern.

"Take them back to the Moot Hall," he ordered. "Secure them in the loft and set Bosa to watch. Then get back here, for I will need every man. I do not know how many are in the gatehouse, or what they might do when they learn they are trapped like rats."

"Can they break through the Keep's defense, lord?" Murdac asked.

"The portcullis was lowered in time so they will find it very difficult," Godwin answered. "Yet, with enough time, it can be done." His eyes glinted. "But they shall not get it."

Osbern ushered the ragtag band off to the Moot Hall while Godwin cautiously led his knights up the rise. The fog was lifting as fast as it had descended, exposing them as they made their ascent.

A volley of arrows flew at them as they neared the gatehouse, harmlessly bouncing off their raised shields, or whizzing past, well off their mark. The men who loosed them ran deeper into the narrow tunnel when they saw their weapons were useless.

Godwin's men huddled at each side of the doorway, careful not to expose themselves to the black opening. As Godwin joined those on the west side, he was brought up short by the sight of Anlaf. His knight was lying on the ground a short distance from the gatehouse.

It looked as though he had been bludgeoned with a blunt weapon, and Godwin thought at first he must be dead. As he grimly stooped over his knight, though, the man's head wobbled back and forth, as if still trying to ward off blows. "Rest easy, Anlaf," Godwin said gently, signaling Eoban to help him hoist the injured man. They laid him along the outer wall of the gatehouse, the only shelter on the hillside. Eoban covered him with his cloak.

"We cannot tend him now, I fear," Godwin said, keeping an eye on the gatehouse entrance, listening for movement within.

Eoban looked distraught and clearly reluctant to leave the injured man's side. Godwin knelt quickly to put a hand on Anlaf's forehead. His eyes opened at once. "Good man," he said softly. "Stay with me, Anlaf.

You are needed here still." The knight nodded once, not taking his eyes from Godwin's. His lips moved as he tried to speak. "Stay quiet," Godwin told him. "I must go, but Eoban will remain at your side."

Godwin stood up. As he did, he heard a strangely familiar tinkling sound coming from a shroud of fog still clinging to a distant segment of the hillside. Straining to see, he was shocked by what emerged: it was Constance's horse, prancing nervously on the slope, reins dragging.

Dear God, he thought, was Constance inside the Keep?

He hurried back to the entrance, calling, "You in there. Drop your weapons and come out. You are trapped. End this folly now, before more blood is spilled."

Shouts could be heard, angry voices raised in disagreement. They were distant though, and Godwin thought the attackers must be clustered far within, at the portcullis. He could get no sense of their numbers, but was heartened by the sounds of discord.

Finally, an angry voice drowned out all others, coming nearer to the entrance, shouting, "We'll not surrender fore we 'ave justice!"

It was Grendel, the root of all evil in this town, Godwin was beginning to think. At the same time, he was relieved, for Grendel was no military strategist. Matters might have been far different if Havelok had led this assault. "Grendel," he shouted. "End this before more lives are lost, including your own! This is not the way to justice!"

"Whilst yer the bailiff, there can be no justice!" he shouted back. A thunderous clamor of voices rose up behind him, signaling angry agreement with the ringleader.

"There is no way out, Grendel. You have no provisions. You cannot last long in there. I will starve you out if need be. Nor will you breach the iron portcullis. Far better soldiers than you have attempted it and failed."

"We won't give way!" Grendel screamed. "God's our ally! He'll cum to our aid!" Then he lowered his voice to a menacing growl, saying, "Will you even battle *Him* fer the sake of yer precious Jews? And never forget, they, too, are 'ere. Not within my grasp, not yet. But starve us and ye starve them also."

Godwin did not answer, but stood considering his options. He could rush the gatehouse and likely win the day, but at the cost of more knights, no doubt, for they would be at a great disadvantage while their eyes adjusted to the dimness, trying to fight unknown numbers in the narrow passageway.

No, he did not favor that option. Best to hold back for now. If there was discord in the ranks of the besiegers, it would only grow with time. Neither did he worry that those inside the Keep would go without food and water. If necessary, these could be hoisted through the window slits. Constance and the Jews were safe for now.

Beorn, too, was secure in his perch over the gatehouse. The hatch was solid iron, almost impossible to breach. Godwin knew the besiegers had not the tools to penetrate the chamber and raise the portcullis, nor any of the equipment required to win a siege. Except for fire.

This was Godwin's greatest concern—that they would attempt to set fire to the oaken portions of the portcullis, and then the great door itself. It would be very risky for the attackers, for the passageway could quickly fill with smoke, forcing them out of the gatehouse before they achieved their goal. Yet it was also possible that the wood would catch quickly, especially if doused with oil from the lamps that hung throughout the passageway. The vigorous arguing that he and his knights could hear probably centered on this very issue: to burn or not to burn.

Godwin had much experience in siege warfare and knew he had the advantage. The greatest risk for besiegers was failing in their initial assault, as Grendel and his followers had, forcing them to contend with reinforcements under very awkward cover. But this was no company of seasoned soldiers Godwin was battling, but an odd assortment of angry men whose actions were unpredictable. He must weigh his decisions carefully.

No attempt had been made on the Keep in his lifetime, not since the skirmishes with the Scots. Its function as a defensive fortress was but a distant memory, as it was now only a convenient place to store goods and temporarily house criminals. Few efforts had been made in recent years to keep its defenses shored up.

Godwin considered all these things before deciding that at the first sign of fire he would order his men to attack. He could not risk the besiegers getting into the Keep, for their intentions were clear: to execute the Jews. He would try to keep them occupied with negotiations in the meantime and hope that their own disagreements would bring about their defeat.

Osbern came panting up the hill just then, reporting that the prisoners were secure in the loft of the Moot Hall, guarded by Bosa and Eilaf. Godwin sent the knight back into town for a litter and some lengths of rope. "When you return, help Eoban get Anlaf to the hospital so that the canons and Fara can tend his wounds. Then the two of you return as quickly as you can."

Osbern turned to make for town once more, and Godwin went back to the entrance, calling to the besiegers, "Listen, you men. Give up now and your punishment will be made lighter. Force an attack, and I will spare you nothing. There is still time to end this peacefully. Think carefully! You are farmers and craftsmen, no match for my knights. You risk losing everything—your lives, your trades. Think of your families!"

There was more quarreling, and it was clear that many were losing their nerve. Doubtless they had been convinced by Grendel that the attack would be accomplished swiftly, "justice" meted out before Godwin and his knights could arrive. Perhaps they had even hoped to remain anonymous, attacking suddenly at an opportune moment before slinking back into the mist. Now they were cornered like rodents, at dire risk of dying in a melee, or being hanged for their participation in the assault. Even if they achieved their purpose and won the Keep, they would eventually be captured and punished, but for a far more serious crime. However, Godwin was determined that it would not get that far. No matter what, they would not enter the Keep.

He and his men waited, letting doubt and hesitation gnaw away at the besiegers' confidence. Osbern arrived with the litter and rope, giving the latter to Godwin. Then he and Eoban carried Anlaf down the rise toward the hospital of St. Giles. A crowd of people had gathered at a safe distance to watch the scene on the hill. It parted to let the litter pass.

They could hear Grendel again, shouting, urging, trying to compel his followers to remain steadfast. Godwin heard snatches of his passionately delivered argument, phrases like, "Light the fire of judgment . . . Divine wrath. . . . He'll not forsake us."

But his coconspirators were abandoning him. Godwin and his knights, standing ready with their swords, could hear a mob approaching the mouth of the doorway.

"Leave your weapons behind and come out slowly, one at a time," Godwin shouted.

He and his knights heard the clatter of various implements dropping. Beyond the yielding men, still deep inside the passageway, Grendel was shouting, "No, no!"

The besiegers filed out of the gatehouse, some hanging their heads in shame, others looking defiant still, but grimly resigned to their failure. There were some twenty men, and Godwin was surprised by some of the faces among them.

There was one man in particular, old Fergus, whom Godwin was especially dismayed to see. He was a gentle soul, once in minor orders, now a farmer who tilled a small toft at the southern edge of the shire. He sold mushrooms at the Market every autumn, and Godwin always looked forward to those tasty morsels as well as the bits of conversation he shared with Fergus.

He was a man who viewed life differently from most, in ways that Godwin found intriguing. Once, many years ago, he had flatly denied to Godwin that John was his king. "How can you deny him," Godwin had asked. "Does he not sit upon England's throne?" Fergus had replied, "A king must trample all injustice underfoot, to throw it down and crush it utterly. John does this not, indeed, he is the wellspring of inequity, violating his sacred duty to protect the poor and humble. I owe him nothing, least of all my fealty." Godwin had gone away feeling slightly uncomfortable (were these utterings not treason?), yet he had contemplated Fergus's words for many days. Could a king be rejected by his people because he did not adhere to the duties and obligations of his office? What of lineage? Do not the sons of kings become kings themselves because their blood makes them royal? As it turned out, Fergus had been right. John had indeed been forced by his rebellious barons to mend his tyrannical ways.

Never would Godwin have guessed that Fergus harbored such hatred in his heart. He watched sadly as the man was quickly bound up with the others by the rope Osbern had supplied. There was little fight in them now, though, and Godwin and his knights turned their attention to Grendel.

With Godwin leading, they slowly entered the passage, allowing their eyes to adjust to the dimness. Ahead, they could hear Grendel, muttering incomprehensibly. The words echoed eerily, like an evil chant offered up to something in the darkness. A few of his knights exchanged nervous glances. The man has surely lost his mind, Godwin thought with a shudder.

They steadily made their way toward the portcullis. It was almost dark; many of the lamps that hung in the passageway were missing. There was faint light ahead of them, though, and drawing nearer the end of the corridor, they could see Grendel working busily. He had stacked all the lamps he could gather against the oaken sections of the barrier and was reaching overhead, trying to grasp a lamp that hung from the ceiling above him.

"Stop there, Grendel!" Godwin shouted.

Grendel paid no heed and gave the lamp a great tug, spilling the oil onto his face and arms. Without warning, his entire body was instantly engulfed by flames as the wick from above fell, lighting him up like a huge torch.

The passageway was brilliantly lit by his flaming body, and Godwin and his knights were momentarily rooted by horror as they watched a blazing Grendel flail his arms and scream in terror. Then they desperately cast about for anything they could lay hands on to douse the flames, choking on the smoke and the stench of burning flesh.

They found a pile of blankets and snatched them up as they ran toward the burning man. "Hurry, before he sets off the other lamps," Godwin shouted, seeing how Grendel was backing away from them.

But he fell forward instead, and the knights rushed to smother the flaming body. When the fire was quenched, Grendel was dead.

The knights carried him outside, gulping in the fresh

air as they emerged with their grisly burden. Grendel's roped comrades stared in horror while the crowd of onlookers, now at the foot of the rise, gasped in unison.

Godwin stared sadly at the charred remains, a man consumed by his own hatred. Then he instructed some knights to escort the captured men to the Moot Hall. Two others were given the task of carrying Grendel to the priory. He himself went back into the gatehouse, holding his cloak to his mouth, for the stench was unbearable. At the door, he shouted, "Hoy in there! This is Godwin. All is well now!"

When they raised the portcullis, a very relieved Chadd opened the great oaken door. Godwin looked for Constance first, finding her at the far side of the hall with the other women and the children.

Then he told them what had happened, ending his account with Grendel's gruesome death. Constance asked, "Was it Grendel, Godwin? Was he Alfred's killer?"

"I'm not certain," he answered. "Obviously he wanted to see the Jews destroyed, yet I'm not convinced that he killed Alfred. . . .

"In any case," Godwin went on, "if he was the murderer, we need more evidence to prove it, for the little we have will not satisfy the archbishop."

"But with the man dead, how can we ever discover the truth?" Jacob asked.

"We may have located someone who can help us," Godwin answered, describing the discovery of the wandering beggar by Wulfstan and William the Welshman. "It seems he knows something about Alfred's death, but will speak only to me. I was about to make for Knitsley when the Keep was attacked. It is too late to go today. I must deal with the rebels, but I will set out at dawn. Finally," Godwin said, rubbing his hands together, "we may get some answers!"

Fourteen ☩

The beggar carefully lowered his feeble frame onto the narrow pallet, pulling a coarse blanket over him. The effort taxed him, and he lay gasping for a time, the rattling of his chest echoing in the silent chamber. He gazed about the tiny room, fastening his attention upon its spare furnishings, refusing to acknowledge the bodily pains that were stubbornly demanding his attention.

The nuns had provided him with a small guest room in their convent, sufficiently outfitted with bed, chair, and water-filled basin. It would seem a dreary place to most, but to the beggar it was splendid. He rarely slept under a roof, usually making his bed out of bracken with only treetops and the vault of the heavens to shelter him.

No need to keep an ear cocked for wild beasts, he relished, nor worry that the weather might turn foul. On this night, the harder the wind blew the more peacefully he would sleep. And despite his weariness, he struggled to stay awake, wanting to savor every moment of this gift from God.

He had lived in a proper house once, long ago. Nothing lavish, but a goodly home sheltering his family and their beasts within its double bays. Like the room he lay in now, it had been spare in its adornments, yet when he recalled his childhood home, it seemed not wanting, but crowded with happy memories of loving parents, trusty kin, plenty to eat.

Breathing deeply, sending up a few dry coughs, he could still recall the mingling aromas that permeated that distant home. There was the sharp, pungent tang of pigs and sheep, the savory smells of his mother's cooking, the smoky odor of damp wood and peat burning, the sourness of sweating bodies fresh from a day's work.

His mind strayed next along the path that led from childhood to his adult years, from innocence and security to the harsh realities of a precarious existence. He tried to resist these memories—why travel that hard road again, he chided himself. But the course was deeply incised in his recollections; he could not recall the childhood years without remembering the painful ones that came after.

The sudden death of his parents was the first tragic milestone, followed by the loss of his home to a covetous uncle who drove him off, anxious to be rid of a competing heir. After that, he had dwelled with various duty-minded kinfolk, working hard to earn his bread and board. Yet in time, he had no more blood relatives to call on, and he entered into his darkest years. These were cruelest because loss and regret were bitterly fresh, his helplessness paralyzing. In time, though, he came to accept his destiny, even took interest and pushed forward.

He was not now bitter over the route his life had taken. He did not angrily examine each downward turn that composed his existence so that he might assign blame. Rather, he dispassionately recalled events to see whether an alternate course had ever presented itself, a moment when he could have taken a new direction to a different sort of life. He never found one, but always came away thinking that his life's span was like an arduous trek down a deeply rutted road. Powerless to turn left or right, the only course accessible had been to journey forward in the relentless tract, or stop altogether.

No, he had not given up, but had struggled to acquire the skills necessary to survive. He had learned how to travel the hard road, how to forage for food in wild places and beg for it in civilized. He became skilled at faking afflictions in exchange for sympathetic offerings, taking pride that he could inspire charity and openhandedness in even the most mean and tightfisted. Of late, though, there was no need to pretend.

He had always made sure donors went away feeling that their gifts had been worthily bestowed. Being fairminded, he viewed begging as a transaction of sorts; he acquired life-sustaining contributions while the benefactor received a lighter conscience, a more buoyant spirit, if only for a time. Priceless gifts really.

He had learned through the years that good Christians were ever anxious to accrue points in the Book of Good Works, lest they come up short on judgment day, and the beggar was willing to provide the means to a greater tally. Other vital spiritual services he generously provided as well, like his recent miracle in Hexham. Some might call him a charlatan, but he saw himself as bringing confirmation of the divine to those in need, confirmation that God still cared enough to intercede in their small lives. Was this not a worthy calling, bringing hope and reassurance to his fellow man?

The greatest burden he carried was the prospect of dying unshriven, without a proper burial. The notion troubled him greatly, for he knew that those who died irreligiously were doomed to wander the earth indefinitely, hounded by the living who were justifiably terrified by the itinerant roamings of corpses. Such a death seemed all too like his living state, and it was unbearable to think he might have to endure this manner of existence forever. In death he *must* find escape, and so he sought out friendly priests whenever he could to make his confession. The beggar hoped that this would be sufficient, that infrequent absolution would allow him passage from this world. As an added precaution, he sent a prayer up to St. Katherine each night, for she had powerful influence in the hour of one's death.

A worrisome and difficult life it was, yes, but he had claim to pleasant memories as well, a small store he called upon to cheer him when the nights were especially dark. His most precious were the memories of a year spent living in the wild with a hermit. Dwelling in a woodshed, he had tended the holy man's shack, gathering food and fuel for him.

The hermit's name was Raven. Neither a monk nor priest was he, only a simple potter in the fiery clutch of the Holy Spirit. It had seized him one day as he sat at his wheel, compelling him to sell all that he owned to benefit his poor parish church. He then determined to follow the path of the apostles, to wander Christendom, destitute and unencumbered, spreading the word of Christ.

The parish priest, however, had wisely persuaded Raven to pursue a holy life in a tiny cottage his church owned, set in the middle of a vast forest. It had been the home of a hermit recently passed away. The priest had known that despite the Holy Spirit burning at his side, Raven would not survive long on the roads and byways with their knaves and thieves. He was far better off, the priest deemed, in the forest.

It happened that the beggar passed through this town and was asked by the priest to carry supplies to his newly minted hermit and to see how he fared alone in the great forest. The priest was beginning to fret, for he knew Raven was not a robust man. He had assumed that his passions would cool, that he would return to town and potting wheel once he sampled the arduous life of poverty and solitude. Only Raven had not.

And a good thing it was that the beggar sought him, for when he found Raven, he had but his soul left, so starved and ill he was. Yet he was steadfast in his new-found love, and the beggar stayed on to nurse the besotted man, marveling at how quickly he recovered. Then, at the hermit's insistence, he stayed on permanently, making his home in the tiny woodshed.

They became fast, yet unobtrusive friends, each respecting the other's need for solitude and isolation— Raven because it brought him closer to God, the beggar because it was the only way he knew. They passed contented days together, the beggar seeing to their corporeal needs, the hermit to their spiritual.

Raven's ways were strange and mysterious to the beggar, like nothing he had ever witnessed. Marks of his extreme piety, he reasoned. The man tonsured himself, not in the common fashion, but by shaving his head to make a line from ear to ear behind which the hair was left to grow long. He wore a rough sack for a garment and refused to bathe, except once a month, on a certain night, by the light of a full moon. If clouds obscured the moon on the appointed evening, then he postponed his ablutions for another month.

A good deal of Raven's time was spent in prayer, accompanied by gestures of adoration, prostrations and genuflections. He would often lie face-down before the tiny altar in his shack with arms held outstretched to form a cross. Or he would kneel the day through, genuflecting up to two hundred times; his knees finally grew so enlarged that Raven was forced to hobble about with a stick like a crippled man.

One day he discovered a Bible in the cottage, and took to poring over the text, though he was not skilled in Latin. It was a fabulous book, richly ornamented with luminous lettering of gold and silver. A priceless object, the beggar knew, guessing that it had belonged to the deceased hermit. A gift from a wealthy patron, perhaps.

Raven was captivated by the holy book. To him, the exquisitely strange letters seemed like magical markings, potent, like secret knowledge. Just staring at the beautiful script or running his fingers over the letters brought a faraway look to his eyes, taking him closer to the spiritual realm he pined for. And when he learned that the beggar had some skill in reading, imparted to him long ago by his mother, he was eager for instruction, eager to penetrate the book's mysteries.

So the beggar had taught Raven how to read the holy script, how to render the strange words into everyday speech. They began with the *paternoster*, which became a kind of primer for the hermit, his key to deciphering all the words of the gospel. Raven learned so quickly that the beggar thought the Holy Spirit must be guiding him once more, and it was not long before the pupil exceeded the skills of his teacher.

Once a verse or passage was mastered, Raven would repeat it over and over like an incantation. The Book of John he found especially compelling and for many a day he repeated its opening verse: In the beginning was the word, and the word was with God, and the word was God. Over and over he said these words, varying their pitch and rhythm. He seemed intoxicated by their meaning, shouting them at the trees in the forest, uttering them over his bread at supper. The beggar wondered at his intent, then grew so weary of the declaration that he went off on a prolonged journey to forage for food.

Words and book alike were revered by Raven, and the holy text never left his side. Yet, as he drank in the book's knowledge, filled his spirit with words, he weakened in the flesh, despite the beggar's desperate ministrations. Raven seemed to deplete his body of all physical strength until his spirit finally took to its wings and left this earth. The beggar buried him with his precious book.

He could have stayed on in the woodshed, he knew, or even taken up residence in the shack, but the place had an eerie quality without Raven. The beggar would have been comforted by a sense of his friend's lingering presence, but nothing remained. It was oddly bereft, as if Raven had consumed all the ethereal qualities, leaving the place devoid of its spiritual component. No birds came around after Raven died, and it was oppressively quiet. The beggar grew eager to move on.

Now, as his frail body began to relax, he let go his memories, and drowsiness crept over him like a rising tide. So pervasive were its effects, he gave up all thought of beating it back, and reached a hand, regretfully, to douse the candle stub's flame. But he pulled his arm back again thinking, why not let it burn? A delightful extravagance that he could later recall and savor.

I am coming, I am coming, he said wearily to the dream voices that beckoned. The pain that wracked his body by day slowly receded as his mind finally gave in to the irresistible pull of the current washing over him, carrying him into the blessed slumbering sea of forgetfulness.

His eyes flew open suddenly. What noise was that? he wondered, aches and pains flooding back into his limbs. Even the great scar upon his forehead throbbed in time with his quickening heartbeat.

He lay very still, listening, just as he had done countless nights in the open forest. Then he chuckled quietly and shook his head. I no longer know how to live among the civilized, he chided himself. It is only the kindly nuns, moving about their convent.

He let sleep wash over him again, giving himself up completely now, never hearing the latch upon the door lift, nor the quiet footfalls approaching his cot.

Sleepily, he half-opened his eyes, without fear. He was almost over the boundary to the other world. A nun, he thought, come to pray at my bedside. The dark figure loomed, and his lingering consciousness felt grateful for her pious devotion.

Something glittered in the darkness, making the sign of the cross over his body. "I am blessed," he murmured. A bright shaft of light plunged into his heart, and he heard a raven beckoning, saw black wings beating the air. Then his pain was gone forever.

FifTeen ✠

"You were told to keep him safe!" Godwin roared when Wulfstan and William gave him the news. He had just arrived at the convent, a small house in the woods outside Knitsley. They were standing just outside its gate, Godwin still holding Saedraca's reins. "Now you say he's dead, murdered in the night as you slumbered nearby! By God's eyeballs, Wulfstan! I ought to have you flogged!"

The knight's blue eyes flashed. "The blame is not mine! How was I to know that someone wanted him dead? I worried he might die of his illness, but I never expected someone to steal into the convent by night and put a knife through his heart!"

"Nor did I, Wulfstan," Godwin said, his anger suddenly gone, replaced by a too familiar feeling of helplessness. "Or I would have warned you. Forgive my rash words."

Godwin was stunned by the news of the beggar's murder. Another death! How many did that make in little over a week? First Alfred, then the thief at the church, next Grendel, and now the beggar. How did they relate to one another? Did they? Godwin felt as if he had the pieces of a bizarre puzzle scattered at his feet, at a loss as to how they fit together. "Wulfstan, William—did the beggar say any more to you? Give you any clue as to what he knew of Alfred's death?"

They shook their heads, and Godwin sighed, saying, "Come, take me to him then."

They passed through the gates into a small orchard that fronted the convent. Godwin secured his horse and sent William to fetch water and hay for the beast. He had ridden hard, eager to learn the beggar's secret.

After yesterday's turmoil, he had been reluctant to leave Hexham, even for a day. Those involved in the plot had been fined according to the law and sent home, and Godwin did not worry much about another attack with their ringleader Grendel dead. But he had taken precautions nonetheless. No longer were his knights posted outside, vulnerable to assault; they were positioned at the battlements above and in the watchtower. The portcullis would remain down at all times.

As they entered the convent, Godwin saw that the house was in upheaval, the sedate routine of the cloister brutally disrupted by the murder. Nuns scurried about, whispering to one another as they passed in the corridors. A tall woman, thin as a willow whip, came forward to meet Godwin. "I am the prioress of Knitsley Convent, lord. Sister Edith is my name." She spoke gravely, tilting her head forward slightly to keep her eyes downcast. "I deeply regret the unspeakable crime that took place here last night. Our house has failed in its sanctuary."

Godwin could see that she was profoundly disturbed by the death of the beggar. "Prioress," he said. "You welcomed a stranger, opened your doors to him. The blame is not yours if evil followed him in."

Sister Edith looked up to gaze directly at Godwin, and he knew that his words did not ease her mind. "Why would someone wish to see a harmless old man dead?" she asked. "He was ill, no threat to anyone."

"It was an evil act," said Godwin. "And I will do all within my power to find the one responsible. Can you tell me, Prioress, did any of your sisters see or hear anything during the night?"

"No one has come forward to report any disturbances. To my knowledge, all was quiet after nightfall. We arose, as always, for Matins and Lauds. Nothing unusual was heard or seen."

"Did you or any of the sisters speak with the beggar?"

"I do not believe any other than myself had conversation with him. When the party arrived yesterday, the beggar was taken to a guest room where I brought him a tonic of fennel and rosemary to ease his fever and cough. He thanked me many times, but said nothing else." Sister Edith looked intently at Godwin. "You think he had some knowledge that put him in danger, lord? That he may have been aware of his peril?"

"No," Godwin answered. "I doubt he worried that someone stalked him, or he would have been more guarded. He would have alerted my knights, I think." But, thought Godwin, he obviously had information that someone wanted to keep hidden, knowledge so damning that murder had been committed to keep it secret.

What could a seemingly harmless beggar possibly know? Godwin wondered. Did he see something, witness Alfred's murder perhaps? No, that couldn't be, or he would have been aware of his danger. He had information, some piece of the puzzle, that much was clear, but he did not understand its significance, perhaps. And why had he been unwilling to speak with Wulfstan and William? Godwin heaved a depressed sigh, realizing that these questions might never be answered. Someone had reached the beggar before Godwin and silenced him forever.

Sister Edith led him down a brightly illuminated hallway. At the end, she opened a door into a tiny chamber and stepped aside so that Godwin and Wulfstan could pass through.

The bailiff went to the body first. There were no indications that the man struggled for his life, rather, it looked as though he had lain quietly while someone stood over him and put a dagger through his heart. He had bled profusely; his tattered tunic and blanket were soaked. Yet he must have died fairly quickly, for it did not seem as though he had writhed about in pain on the pallet. A gentle smile rested upon his lips.

Turning to glance around the tiny room, he asked Sister Edith, "Where are his goods?"

From the doorway, for the room was too small to accommodate them all, she said, "Bundled beneath his head, I think."

Godwin gently extracted a rolled-up cloak that had been fashioned into a rough pillow. Unwinding the threadbare, hooded garment, he found a small pouch filled with coin. He spilled its contents into his hand, and Wulfstan whistled at the beggar's hoard. "A sizable sum for an almsman," he said.

"Indeed . . ." Godwin said thoughtfully. "He had a recent windfall, I'd guess." Looking at his deputy, he asked, "Is this all the man carried, Wulfstan? His cloak and this pouch?"

"I never saw the pouch," he replied. "Only the cloak—nothing more."

Godwin nodded, then looked around hopefully. But there was nothing else, no clues to be found in the tiny room.

Sister Edith still waited in the doorway, and Godwin said to her, "Prioress, we must give thought to providing this man a burial. Have you a place here at the convent that could accommodate him?" Godwin waited for her reply, knowing she would object to burying an unshriven Christian on holy ground.

But Sister Edith said, "We failed in our sanctuary. The least we can do is give him a proper funeral."

Godwin was surprised, for he had always known the devout to be unshakable in their convictions when it came to the manner of one's death. "It does not concern you that he died unshriven? That he was not absolved of his sins?" he asked.

"He did not receive last rights, no, but he made his confession last evening to a priest." She smiled faintly. "It is safe to assume, I think, that he committed no sins between Compline and Prime."

"He gave confession to a priest?" Godwin asked sharply.

"Yes, I forgot to mention. It was the first request he made after he arrived yesterday. I sent one of the sisters to the parish church in Knitsley to fetch the priest. He comes once a month to hear our confessions and was not due for another two weeks. But I felt the man's request should be fulfilled if at all possible. Father Anselm arrived just before Vespers to hear the beggar's confession. He broke bread with us and was gone by Compline."

"I must speak with this Father Anselm," Godwin said, his hope rekindling. Turning to his deputy, he ordered, "Wulfstan, fetch the horses. We must go to Knitsley!"

Godwin and his knights hastily prepared to leave the convent. Before they rode off, he placed the pouch of coins in Sister Edith's hands. "Keep this," he said, "for your kindness and Christian devotion to those in need."

She stared at the pouch, which rested like an offering in the palms of her outstretched hands. "Much good can be done with so large a sum," she said in her grave voice. "But we will also use some to buy the beggar a goodly coffin, and to enter his name in our prayer lists. The sisters will pray for his soul daily from this day forward, for as long as this house stands."

* * *

They swiftly rode the short distance to Knitsley, a small village that rarely saw visitors, only those few who turned aside for a respite during their travels to or from the cathedral city of Durham. The parish church was easy to find, for it was situated at the heart of the community. An exquisite little church, ancient by the looks of it, it possessed little in the way of grandeur, but a great deal of charm. And the villagers obviously took great pride in their place of worship; the grounds were meticulously tended, the structure in excellent repair.

Godwin instructed his knights to remain outside, knowing the priest would be reluctant to divulge anything the beggar revealed in confession, and even more so with Wulfstan and William standing nearby.

He did not relish asking a man to break a sacred trust, yet were not the lives of several individuals more important than a dead man's confession? The rules must be broken when circumstances demanded it, and Godwin was becoming desperate enough to break them all.

He entered the church through the single west door to find himself in a tiny nave, no larger than twenty-five paces by fifteen, he reckoned. The morning sun softly illuminated the small room through the clerestory windows. Indeed, the air this morning had a familiar, benevolent warmth to it; at some moment, when he had not been paying attention, spring had arrived.

Beyond the apse, a mere nook housing a small altar, stood the priest. He was placing new candles in their holders.

Upon hearing Godwin enter his church, he turned with a welcoming smile and stepped forward to meet his visitor. Yet when Godwin introduced himself and briefly explained the purpose of his visit, the priest frowned.

He was about thirty years old, Godwin guessed. Not long a priest, certainly. "Father Anslem," he said. "I must know what the beggar said concerning Alfred. He was planning to reveal his information to me himself, but I came too late." Godwin was suddenly struck by a realization, but he put the thought aside for the moment. "Please, I know it is against the precepts of the Church, but can you not make an exception in this case?"

The young man studied Godwin anxiously, clearly torn. "If only my bishop were here to advise me," he said. Then, with more assurance, "But he is not, so I must act as my heart bids. I will reveal the man's confession to you, Lord Godwin." Father Anselm looked up to one of the brightly lit windows, as if looking for additional guidance, then said, "I have been troubled since I heard this man's confession, for though he spoke naught of murder, nor did he mention any names, one thing he confessed was most disturbing. I granted absolution, for it was easy to forgive a man in his poor circumstances. But the other, the one who bought his services, hired him to perform the miracle. I fear he must answer directly to God."

Sixteen ✠

Constance was riding to Hexham once again, this time at the summons of Prior Morel. Beside her rode Cynwyse, perched awkwardly atop a gentle old cob. Unlike Constance, the cook did not take pleasure from riding; however, yesterday's siege and her mistress's inadvertent involvement had distressed her considerably, and she had vowed not to let Constance out of her sight until the affair with the Jews was concluded.

Constance assured her that she required no chaperone, but Cynwyse would brook no argument. She was going and that was that. If Constance didn't like it, she could take it up with St. Peter.

"By God's mercy, Cynwyse!" Constance had cried as they stood in the stables, making ready to depart. "Sometimes you deal with me as if I were no older than Aldwin! One would wonder who the mistress of this house is!"

Cynwyse had made no reply, but blithely went about her preparations. This entailed standing before her horse and gravely asking its permission to mount; for Cynwyse firmly held that horses were honorable beasts, that sitting one had everything to do with its good graces and nothing to do with the rider. If the horse agreed to carry you, nothing could tear you from its saddle, save your own will. By the same token, if one sat a horse against its will, the insolent rider would be brutally dispatched at the first opportunity. As a result, though the cook did not relish riding (heights troubled her), she did so with surprising confidence, sure her mount would never allow a mishap.

They did not hurry, content to let the horses set the pace. Constance was not particularly eager to meet with the prior again; her initial impressions of the man were not terribly favorable. Then she reminded herself that it was in the forbidding crypt, after all, that she had first met him, not an appropriate atmosphere for making a new acquaintance. No doubt she would find him more amenable aboveground, in the light of day. She was curious about his summons, wondering at his reasons.

He's probably seeking a donation to help with repairs, she thought, then turned her attention to the country-side. It was a fine morning. The bitter north wind had at last retreated, and in its place was a mild southerly, a gentle breeze redolent with the freshness of a new grow-ing season come at last. Time finally to sow seeds with the waxing moon, to begin the labor that would coax her flower garden to its midsummer splendor.

Looking about, she marveled at the changes being wrought by the milder air, almost overnight it seemed. Everywhere the land was newly blanketed by a growth of tender green. New primroses starred the lane, and diminutive leaves, tightly wound buds just days before, had swelled and unfurled to bedeck the trees with their dainty foliage. In the fields and meadows, thick blades of emerald grass were suddenly succeeding winter's drab brown. "Spring is late this year, Cynwyse, but was she not worth the wait?" Constance called. "Smell the air and hear the birdsong! Are they not intoxicating?"

"Aye, they are, mistress," the cook agreed, smiling.

"Winter's finally given in, that stubborn old brute."

"Yes," Constance agreed. "He has wearied us all by his persistence."

"At least we had warning and prepared ourselves for a long one," the cook replied. "But bless my bread, not even my onions told me the winter would be so cold and harry us so long!"

Constance smiled, thinking how the cook could do wonders with an onion, from preparing a savory stew to foretelling the future. One of her many rhymes sang:

> *Onion skin very thin, mild weather coming in,*
> *Onion skin thick and tough, coming winter*
> *cold and rough.*

Last autumn's harvest of onions had indeed revealed skins that were thick and coarse, prompting Cynwyse to double their stores for the coming winter. The staff had been ordered to gather all the wood and kindling they could lay hands on and to put up plenty of feed for the horses and stock animals. Nor did Hereberht bristle at her violation of his domain, for Cynwyse was never known to be wrong in such matters.

The next seasonal harbinger the cook awaited was Candlemas Day:

> *If Candlemas Day be fair and bright,*
> *Winter will have another flight,*
> *If Candlemas Day be clouds and rain,*
> *Winter be gone and will not come again.*

To the disappointment of all, February second had been unseasonably fair, accurately predicting a resurgence of winter.

"When this business is behind us, ye will want to work the garden, I expect," Cynwyse said as they crossed over the bridge.

Constance smiled, recalling the cook's early suspicion of a mistress who dirtied herself in the soil. Aidan, too, had been somewhat surprised at his bride's penchant for gardening. It had perplexed and amused him when he brought his wife home to Bordweal, finding that she was far more interested in exploring the grounds than the inside of her new home. No trousseau had been unpacked that day. Instead, Constance had eagerly delved into a wooden box brought with her from Wells, carefully unwrapping fleshy roots and bulbs wrapped in moist sackcloth. Her treasures, she had explained as he looked on curiously, many collected from all over Christendom by family and friends: roses, peony roots, and lavender from France and Spain, iris and jasmine from the Holy Land; old favorites from her mother's garden—columbine, hyacinth, red poppy, and hollyhock.

She felt a familiar stirring. "Yes, I believe I will, Cynwyse."

They left the horses at Hexham's stable, packed today with all manner of beasts. More visitors from abroad, Constance realized. They had agreed to part company for an hour or so, that each might go about their errands. The cook had business with the weaver, then Fara. She needed spices for her pantry, too, and water from the cooling trough in Lioba's metal shop, for its healing properties were powerful, a mainstay of her charms and remedies. Once her chores were finished, she would meet Constance in the church courtyard.

But now Cynwyse wavered, clearly reluctant to let her mistress out of sight. "These errands," she said, "they could wait. . . ."

"Cynwyse!" Constance cried. "It is our friends the Jews who need safekeeping, not I! I am only going to the priory. There is no safer place in Hexham!"

But the cook paid her no heed, only stood quietly

looking about through narrowed, watchful eyes. The signs must have been favorable because her expression soon cleared and she said briskly, "Ye best go, mistress. I hear he's most adamant about punctuality, that one."

Constance laughed, her irritation gone. "You are a riddle at times, Cynwyse, but how I adore you!" She gave her a quick hug, then headed up Gilesgate to the priory, finding the thoroughfare packed with pilgrims. Some wore the traditional garb of penitents, flowing robes that resembled the monastic habit. Others were more gaily attired in bright colors. Yet all wore the cross as a sign of their expiative mission.

Constance struggled against the crowd, feeling like a fish fighting its way upstream. To her relief, she was able to find a favorable current: a large party of pilgrims that looked to be heading for St. Andrews. Constance fell in behind, chagrined by Hexham's growing fame. It must be this way always, she thought, in towns like Canterbury where churches have claim to powerful saints.

How did the townspeople endure it, she wondered. The constant flow of visitors increased the prosperity of all, she supposed, but did it compensate for the jostled turmoil they caused?

Perhaps it is only me who feels thusly, accustomed to a more sedate way of life, she thought. No one else seemed particularly bothered by the heavy traffic in the narrow lane. Indeed, there was an air of excitement and festivity, as if this Saturday were one of the year's major feast days.

She squeezed through the priory gates, spilling toward the church courtyard with the rest. She assumed that Brother Michael was still at his post in the gatehouse, yet the crowds were far too great now for each visitor to be politely questioned and directed. Constance tried to veer that way, to ask the gatekeeper where she might find the prior, but to no avail; she was helpless to go in any direction other than the one dictated by the mob.

She was deposited in the courtyard, jammed with the curious and penitent alike. How would she ever find Cynwyse? The priory would need to take measures for managing visitors, she thought, if numbers continued to increase this way. Looking about, she saw that the west front had been buttressed with timbers and the blocks of stone cleared away. Then, as she continued to look around, Constance realized that the increased congestion was due in part to the fact that no one was being admitted to the church. What could this mean? Was Alfred's sanctity on hold? She asked those around her why the church was closed, but no one could say. Relief washed over her. Had the prior finally recognized the peril he brought to the Jews by encouraging the cult of Alfred?

Constance looked at the excited, expectant faces surrounding her. But was it not beyond Morel's control? Could these people now be convinced that it was all a misunderstanding, that Alfred had mistakenly been taken for a holy saint? After hearing the tale of his tragic martyrdom and the fabulous stories of his so-called miracles, would people accept a much less hallowed version of Alfred's death?

She struggled to the edge of the courtyard, toward the row of private apartments flanking the east side. Surely one of these belonged to the prior, she thought, looking around in vain for a canon to direct her.

Suddenly, there was a great heave as the crowd expanded to accommodate yet another large party pressing through the gates. Constance found herself pushed against the wall of a dwelling, its coarse siding leaving splinters in her hands as she was pressed against the dry wood. "Please," she called out, "I will be crushed!"

No one even acknowledged her, and a surge of anger

welled up inside her. Surely the prior knew she would encounter difficulties in coming here. Why had he not sent a canon to lead her?

She was momentarily tempted to disregard his summons and stalk off, but she wanted to find out what was happening, and her meeting with the prior was an opportunity to gain information firsthand. *If* she could reach him.

Biting her lower lip, she now realized that she must get to the church. For surely the prior would be there—not holed up in his private chamber. Yet the north transept door was on the other side of the courtyard. How to cross? She firmly tapped the broad shoulders directly in front of her. The man turned, a hulking thing with no teeth. Yet the eyes were gentle and politely inquiring.

"I must pass. Will you step aside, please?" she asked.

He answered her with a toothless grin, but stepped aside as best he could, indifferently heaving his bulk at those who stood nearby. This sent up a flurry of resentful cries, but Constance ignored them as she hastily moved forward. But she faltered at the sight of an endless sea of backs. This would take all day, she realized, and stepped back to the wall in dismay. If stuck, she felt safer anchored against the wooden structure than floating helplessly in that surging body of souls.

All of a sudden, a door, not an arm's length away, was yanked open. A man appeared, fully armed for battle. "Back," he yelled, waving a sword. "Disturbers of my peace, away with you!" The people nearest cringed away, yet there was little ground for them to gain, and the sword came perilously close to some. The knight cared not, for he sprang forward again, crying, "Back, I tell you, or meet Faerwundor!"

"Sir!" Constance shouted. "Can you not see? They have nowhere to go! Put up your sword at once before someone is injured."

The man wheeled around to face her, and she saw that there was something very unusual about him. It was his eyes: one stared at her intensely, taking in the rich cloak and hampered position against the wall; the other gazed off in a different direction, looking over the heads of the people in the courtyard. "Are you in distress, lady?" he asked eagerly. "I am Sir Havelok," he said, bowing low. "At your eternal service."

Knowing it was rude to gape as she did, Constance could not seem to help herself, so extraordinary were his eyes. The one was now regarding her with concern, the other utterly indifferent.

Constance spoke to the eye that looked back, saying, "I am Lady Constance. I was trying to see my way to the church," she explained. "The prior requested a meeting, yet I am finding it impossible to cross the courtyard."

"Did he not send an escort?" he asked with exaggerated outrage.

She shook her head, suddenly overwhelmed by the entire situation, wishing that she were back at her peaceful Bordweal. To her dismay, tears sprang to her eyes.

The knight looked truly distraught now, and Constance regretted her momentary weakness. She hastily brushed away the tears and collected herself, saying, "I am fine, sir, truly. There is no need for concern."

But Havelok was already springing into action, taking matters in hand. "Come," he said, lightly taking her arm, as if she were as fragile as the finest piece of porcelain. "You will take your ease inside for a moment. Then I shall see you through this rabble of rustics." He looked around disdainfully, and those nearby shrank from his contemptuous glare. "I had no idea it would come to this," he said as he led her to his door.

Constance hesitated, the speculations she and Godwin had made concerning Havelok fresh in her mind. She had been convinced that the knight was a likely suspect in the murder, but now that she faced him, the idea seemed ridiculous, though she was not sure why. He had a temper, that much was clear. But there was also a gentle quality to him, and she found his chivalrous nature rather touching.

Still, it was certainly conceivable that Sir Havelok was a murderer. And if this was the case, would it not be foolish to put herself at risk by entering alone into his chamber? Yet, she was eager to learn more about him and with a large crowd just outside the door, Constance decided that it would be safe enough. She nodded to the knight who stood awkwardly by, awaiting her consent.

He led her inside, and Constance gratefully accepted the bench and ale he offered. "I have no wine at the moment," he said, looking so embarrassed that she hastily assured him she preferred ale.

She drank the brew down, feeling much better for it. "Thank you for your kindness, sir. You are a credit to your brotherhood, and I am grateful."

Havelok's face turned pink with pleasure. "Any gentleman would have done the same, lady," he said.

"I know you have not been long at St. Andrews," she said. "Are you content with your new home, sir?"

An irritated look crossed his features. "It will serve," he said.

"Only just it sounds," Constance answered with an encouraging smile. "Are you finding the cloister too sedate after military service?"

"Bah!" he shouted, then blushed at this unseemly outburst. "My pardon, lady. It is only that the canons here, well, they are anything but sedate in their lifestyle."

"True," conceded Constance. "They have not been as contemplative as most who seek the monastic life, but they are not Benedictines, after all, but Augustinians." Constance felt the need to defend her local monastic community. "They serve through good works and service to others."

"They serve only themselves," said Havelok, adding quickly, "I do not mean to contradict you, lady, but, my close proximity to them has shown me their true nature. They have squandered the resources of this priory. Had I known it was impoverished, I would have retired to another house, one more befitting my knighthood." He pointed sadly to the jug of ale. "Now I must go without, for I cannot demand more than the priory has, though it may be due."

"Now that Prior Morel has taken charge," she said, "perhaps the priory will be more to your liking."

"Oh yes," agreed Havelok, keen eye straying to the door, which he had left partially open. "The canons are now a model of subservience, at least in his presence. The prior has indeed brought order, though it is difficult to appreciate." He gestured to the crowd beyond his door. "Prosperity has come in his wake as well," he added with a strange smile. "Soon, I will not have to go without wine or anything else. I will live comfortably, as I deserve."

"You are speaking of Alfred?" Constance asked. "And the silver his fame will draw to St. Andrews?"

"St. Alfred we will name him soon, our saint-martyr," he answered. "Yes, it is thanks to him that this priory will one day be great, its holy shrine known throughout Christendom."

"It will have nothing to do with Alfred," Constance said coldly, rising from her chair.

He jumped up as well, crying, "I have offended you! My pardon, lady. I meant no disrespect to the boy. I should not have spoken so crudely of silver and fame!" He hurried on, "I envy him his honorable death, truly I do, spilling his life's blood for Christendom." He waved an arm at the door. "The rest is but a lucky consequence." Misunderstanding her chilly withdrawal, he declared, "He will be avenged, rest assured, lady. The Jews will pay with their lives."

"The Jews did not kill Alfred! I would stake my life on their innocence!"

The knight looked at once wounded by the harshness of her voice and puzzled by her words. But he made no reply, only kept one eye miserably on the floor. Constance regretted her sharpness, for it was not entirely his fault; he was obviously caught up in the same sentiment that was raging through this town like an evil plague. Or feigning to be, she thought. Still, she was more gentle when she said, "Please, Sir Havelok, can you assist me to the church? I am late to my meeting with the prior."

Once again he said nothing, fearful perhaps of another blunder. He decided to let actions speak in his stead, she realized with a faint smile, for he opened the door with a grand flourish and stepped back with a bow to let her pass. Then he took up his sword and bounded into action.

Constance felt a bit guilty over his method of escorting her, for Havelok's means of persuading the crowd to part was frightening to behold. With sword high, he cried, "Back, back, I say, or Faerwundor will hew a path through your insolent flesh!" He fervently brandished his sword, like a crusader amidst an army of infidels. He was terrible to behold, and none denied his request, but dived frantically from his path. Constance marveled at the power of his command, feeling as the Jews must have when they followed Moses out of bondage, the Red Sea miraculously parting at the patriarch's bidding.

Within minutes, they were standing before the north transept door, and Constance was thanking the gallant knight who had rescued her. He bowed low once more, pride smoldering in his eyes. She watched as he made his way back, not having to raise his sword this time, for all smartly stepped aside at the mere sight of Sir Havelok.

Brother Mark and Brother Thomas were posted at the north door, apparently watching for Constance, for when they saw her, she was whisked inside.

When the door was shut behind her, firmly locking out the convivial clamor of the courtyard, Constance stood a moment, overwhelmed by the tranquil majesty that suddenly enveloped her. She had been in the cathedral countless times, yet never before had she so powerfully sensed its spiritual potency. She gazed up at the vaults that seemed to border the heavens, imagining that God must reside somewhere in that echoing vastness. Perhaps He came on those splendid shafts of light arcing through the lofty windows.

"Lady Constance, the prior is expecting you," Brother Mark said in his breathless way. "He hoped you would not mind meeting in the church?" The canon's boyish face looked both anxious and hopeful, like one who always expects a reprimand while praying it never comes. "He is so busy, you see, overseeing preparations for tomorrow's great event. And the courtyard," he babbled on, "well, you saw yourself. It is difficult to go anywhere. We are besieged!"

Several testy replies came to mind, but Constance only said, "It matters not where I meet the prior, Brother Mark."

The canon's reference to "tomorrow's great event" made her uneasy. What event could this be? she wondered as he led her past Alfred's sanctuary, filled with black-robed canons, then toward the crossing, where the nave and transept met.

As they rounded the turn into the choir, Brother Mark said, "The prior will be here shortly, lady. He was called away by a man of the archbishop's. He will soon return, though. He knows you await him."

He quickly bowed away before Constance could put a question to him. She took a seat in an ornately carved chair, one in a long row that accommodated the canons during Mass and their offices of prayer. She often saw them slumber away the service here and wondered how they managed it, so cold and hard were these chairs. She shifted about and pulled her cloak closer, shivering. Spring may have arrived in the secular world, but it was still winter inside the cathedral.

She felt her lower back going numb, and abruptly stood, deciding that she would rather move and keep warm than take her ease awaiting the prior. She started toward the high altar, but stopped when she saw a canon stretched out on the floor, face-down upon the stone paving with arms outstretched to form a cross. Shiny blond locks told her this must be Brother Elias, atoning for some serious transgression, though she had trouble believing he was capable of any.

She wandered back toward the crossing and around to Alfred's sanctuary, curious about the canons' activities there. Standing before the stone grill fronting the tiny chapel, she craned to catch a glimpse of what went on, but to her frustration could only see the brothers' robed backs. Then they parted to finally reveal what they were about.

They had removed Alfred from his grand sarcophagus and to her relief were just finishing, wrapping him in a linen cloth of a coarse texture. It had a dullish sheen to it, and Constance thought it must be coated with wax. On a nearby table lay a pile a silken robes and wrappings, the exotic likes of which she had never seen. Far beyond the resources of our local weaver, she thought. Finery from the East, no doubt, and Constance wondered how the penurious priory had procured such lavish accouterments.

So this was why the church was closed to pilgrims.

The canons were preparing the body—but for what? Then, with Alfred securely encased in linen, the silken garments were carefully unfolded to go on next. Constance saw that they were exquisitely cut, designed to fit a child, a princeling perhaps. Arrayed to their satisfaction, Alfred was then reverentially placed back in his sarcophagus.

"Lady Constance," an exultant voice behind her boomed.

She jumped and turned to see Prior Morel looming. She had not heard his approach.

"My deepest apologies for keeping you waiting," he said.

The prior looked anything but contrite, Constance noted irritably. Indeed, he seemed to be bursting with gladness, a smile playing on his lips that was at odds with an otherwise severe countenance. She was reminded of the grinning demons above the west door, and took a step backward.

"It is inexcusable," he said jubilantly, his brimming smile now overflowing to a full-fledged smirk.

She stared at him, baffled by his unaccountable mirth and good cheer.

Prior Morel saw her discomfort and said, "Forgive me." He put a hand to his lips, his face registering surprise when he found the smile there. He removed it at once. "I have just been given some favorable news," he explained. "I am very pleased." The unwelcome grin crept back.

"You've had word from the archbishop?"

A flicker of annoyance passed over the prior's face as he no doubt found her inquiry too forward. But his exultation impelled him to overlook her boorish behavior, for he clapped his hands together in a childish gesture, exclaiming, "Better!"

Constance waited uneasily, wondering if he was going to share his news, yet unsure she wanted to hear it.

"Actually, it concerns the purpose of my asking you here today. But come, let us sit." He urged her back to the choir. When they were seated, he continued, "As a patron of St. Andrews, I wanted to invite you personally to tomorrow's momentous event. It is only proper that our most generous benefactor hold a place of honor at the ritual." He paused dramatically.

"Pray tell, what event do you speak of, Prior?"

"Alfred is to be translated to the high altar at Mass tomorrow!" he proclaimed triumphantly. "There he will lie to become St. Andrew's new patron saint! The archbishop has sanctioned it—as I knew he would. St. Alfred will be no less a saint than Thomas à Becket!" He clapped his hands again.

Constance jumped up, crying, "You must not! If Alfred is made a saint tomorrow, no one will ever believe the Jews are innocent!"

"But they are guilty," he said, frowning at her outburst.

"How can you be so certain?" demanded Constance. "Nothing has been proven!"

"Proof," he sneered, rising to stand beside her. "Why seek proof when we know that all Jews bear guilt?"

"What madness is this, Prior? Are you saying that all Jews bear guilt in Alfred's murder?"

He cast upon her a faint, sad smile, as if sorry for the intellectual challenges her tiny mind grappled with. Then he thought for a moment, struggling for a way, it seemed to Constance, to bring his towering intellect down to a level she could comprehend.

"Lady Constance," he began. "The central truths of the Christian Church are brilliantly self-evident to all, even the most backward of humanity." He watched her carefully, making sure his words penetrated. "The Jews willfully reject reason, the truths announced and expounded in their own sacred books. Why?" he asked.

"What has this—"

"Because," he interrupted. "They share not in humanity, but are creatures of Satan. Not individuals, but evil sent within to test us in our faith."

Constance was too stunned to reply at first. Finally she managed to say, "These are wicked things you say, Prior, and I'll not stand here and debate you. The Jews are innocent, and Godwin will prove it. You would be wise to put off tomorrow's ritual, for when it becomes known that the Jews are innocent, that Alfred is no saint—" She stopped abruptly, struck by a realization that sent her mind reeling.

Prior Morel was smiling again, shaking his head in pity. "Godwin," he said. "You have not fallen prey to his rantings, I hope?" He watched her closely. "Ah," he said, though she was not sure what he comprehended. "So it is like that. Well, I'm afraid I must tell you, lady, that his is a twisted crusade. And hopeless, for the Jews shall be dead soon."

"What are you saying?" Constance demanded.

"They are to be hanged today. The archbishop's retinue has arrived. Even now they are building a scaffold in the square."

"The Jews are safe in the Keep," she insisted.

"The Keep?" he snorted. "Do you think that God's vengeance can be held back by a pile of stone?"

"No!" she cried. "This cannot happen! It must be stopped!"

"Oh it's far too late, lady. You see, I've just had word from the captain of the retinue. The Jews have confessed to killing Alfred."

SEVENTEEN ✝

Godwin rode like a gale from Knitsley, Saedraca's hooves tearing madly at the road as he frantically urged the horse on. Great clods of earth flew up in his wake as Wulfstan and William fought to keep up with their lord. But no beast could rival Saedraca's swiftness, and the knights fell farther and farther behind.

He must get back to Hexham. A sense of urgency had been mounting all morning, culminating with Father Anselm's revelation. And the moment Godwin heard what the beggar had confessed to the priest, even before the pieces of the puzzle began falling together in his mind, he had known that if he did not return to Hexham with the greatest possible speed, the consequences could be deadly.

As he bent over the horse's flying mane, keeping a watchful eye out for travelers on foot, Godwin cursed his slow-wittedness. The signs had been there all along—why hadn't he put it together? Why hadn't he investigated the first miracle, coming as it did so quickly after Alfred's death? He should have suspected a connection, should have sought the crippled man who claimed to be cured. Then he would have learned sooner that the beggar and the man healed were one in the same. He might have saved the man's life. But he had dismissed the event, never suspecting that a closer scrutiny would uncover the bare outlines of a wicked plot. For the first miracle, he now realized, was the act, after the ritual slaying itself, that set in motion a whole series of events. It was the moment when most everyone became convinced that the Jews murdered Alfred.

He slowed Saedraca to round a sharp bend in the narrow, tree-lined road. He was well beyond the cultivated lands bordering Knitsley now, halfway home. The next stretch of road ran straight through dense woods, and Godwin slackened his grip on the reins. Rising a fraction from the saddle to crouch over the horse's powerful neck, Saedraca instantly heeded his cue and soared ahead like a loosed arrow.

Turning in his saddle, he saw William and Wulfstan just rounding the bend. Better to head straight for the Keep, he decided. Had he suspected the identity of Alfred's murderer before, he would never have left Hexham; for even the Keep could not withstand the power that one could summon.

Godwin passed into the forests of southern Hexhamshire, his horse showing no signs of weariness. Then, as he approached one of the thoroughfare's main intersections, where east and west roads join the southerly route, he was forced to slow his pace. Other travelers were about, some on horseback, many on foot. He threaded his way past, noting that most were traveling toward Hexham.

Wulfstan seized this opportunity to catch up to his lord and heedlessly pounded his horse through the groups of travelers, a streak of silvery mail in the bright sunlight. They shouted angrily, snatching up unwary children, shaking fists at his indifferent back. William followed the path opened by the deputy at a slightly less reckless pace, yet determined not to be left behind.

"Lord Godwin!" Wulfstan cried as he caught up to

the bailiff. "What have you learned? Why do we ride for Hexham as if Satan himself pursued us?"

But Godwin only motioned them on, shouting, "To the Keep!"

They thundered into Hexham, Godwin veering them toward the citadel. But when they reached the Keep, he pulled Saedraca up short to stare in amazement. Wulfstan and William swerved to a stop behind. "By the Virgin!" the deputy cried. "The Keep's fallen!"

Godwin was off his horse with sword drawn in one swift motion. Wulfstan and William ran up the rise after him, toward the northwest corner where once the watchtower had sat perched atop the unscalable walls. Now the tower was but a tumble of massive stone, the walls below it torn open to show a gaping breach.

It was immediately apparent to Godwin what had happened. Scorched stone and timber and tunneled earth indicated that some force, a fairly large one to have accomplished this in one morning, undermined the northwest corner of the structure by tunneling a space beneath. A roof of sorts was created by timbers and the space filled with some combustible material— brush it looked like. The excavation was then fired, and the combination of heat and weakness to the foundation, plus the weight of the tower, had brought down the walls. Godwin almost admired the directness and simplicity of the assault. A professional job, certainly.

They hurriedly picked their way through stone and debris to enter the fortress, afraid of what they might find. To Godwin's relief, his men were alive and well, only trussed up and gagged, their swords and arms heaped in a far corner. The Jews were gone.

Hastily, they freed their comrades, and as soon as Eoban's gag was off, he cried, "My lord, it was the archbishop's men! They arrived just after daybreak and had us by midmorning! There was nothing we could do!" His voice was hoarse with dryness.

"William, fetch water!" called Godwin. Then turning back to Eoban, "What of the Jews? Where are they? Have they been harmed?"

Eoban gulped down some water before saying, "They were taken away—to the Moot Hall, I think. They mean to hang them, lord!"

Dear God, he thought, was he too late? And Bosa and Eilaf were in the Moot Hall—what had befallen them? Godwin was running back through the breach, calling, "Hurry, men! Take up your swords and follow me!"

They sped through deserted streets toward Market Square. When they arrived, they found it teeming with onlookers, so many that the gathering overflowed the square and backed up Gate Street to converge with those trying to exit the priory precinct.

All in the square were gazing expectantly at a scaffold, hastily erected by the looks of it, standing at the center of the square. The gathering looked eager and excited, as if treated unexpectedly to a rare delight, like a holiday passion play. Upon the platform, standing before three nooses, stood Isaac, Jacob, and Samuel. A retinue of some forty knights ringed the scaffolding with swords drawn and pointed outward.

Isaac wore his usual composed expression, ready to meet his God with dignity. Jacob, too, was calm, staring disdainfully at the crowd. His face was swollen and blood trickled from his nose and mouth, stained his shirt front. Samuel looked stunned, utterly bewildered by his position before a hanging rope.

"Stop!" Godwin shouted, raising his sword high, thrusting through the mob. His knights followed closely. The people turned and saw their bailiff's fury, then hastily moved away to give him and his men a wide berth. "Stop!" Godwin commanded again. "Release those men at once!"

A ripple of alarm went through the crowd, which

edged even farther from the now opposing retinues.

A knight stood on the platform, two others beside him, shouting, "These are the archbishop's men and I am their captain. The Jews will not be released!" He answered Godwin with his own ringing sword. "We were sent to act in your stead, Godwin. I am here to bring justice since you have failed!"

"Hanging the Jews will not bring justice, for they are innocent!" Godwin shouted back, closing the distance to the platform. His words brought an angry murmur from the people. The archbishop's knights leveled their swords at his breast as he approached. Godwin's men rushed forward to level their own.

He looked up to see the Jews keenly watching him. Then addressing the captain, he said, "I have proof of their innocence. Let us lower our swords and stop this madness. Hear me out and you will learn that I speak the truth." Godwin's mind raced. He did not actually have "proof," only the barest grip on the tiniest of threads that could unravel the whole plot. He could gather evidence, perhaps, now that he knew where to look. . . .

"I have all the proof I need," the captain shouted, glaring down at Godwin. "I have the Jews' confession!"

The crowd cried out triumphantly. Godwin stood stunned, looking frantically up at the faces of his friends on the platform. But they revealed nothing, only stared back helplessly.

No, it is false! his mind screamed. "Jacob," he called out. "Why have you confessed? How did they make you say it?" Jacob said nothing, only gazed back at Godwin with a resigned expression that said he was reconciled to his fate. Godwin stared at his battered face, his bloodstained clothes.

"No more time shall be wasted," the captain shouted, gesturing to the two knights beside him. They pushed the heads of the Jews into the nooses and cinched them tight, then roughly led them to the edge of the platform.

Godwin was about to give his men the signal to fight. They were outnumbered two to one and would most certainly die in the melee, along with the Jews. Yet no more choices were left to him. He would not stand by and watch innocent men die. From behind, he could hear Wulfstan's low growl, his customary preamble to assault.

"Godwin!" came a voice from the crowd. It was Constance, pushing her way toward him. "Wait!" she called out. "It is a lie! The confession is false!"

The captain stared coldly down at Constance. "Take this ranting woman away," he commanded.

His knights stepped forward to obey and met Godwin's lance. Constance shouted, "Isaac, Jacob, and Samuel, they were forced to strike a bargain with that devil." She pointed up at the captain. "He spared the lives of their wives and children in exchange for a confession to Alfred's murder!"

Another murmur went through the crowd, and the captain glanced nervously around. Godwin pulled Constance close to his side. "Where are they now, Constance?" he asked. "The women and children, are they safe?"

"Safe at Bordweal with Cynwyse by this time," she answered.

Turning back to the captain, Godwin shouted, "I see the way of it now! You tried beating a confession from the Jews first, to no avail. Then you threatened what they hold most precious and finally had your way!" He glared contemptuously at the captain. "Our law does not tolerate such methods, Captain, as well you know! Now hear me out so that justice may *truly* be served."

"I have my orders," he answered quietly. "The oath I have sworn to my liege-lord is the only law I follow." Louder, he said, "Now stand down, Godwin, or you and your knights will fall alongside these Jews."

The crowd shrank back, seeing that a confrontation was inevitable. Godwin quickly pushed Constance behind him. "Move away!" he told her.

Then he turned to face his enemies, and as he did, he saw the prior striding toward the square, black robes billowing. A little way behind came an eager Havelok, dressed for battle. When the knight reached the square, he intently studied the situation, seeming to size up strengths and weaknesses. Then he thrust his way through the crowd to arrive at Godwin's side. "May I serve you, Lord Godwin?" he asked, solemnly offering Faerwundor.

Godwin nodded, then briefly cupped a hand over the offered sword's hilt, hastily executing the ritual. He made room for the knight beside him, but had little time to wonder at this new allegiance, for the archbishop's retinue had raised their own swords, poised for battle. The bailiff tried one last time. "Stop this madness, Captain, and listen to what I have to say!"

"Yes!" a deep voice rang out over the crowd. "Let us hear what my nephew Lord Godwin has to say!"

Everyone turned around to see Lord Eilan emerging from Hawk's Lane, mounted on a great horse. He was followed by Waldeve and a large company of knights who drew up behind Godwin and his men.

"Lord Eilan . . . " the captain stammered, recognizing Earl Gospatric's brother-in-law.

"Name yourself," Eilan commanded. "Who dares to stand in opposition to my kinsman?"

"Ranulf of Anjou," he answered, then hastily added, "Captain of the knights of the most holy Archbishop of York."

"Ranulf of Anjou!" Lord Eilan spat out. "So your kin cower across the waters in France? No matter—my reach is long. They, too, shall know my vengeance at your affront, for my revenge will not halt with you, Ranulf of Anjou!"

"I must do what my lord has bid," he said, greatly alarmed. All knew of Lord Eilan's far-reaching power. "I meant no disrespect to your kinsmen."

"Disrespect?" Eilan shouted. "I have just come from the Keep. What you did there is no mere discourtesy, but a declaration of war!"

"But I must abide by my sworn oath," the captain protested. "The archbishop commanded me to hang the Jews. I cannot disobey."

Prior Morel drove his lean frame through the crowd, sharp elbows jabbing and propelling him to the scaffold. "The captain is right," he called in his imperious voice. "It is his duty to carry out his lord's command."

Lord Eilan did not acknowledge the prior, only stared disdainfully at Ranulf of Anjou. "You would take the lives of these men when you know not whether they are guilty? Would you slay an innocent child because your lord commanded it? Can you not judge right from wrong? If your lord commands you do wrong, it is your duty to disobey, to renounce your sworn oath. For lordship is not one way, but a mutual agreement between the honorable. If one dishonors the other, the bond must be disavowed."

"He cannot judge properly, for he has not all the facts," countered Morel. "He must trust and obey his master, else chaos will reign."

Ranulf of Anjou had no immediate reply to the debate, caught up as he was in the practical issues at hand. Nervously he sized up the opposing force, newly swollen, seeing that the numbers were now quite even. He decided to give discourse a chance, asking impatiently, "What is it you have to say, Lord Godwin? What proof do you have that the Jews are innocent?"

Before Godwin could answer, Constance rushed over to whisper in his ear. Then she quickly made off into the crowd toward Gate Street. Looking up at the captain again, Godwin said, "The story of Alfred's death is a twisted tale. A brutal slaying it was by an evil man who even now walks among us, his wickedness cunningly concealed."

The crowd was very quiet, listening intently as Godwin continued, "The manner in which the boy was slain led most to believe the Jews were responsible, though never was there proof, only deeply held suspicion of the sons of Israel."

"A witness saw the boy go into a Jew's house," someone from the crowd shouted.

"Grendel's testimony was a lie, and he is dead," Godwin announced. "There are no other witnesses, and not a scrap of evidence that points to the guilt of the Jews."

Morel said, "The manner of the boy's death is evidence enough. He was crucified. No Christian would do that to another! The miracles, too, are evidence that the boy suffered a martyr's death. It is plain to all, save you. Must God write it up in a writ, Lord Godwin, to make you see the truth?"

A great murmur of agreement rang through the square before it grew deadly quiet again as everyone waited for the bailiff to reply.

Godwin turned as the crowd parted to let Ada and Gamel move closer to the scaffold, everyone acknowledging their primacy in the matter. Lord Eilan leaned tautly over his horse, listening intently with the rest.

Godwin said, "Alfred was killed by way of a mock crucifixion for this purpose: to cast the guilt for the crime upon the Jews."

The captain rolled his eyes as a roar of dissent went through the crowd. "Not proof is this! Nonsense and guesswork, I call it. Many, doubtless, long to see the Jews suffer. Can you blame them? But who would kill an innocent Christian to bring it about?"

"More than you realize, perhaps," Godwin answered quietly. Then he turned to meet the prior's gaze. "That the Jews would stand accused was but a happy, yet necessary consequence of the murder. The true motive for killing Alfred was his sainthood. Our murderer greatly desired a new saint for Hexham, and so he set about to make one."

The people in the square exploded in shocked protest. The captain threw up his arms and his knights looked at each other doubtfully. Only Lord Eilan sat impassive, his eyes narrowing on the prior.

"Blasphemy," cried Prior Morel, arching a long arm at Godwin. "He is mad! No *man* can make a saint!"

"But did you not try?" Godwin asked him. "Were you not displeased with your ignominious posting at the priory of St. Andrews? You, who once was called abbot, now a prior? Did you not conceive a way to bring fame and prosperity to your impoverished monastery?"

Morel was white with rage. He looked from Lord Eilan to the captain, saying, "Do you hear him? Beware, this is no man, but Satan himself! We must stop our ears, else our souls be in peril!"

People nervously made the sign of the cross. Lord Eilan wore a deep frown. Ranulf of Anjou stood on the platform, looking uncertainly from the prior to Godwin. Then amazement dawned as he comprehended the bailiff's accusation. "You accuse the prior—" he started. But the notion was clearly too farfetched to contemplate, for he shook his head suddenly and laughed. "An ingenious plot indeed, Lord Godwin! What an inventive mind you have! But what of the miracles we heard tell of in York? Did the murderer summon the aid of God as well to help him in this fiendish plot?"

"Many have aided the murderer, though unwittingly, in his scheme to win a saint and destroy the Jews, but not the Divine. The first miracle was a fake," Godwin announced.

Shouts of denial went up, and the captain heaved a great sigh, saying, "Again, I ask what proof you have?"

Godwin answered loudly, so that all could hear. "The man who claimed to be cured at Alfred's tomb was *hired* to play the role of a crippled penitent miraculously cured."

The loudest clamor yet rippled through the square, and the prior turned to Godwin, demanding, "And where is this man now? Bring him forth and let us hear from his own lips that he is a fraud."

"He is dead," Godwin said, staring coldly at the prior. "Murdered before I could reach him."

"Murdered?" the captain asked, frowning.

"Yes," Godwin answered. "While he slept last night at a convent in Knitsley. Alfred's murderer killed once more to keep the poor man from ever revealing the truth. But we are fortunate that this harmless beggar, though a fraud, was a penitent man, deeply religious in his own way. He confessed his deed to a priest before he was killed."

The captain was taking Godwin more seriously now, asking, "He told a priest that he was hired to feign a miracle in Hexham?"

Godwin nodded.

"Did he give the priest a name? Say who hired him?"

"He did not," Godwin admitted.

Morel pounced. "Then what proof have you? How can you be sure that the man cured by Alfred is the one you claim confessed to the priest?"

Godwin looked out at the crowd, shouting, "Who was at the church when the crippled man was cured?" Hands waved everywhere. "Tell me what he looked like, if you can."

Everyone shouted, "A scar! A scar!" and pointed to their faces.

"He had a great scar upon his forehead," Godwin

explained. "It was the same man."

The captain said, "He could have been acting alone, a perverse man who goes about defrauding good Christians."

"He admitted in holy confession he had been hired, and he was murdered before he could point a finger at his employer. That he is dead is proof enough."

"Indeed, it is suspicious," the captain admitted, avoiding the prior's gaze. "Yet, without evidence or witness testimony. . . ."

"When I was told of the beggar's whereabouts, three others were present to hear the location: Prior Morel, Brother Elias, and Sir Havelok. I suspect that if we question the canons of St. Andrews, we will find that the prior took an unexpected trip yesterday evening. Also, a large sum of money was found in the beggar's possession. I doubt either the canon or the knight could afford to pay such a fee. All the evidence points to our prior."

Havelok said, "I saw the prior ride off alone last evening. I was with Brother Mark—he can say the same."

The captain looked at Morel. "Prior?" he asked. "What have you to say? Do you deny these accusations?"

"Of course! They are utterly false!" Morel exploded. "Yes I had an errand to attend yesterday—some fallow fields to inspect. What of it? I am a busy man, with a priory to manage. I go on many errands. As for the rest, the bailiff has not a shred of evidence, but is so desperate to save his vile friends that he offers only this wild tale—"

"The evidence you desire, Captain," Godwin interrupted, pointing into the crowd, "is coming our way now."

The people parted to let Constance approach the scaffold. She was followed closely by Brother Elias, who trailed her miserably with head hanging, a small bundle cradled in his arms. They passed Ada, and when the woman saw what the brother held, she cried out, then covered her mouth to stifle anguished sobs.

"What is this?" the captain asked.

Godwin said, very gently, "Tell us, Ada. What does Brother Elias carry?"

"It is Alfred's cloak," she cried. "The one he last wore. The cloak his killer took."

"And where was this cloak found?" Godwin asked, turning to Constance and the canon.

Brother Elias kept his eyes on the ground, unable to look at his master. "I discovered it in the prior's bed-chamber, behind his private altar."

There was a collective gasp. Godwin loudly demanded, "How do you account for this, Morel? The same cloak that was taken from the boy when he was murdered. How did you come to possess it?"

The prior waved contemptuously at Ada. "She is mistaken. We collected all the boy's possessions after it had become clear he was marked for sanctity. This cloak was among them, and I took it for my own private relic. A selfish act, I grant you, but not a murderer does it make me."

"No," Ada cried. "It is the same cloak he wore when I sent him off to Corbridge! I wove it myself for him not three months ago. I am not mistaken!"

"She is wrong, I assure you," Morel said confidently. "Stricken by grief. It is easy to understand her confusion," he indulgently conceded.

"I fear she is not mistaken," a jovial voice boomed from somewhere beyond the gathering in the square.

Once again, the crowd whirled around to see the archbishop's chief man, Fulk, serenely riding into the square. "I have just come from the prior's last post, a town away in the south," he called out, merry eyes on Godwin. They danced over to rest on Morel. "There I learned of a similar murder and the same accusation against the local Jews. Is this not a strange coincidence, Prior?"

Morel's eyes darted around the square. "Not a coincidence," he said, turning to face the crowd with arms raised high, speaking directly to his followers. "Only more proof that Jews in all places murder innocent Christians—" He stopped abruptly, seeing how people were backing away, staring in horror. "Do not listen to them!" he shouted. "They speak lies! Godwin and his minions are in league with the vermin Jews!" The square was deadly quiet now as all stood rooted, eyes fixed on the prior.

"Listen only to your hearts, to what you know to be true of all Jews! Guilty from birth they are! What does it matter if *these* did not kill the child? They are Jews and that is guilt enough." The people gaped, shrinking from his words. "Do not look at me so!" he roared, spinning on his heel to face them all, seeing the same look of revulsion on each face.

Something seemed to die in the prior then, a glowing taper suddenly snuffed out. "Yes, I killed the boy," he quietly admitted. "As our patriarch Abraham, I would do anything my Lord commands." Morel turned to Gamel and Ada. "He was so like Isaac, too, trusting and gentle as a lamb. But the angel of the Lord came not to stay my hand."

EIGHTEEN ☩

"Will you tell us, Constance and Godwin," Lord Eilan was saying, looking from his daughter-in-law to nephew, "how you were able to determine the prior's guilt? It seems you both arrived at the same conclusion, but by different routes."

They had all gathered at Bordweal—the Jews, Godwin, and his knights, including the newest in his service, Sir Havelok. Lord Eilan and his retinue were there, too, along with Fulk. Fara and Gwyn had been summoned to dress the various wounds with salves of comfrey and ointments of crushed mandrake leaves.

Jacob bore the worst, but Bosa and Eilaf had suffered injuries as well in a valiant attempt to defend the Moot Hall. The archbishop's knights had easily overwhelmed their defensive efforts, taking the two captive. They had not been severely dealt with, though, only roughed about and tied up. Still, they bore angry burns from chafing ropes, and the healers carefully tended the wounds lest infection set in.

After Prior Morel had confessed to killing Alfred, he had been led away by Captain Ranulf of Anjou to be dealt with by the archbishop's court. He bore himself proudly as ever, and mindful of his responsibilities to the end, he directed his final words to Brother Elias, who stood nearby in abject misery. "I leave the priory in your hands, Brother—do not fail me. And keep your eyes on that sorry lot of canons!" Brother Elias had nodded his obedience, never meeting the prior's stern gaze.

A more sedate crowd, already diminishing at its fringes, had watched as Isaac, Jacob, and Samuel were released from their fetters. The Jews insisted on making straight for Bordweal, painfully aware that their wives must be in torment over their presumed fate. And so, looking like a small war-band hastening to battle, the entire company had stormed off to Bordweal, leaving behind a crowd of stunned onlookers.

Now they took their ease upon benches and blankets strewn about the orchard. The day was warm, the air sweet; no one wanted to be shut indoors. Apple blossoms were beginning to swell overhead, enfolding them within a haze of soft pink and the wholesome fragrance of their impending sprays.

Long it had been since Bordweal hosted so great a gathering, and the servants rushed about in breathless haste, seeing to everyone's needs. They were keeping an eager ear cocked as well, listening for details of the events just unfolded in the Market Square, storing them away for a later narration to those not lucky enough to hear the story firsthand.

Cynwyse had been in a state of near panic since leaving Hexham, taking the Jewish women and children to safety at Bordweal as Constance had bid. She had refused to leave her mistress at first, but Constance's stern command had, for once, compelled her to obey.

Once the cook observed her mistress, saw that all had miraculously ended well, she zealously launched herself into the business of feeding guests. Trestle tables were carried from the Hall and set amidst the trees, then dressed with all the victuals she could muster on short notice: the remains of last evening's savory pudding and joint of beef, today's stuffed capons, a heap of fresh bread and butter, egg custard, and apple tarts. Suddenly famished, the company had enthusiastically converged on her offerings.

Godwin stood a little removed, watching his knights pick the platters clean of the last morsels. He himself had little appetite, still taking in the dramatic resolution of Alfred's murder.

He looked over at the Jews, a tight cluster at the center of the gathering. They did not eat with the others, and the women stayed close to the menfolk, eyes rarely straying from them, as if requiring reassurance that they had truly come through the ordeal unscathed.

Not unscathed, Godwin thought, looking across the orchard to his friend. In Jacob he sensed a new graveness, a more thoughtful manner. A brush with death is, of course, a transforming experience, but Godwin suspected that this was not the source of his friend's more sober mien. Jacob's worst suspicions had been confirmed: the hostility and intolerance of his fellow townsmen, only hinted at before, had been fully revealed, its ugly brutality worse than anything he had imagined.

Fulk's melodious voice rang out. "Yes, Constance," he said, flashing her his most irresistible smile, while moving closer to where she sat upon a wooden settee. "How did you determine that it was Morel? It's easy to see how Godwin worked it out, finding out as he did that the first miracle was false." He glanced over at Godwin, giving him a mocking look that said it had been made all too easy for him. "But you had no such advantage," he continued, turning back to Constance. "Yet I hear you knew to look among Morel's belongings for the dead lad's cloak?"

Constance looked up and felt the full force of Fulk's charm as he bent over her. She had to smile back, so compelling was his appeal. Then she looked beyond him, her eyes seeking another, and Godwin came across the orchard to take a seat beside her just as Fulk was about to do the same. "The question has been on my mind as well," Godwin said, smiling up at Fulk.

She spoke haltingly at first, a little shy now that all eyes were upon her. "I think it always bothered me that the priory was benefiting from Alfred's death, winning fame and fortune as it was. But I never considered this the reason behind the boy's murder until I was speaking with Sir Havelok this morning."

All heads turned to find the knight, who was standing uncomfortably at the edge of the orchard.

"We talked of St. Andrew's new fame and prosperity, and I was troubled anew. Later, I watched as the canons dressed Alfred in preparation for his saintly burial beneath the high altar. Something about the lavish vestments troubled me also, and I realized that such garments could not be procured without much cost and foresight. A strange coincidence it seemed that the priory had them in their possession, fashioned as they were for a child, or rather a princeling.

"As Prior Morel spoke to me of Alfred's impending sainthood, I was struck by the idea that Alfred's martyrdom was planned all along, that the fame and prosperity accidentally brought to St. Andrews was no accident, but rather the purpose behind Alfred's slaying and the casting of the guilt upon the Jews."

Godwin nodded, for her reasoning mirrored his own. The orchard was quiet as Constance paused. "These thoughts left me with few to consider," she continued, avoiding meeting Havelok's gaze. "I came to Morel because he stood to gain the most and because something about him was . . . disturbing to me. There was no doubt in my mind that he believed in Alfred's sanctity. He seemed obsessed by it, and it occurred to me that if he was indeed the murderer, he would likely keep the stolen cloak as a precious relic, so lost had he become in his own scheming. But it was Brother Elias who led me to his private altar. He, too, had come to suspect the prior and knew where to look for the garment.

"And I knew that very few could afford the garments that even now adorn Alfred in his tomb. I think that Morel must have brought them with him when he came to Hexham, planning the murder, perhaps, even before he arrived."

Fulk said, "I believe you are right, Constance. It was a murder long planned, its inspiration from a similar murder."

Everyone turned to stare at Fulk, and Godwin asked, "If you suspected him, why did you not come to me right away?"

Fulk considered a moment. "I did not suspect him right away, Godwin. In fact, I was doubtful of your whole pursuit of a mysterious killer." He cast an apologetic smile at the Jews. "Yet your words kept intruding, and I found I could find no pleasure in my respite at Warden Manor." He grinned briefly at Godwin. "There was something oddly familiar about the murder, though I could not think what. It kept nagging until I had a vague recollection of a similar murder in a small town south of York. I decided to travel there to investigate. I asked around and found the circumstances strikingly similar, only the case against the Jews had been dismissed by the king's justices for lack of evidence. People told me that a local abbot, Morel, had been outraged by the dismissal, had lobbied hard for a reconsideration. But he got no satisfaction. After learning this I felt I had enough to at least investigate the possibility of the prior's involvement in the murder here, and I rode to Hexham as swiftly as I could."

"Do you think that Morel killed that other boy also?" Godwin asked.

"Perhaps," Fulk answered. "The murder was never solved. But it may be only that it put the idea in his mind." He considered a moment. "Morel was quite displeased by his appointment to St. Andrews. I remember that he and the archbishop had a great row over it.

"You see, Morel counted himself on the way up, and Hexham was several steps down to his way of thinking. But the archbishop wanted someone capable of turning matters around here, someone who could restore St. Andrews to its former glory. He flattered Morel, telling him he need only apply his considerable talents. Thus cajoled, I think Morel determined to live up to the archbishop's expectations. He probably decided that a saint would be the fastest means to achieve the goal. And the quickest way to make a saint is martyrdom."

"And the archbishop? Did he know of Morel's plot?" Godwin asked.

Fulk raised his brows. "Indeed, Godwin, he is a ruthless and underhanded man, yet I am confident he had no part in the murder."

"Not directly, perhaps," Godwin replied. "Still, he let himself be used by Morel, heeding without question the messages sent by the prior, urging him, as I'm sure they did, to take action against our Jewish friends."

"I'm afraid you're right there," Fulk said. "Morel knew just how to maneuver our lord, playing first on his outrage over a murder within his liberty, then on his desire to lay hands on the debts owed to the Jews, and finally on the prospect of acquiring a new saint."

"Yes," agreed Godwin. "Morel was surely clever, knowing that once the debts were in the archbishop's hands, those owed by St. Andrews, a considerable sum to be sure, would most certainly be forgiven."

Fulk shook his head, admiration in his eyes. "Such

an elegant plot, do you not think? In one brutal act, Morel almost single-handedly dispensed with the priory's debts, while winning a saint and all its attendant fame and riches." More soberly, looking at the Jews, he said, "And he almost destroyed a community of people he loathes."

"Not single-handedly," corrected Godwin. "He had accomplices, unwitting maybe, but that is no excuse for their complicity. The prior knew that if he made the murder look like a crucifixion, people would accuse the Jews of the crime, though it was contrary to all reason. Nor did many disappoint him.

"On the morning of Good Friday, as Alfred was making his way to the rendezvous at the vintner's, Morel must have abducted the boy as he entered the Shambles. He probably saw Alfred pass by the priory gates and followed him down the narrow, darkened street. Once Alfred was strangled and the marks set upon his body, Morel hid the body until he could place it in the south fields."

"Why did he single out Alfred, I wonder?" Constance asked. "And why leave his body in the common fields?"

"We may never know, but I suspect he chose Alfred because of the boy's association with the Jews. Perhaps Morel learned he was leaving Hexham and seized the opportunity to murder him on Good Friday. I'm sure, though, he meant for the body to be discovered on Easter Sunday—it would be more dramatic and lead minds straight to the Jews. Only Alfred was not discovered until Monday." Godwin looked to where Gwyn played with Aldwin and the other children at the far side of the orchard. "But this did not hamper his plan. Indeed, it worked flawlessly, for the Jews were arrested by the townsfolk almost immediately. Morel then hired the beggar to perform the first miracle and set in motion his scheme to create a saint."

"It was Brother Elias who proclaimed the meaning of the first miracle," Havelok observed hesitantly.

"Yes," said Godwin. "And it was an act for which he will pay penance the rest of his days, I think. Yet it was a thought that occurred to everyone as they gathered at the church in the wake of the first miracle. Coming so quickly after the discovery of the body, it was natural to link the two events. Brother Elias merely proclaimed what everyone else was already thinking."

"What of the second miracle, Godwin?" asked Constance. "I can't think how Morel could have been behind the collapse of the west entrance."

"He was not. It was a chance occurrence, easily explained by the run-down condition of the priory. Under normal circumstances, the accident would never have been hailed a miracle, but a tragedy. No doubt there would have been many more miracles had Morel's plot gone undetected."

Isaac asked, "Morel found an accomplice in the beggar. Was he an evil man, Lord Godwin?"

"I do not believe so," he answered. "Nor do those who last spent time with him. He was desperate, perhaps, but also a spiritual man. The priest at Knitsley told me that he often tried to make confession for his sins. He must have gone to St. Andrews for this purpose when he first arrived in Hexham. There he met Morel, who hired him to perform the miracle. But the beggar, I believe, had no knowledge of the prior's involvement in the murder."

"He paid a high price for his ignorance," said Lord Eilan.

"I am to blame," Godwin said, casting his eyes down. "Morel never intended to murder the beggar until I happened upon him through young Corby. I was careless in letting the prior learn the poor man's location. He was easy prey, thanks to me."

Constance reached out a hand to grasp Godwin's,

saying, "You cannot blame yourself for the beggar's death. None of us suspected the prior. He was the last, I think, any would have thought a murderer."

Ivetta said, "And it is thanks to you, Lord Godwin, and to all our steadfast friends," she said, gazing around, "that our men were saved today. For this we shall always be grateful."

"Aye," agreed Isaac, raising his cup to Godwin. "You are a good man, and worthy of your role as keeper of justice."

All raised their cups to Godwin, and as everyone drank to the bailiff, they heard a disturbance in the lane. They looked over to see a large party of townsfolk and farmers arriving at Bordweal, led by Lioba.

They crowded into the orchard, stopping before the Jews, and Lioba spoke for them all, saying, "These folk have come to make amends with Hexham's Jews, if they are willing. Many more feel remorse, though they will not come forward, wishing now for the matter to be forgotten."

A long silence followed, and Godwin wondered what the Jews were thinking. Finally, Isaac inclined his head to solemnly acknowledge the gesture, easing the tension.

Then Cynwyse bustled into the orchard with another platter of food. Seeing the newly arrived party, she cried, "Bless my bread! More of ye? Cum on then, yer welcome here. Have something to eat."

Constance and Godwin strolled from the orchard, ambling across the fields toward the bordering woodland. Cuthbert followed, but when he saw they were heading for the distant trees, thought better of it and changed course for home. Constance turned to watch his progress, an unkempt creature plodding slowly, stopping from time to time to sniff at some unseen object. Her eyes strayed beyond him to the orchard, now crowded with townsfolk and knights, children and servants, then on to the manor house. How fine her home looked in the pale light of spring, she thought. "What is the meaning of Bordweal's name, Godwin?" she asked, turning back to face him where he stood waiting. "I've never thought to ask."

"It means 'Wall of Shields' in the old Saxon tongue," he answered, looking past her to gaze at the hillside manor. "A comely place, yet well fortified, for in days past, dwellings built north of the river were more at risk from Scottish raiders, and defensive works were constantly added." He turned back to her, smiling. "A shining citadel she always looks to me."

"Yes," Constance agreed. "A good home for Aldwin is Bordweal."

"And for you?"

She did not answer right away. "I have considered returning to Wells to be near my kin," she finally said. "But that will never come to pass. There is much to keep me here, though Aidan is dead."

"He would be pleased, I think, to know you remained in the north, tending his beloved Bordweal. It was difficult for him to leave." Godwin looked across the river to the ridge above Hexham, remembering how he and Aidan had paused there, etching into memory the valley, their homes, before turning south, then east.

"I think he went to prove me his worth. The menfolk of my family were crusaders all, you see . . ." Her voice trailed off.

"He would have gone, married to you or no, Constance. Always it was his dream to crusade. Too young we were for King Richard's crusade, but when the call for Damietta came, he was determined to share the glory."

She was silent again, taking in his consoling words as they resumed their walk across the field. When they reached the forest, she asked, "And you, Godwin? Was it your dream as well to be a crusader?"

"Yes," he answered slowly, leaning against a giant oak, its mighty branches long and arching. "It is every boy's dream, one that was stirred by the pope's summons. Yet I've had much experience in war, more than my learned cousin." He smiled again, faintly. "I knew better what to expect."

"And still you went. That is bravery indeed."

"Nay, I followed Aidan's lead is all."

"His protector always," she said, her smile affectionate.

"In that I failed." He stared across the meadow's expanse. "Can you ever forgive me?"

"There is nothing to forgive, Godwin. As you say, he would have gone, heedless of my words or yours. Nor was it for you to ward off every threat. Did you think you could?"

He gave a rueful laugh. "Yes, likely so," he admitted.

"Aidan chose his own way and died defending it. We can have no more regrets, only respect for the choice and honor for the man."

They started back for Bordweal, the westerly sun behind them.

Author's Note

Murder on Good Friday draws on actual thirteenth-century events: accusations of ritual murder. In various towns throughout England, Jews were accused of murder in the suspicious deaths of young Christian boys. Skeptical royal justices often dismissed these charges, but, on occasion, Jews were found guilty and unjustly put to death. In some cases, the child murder victims were even venerated as saints, considered martyrs by their fellow Christians.

A mythology grew up where it was believed that Jews annually murdered a Christian boy by ritually crucifying him. Not unlike the mentality and hysteria that fueled the later witch trials, this phenomenon spread from England throughout the Continent and accusations continued well into the modern period. Today, in England's Lincoln Cathedral, one can still visit the tiny sarcophagus of little Saint Hugh. The Catholic Church no longer venerates him, but his tomb is a powerful testament to the fear and hatred of Jews, past and present.